MW01049497

A FORTUNE OF REVERSAL

The leaving-of-age story of 78-year-old Robert Dodd, who discovers he has not only stopped aging, he is growing younger each day.

After medical science confirmed his "condition" and the news was made public, Bob reluctantly endured the significant drama that accompanied his fifteen minutes of world-wide fame as "The Most Intriguing Man on the Planet."

Seventeen years after the Reversal, Bob is grateful to be mostly forgotten but he is also bored. Living as though there is always a tomorrow is great if you have a minimum level of zest for life, otherwise it can be a bit tedious. Confrontations with "fidiots" behaving badly inspires Bob to finally accept his reality. He decides to steer into the skid and find ways to make his life more interesting.

Then things start to get weird…

STEVE:
MAY YOUR FORTUNES
NEVER BE REVERSED!
ENJOY
Steve Moore
Nov 2023

A Fortune
of Reversal

Steve Moore

A Fortune of Reversal

Copyright © 2020 by Steve Moore
Published by Blue Quest LLC

Cover Art by Indi Martin - Tortoise & Hare Creations
www.tortoiseharecreations.com

Print ISBN-13: 978-1-7360243-1-7
Ebook ISBN-13: 978-1-7360243-0-0

All rights reserved. This book or any portion thereof may not be reproduced or used in any manner whatsoever without the express written permission of the publisher except for the use of brief quotations in a book review.

This book is a work of fiction. Names, characters, places, and events in this book are either products of the author's imagination or are used fictitiously. Any resemblance to actual events, places or persons, living or dead, are purely coincidental.

for Vana
SPT

THIS PAGE

UNINTENTIONALLY

LEFT BLANK

Chapter 1

August 5, 2017
Saturday morning

Today was Bob's ninety-first birthday, and he was fifty-seven years old.

Seventeen years earlier he had known, with absolute certainty, he would never see this day. Now, the concept of absolute certainty had no meaning. He settled back against the cushions of the wicker chair inside the screened-in patio. It was "coffee and couch" time, one of his life's greatest pleasures. He enjoyed the sunrise mix of pinks and blues, and a few wispy clouds. A moment of zen to pause, reflect, and interpret. Especially today.

Wait, I'm still fifty-eight. I'll turn fifty-seven on Monday.

The age-math frequently tripped him up. Sometimes he'd have to grab a scratch pad and work out a time line, just to stay connected to his old self. It would have been much simpler if the Reversal had occurred on his birthday instead of two days later. It didn't really matter, but Bob's engineering mind craved order and precision in the universe. Most of the time he couldn't allow himself to round it off.

On the day he turned seventy-four, Robert Dodd lay in a hospice bed, tripping on morphine and flying through crazy memory-dreams. One of the nurses told him later everyone knew it was his birthday, but no one wished it happy out loud, not with cancer consuming the last of his organs and energies. Most of the staff had hoped he would make it through one more day, but a few admitted to appreciating the ironic life-symmetry of dying on the same calendar day on which you were born. Everyone, though, had wished for him a peaceful, easy passing.

Bob surprised them all and sleep-mumbled for two more days before it was clear the end was near. He was fading, breathing erratically and still babbling softly. Then a last, deep intake of air as his body arched, shuddered, then became still. One nurse confirmed the absence of a pulse and another noted the time, 3:33 pm.

They started to pull the sheet up and over his head but stopped at the gentle whoosh of air being released. Bob's body relaxed and his eyelids twitched. Both nurses watched in astonishment as Bob resumed breathing, shallow and regular. It was not his time after all. Three hours later he was alert enough to ask for water.

Bob sipped his coffee and smiled, remembering the reaction of his nurses to his Monty Python recovery. *"I'm not dead yet! I'm getting better!"* The cancer had failed. Over the next several days he steadily improved, physically and mentally. His liver and kidneys slowly regained their functionality while his mind burned off the fog of near-death and rebooted.

Bob's oncologist, Dr. Roger Kilmore, had no medical explanation for Bob's recovery, calling it a fantastic case of remission. Many of the staff considered it a miracle.

Over the years Bob came to think of it simply as the Reversal.

* * *

Bob backed his SUV into the street and saw his neighbor waving. He pulled to the curb and rolled down the window.

"Hi, Ray. What's up?"

"Hi, Bob, sorry to interrupt. I wanted to let you know I'm leaving again this evening. Flying overnight to Bonn. I'll be gone four or five weeks, and, well…you know." Ray cleared his throat and looked away.

Bob nodded, drumming his fingers on the steering wheel. Ray had shared his worries more than once since he and Betty moved in next door a few years earlier. Ray's job required him to travel overseas several times a year, and Betty often acted strange, even reckless, anytime Ray was away for more than a couple of days. For several months Ray had searched for another job that would not require much travel but so far had no luck.

"Sure, Ray, I understand. I'll keep an eye out and make sure to check on Betty. Germany, huh? Going to have time to visit your family?"

Ray grinned. "Yes! After my work in Bonn, I'm taking vacation time and staying with my brother in Munich. He's planning a big reunion with lots of cousins and their families. My first trip back in fifteen years. It will be great to see them all again. I tried to get Betty to go, but you know how scared she is to fly. No way."

"Right. Well, no worries. I'll be around. Have a great trip and I look forward to hearing about it when you get back."

"Thanks, Bob. I really appreciate it." They shook hands and Bob pulled away just as Betty stepped through the front door with a friendly wave and a huge smile. Bob waved back with no smile at all.

Well, crap. The next few weeks are going to be interesting.

* * *

Springburg, Missouri was a town big enough to have a Costco store but small enough that everyone could drive there in twenty minutes or less. Bob parked as far from the entrance as possible to get in some extra steps despite the hot pavement sizzling in the August sun. He needed a few groceries and was going to pick out a birthday treat for himself at the bakery. On the way to the paper goods he zagged to cut through the hardware and automotive sections. He liked the rubbery, slightly oily smell. It reminded him of trips to the hardware store with his father when he was a boy. Huge riding lawn mowers, ladders, garden hoses and yard tools. Great big tires with impressive tread patterns, the sound of pneumatic tools whizzing from the automotive shop. It was different, better somehow, walking through these aisles. Unlike the bakery and grocery areas, there were no end-stations staffed with friendly part-timers handing out free samples of lemon gelato, cream-cheese spread or gluten-free biscotti. There were only tires in the tire aisle.

Bob heard crying and running feet as he turned the corner. A small child crashed into his legs, bounced back and sat down hard. The girl, maybe three or four years old, sobbed and tried to breathe. Her blond hair was messy, her face streaked with dirt and tears, and her shirt was stained with what looked like chocolate ice cream, maybe one of those free samples.

Bob got down on one knee, keeping a few feet away so he wouldn't scare her. "Hello there. What's wrong?"

She stared at him and wailed.

"Okay, okay. It's all right," he said gently, hoping she would engage and tell him what was going on. The girl continued to cry, interrupting herself with great gulps of air. Something had really upset her.

Probably lost, got separated from Mom or Dad. Someone was bound to be looking for her. It didn't seem right to leave her alone to go and get help, and he didn't want to make it worse by talking her into getting up and following him. He looked through the shelves to the other aisles and saw no one.

He decided he was going to have to leave her alone long enough to find a NEED HELP? station to light up and get an employee headed their way. As he stood up, a dark-haired woman rounded the corner at the far end of the aisle and rushed forward.

"Jasmine! There you are. Oh, honey whatsamatter?" The woman dropped to her knees and pulled the child close. "Momma's here, sweetie, it's okay." She glared up at Bob. "Back off! What did you do to her?" she shouted.

Bob shook his head. "Found her like that. I was just about to go for help." The woman started to get to her feet but failed as the child thrashed wildly, still wailing. Bob noticed a handful of shoppers had gathered at the far end of the aisle to check out the commotion. The woman turned to look, then spun back around.

"What did you do to her?" she yelled again, struggling to keep her grip on Jasmine. The child continued screaming and seemed to become boneless, trying to slump free of her mother's arms and down to the floor.

"Nothing! Why wasn't she with you?" Bob's face flushed. He put his hands in his pockets and tried to appear calm.

"Don't you dare turn this around on me, you pervert! You dragged her back here so you could...to do..." The woman hugged the child fiercely, whispering in her ear. Jasmine gasped for breath and continued to squirm.

Bob looked past the woman. The seed Momma had planted was starting to sprout. The crowd had grown, many shaking their heads and glaring at Bob. He shifted on his feet and tried to think. The woman's aggressiveness had caught him off guard. She was angry and probably embarrassed she had let her kid get away from her. A nightmare that could happen to even the best of mothers.

Bob spotted a blue-vested employee among the onlookers. "Tell you what," he said to the woman. "Let's get this straightened out." He gestured to the worker. "Sir? Would you please call the store manager? It's kind of an emergency."

The man in the vest stepped forward. His name tag read TIM. "I'm one of the managers here, what's the problem?" The woman was still on her knees, trying to control Jasmine.

"This creep grabbed my daughter!" She tightened her grip as the child nearly wriggled free. "What kind of store lets people like him inside?"

A couple of shoppers were holding their cell phones, recording the scene. Bob remained still and said nothing. Tim looked at Bob, then back to the woman, unsure of his next move.

Jasmine ran out of air, temporarily unable to make a sound. She wrenched her body in a great violent twist to escape from her mother's arms and nearly succeeded. She slumped further to the floor, staring up at Bob with huge, frightened eyes. Bob's vision blurred, then went black. He swayed, dizzy and confused, then his vision cleared—

—*and he was in the boy's bathroom standing at the urinal. Bobby had asked Mrs. Bernie if he could go to the restroom on the way outside for recess and she had told him to go ahead, but hurry. He peed as fast as he could, he didn't want to be left behind. He finally finished and started running toward the door while he fastened his jeans. A fiery flash of pain ripped through his body and he screamed. He'd caught himself in the zipper, it hurt more than anything. Bobby frantically tried to pull it free but only made it hurt worse. He had to get help right now! He stepped out of the bathroom and saw Mrs. Bernie and the class down the hall, almost at the door to the playground. He ran-walked to catch up, crying and holding his crotch, every step causing a burning spike of terrible pain.*

A classroom door opened, and a girl stepped out a few feet ahead. Bobby cried out and she froze, right in his path. Bobby juked to his left to avoid running into her and the motion jarred the zipper free. The pain lessened instantly and he stopped running. It still hurt but nothing like before. He carefully finished zipping up and turned back toward the girl. She stared at him with deep brown eyes, large and frightened—

—Bob's mind and vision rocked back, and Jasmine stared up at him with wide, brown eyes as she writhed on the floor, screaming. The woman struggled to get hold of her and calm her down.

Bob reeled, disoriented, and grabbed a shelving fixture to keep from falling. He shook his head to clear his mind. *I'm Bob, not Bobby. I'm in Costco, in the tire aisle.* He realized, without a shred of doubt, that a few seconds earlier he was running through the school hallway in agony, trying to catch up to his third-grade teacher to help him get free from his zipper. *As a child.*

Bob recognized this was absurd but couldn't deny the reality he had just experienced. The residual pain still radiated in his crotch. He was remotely aware of another memory, the fuzzy, normal echo of when it first happened to him back in third grade, eighty-something years ago in the halls of Eastmorland Elementary School in Joplin, Missouri.

Unable to reconcile the two confusing memories, he shifted his focus to the present moment. Jasmine continued to struggle in great distress, and the woman was trying to get to her feet without letting go of the child. Time seemed to thicken and slow, and Bob stared at them both, analyzing, processing. *Something's not right here.* Everything snapped back. Feeling steady again, Bob looked into the woman's eyes, black and sharp. She glared back and instantly, he knew.

Jasmine is not her daughter.

Fake Momma twitched and frowned. The dynamics had changed. She turned away from Bob and with great effort picked up the exhausted child and got to her feet.

Bob turned to the manager. "Tim, please call security. We need to get this straightened out." He glanced up and spotted a camera bubble mounted on the ceiling. "We'll need to check the video recordings."

Tim looked up at the camera and nodded. He spoke quietly into his headset microphone.

The woman shifted Jasmine into a bear hug. "We're leaving now!" she snapped, and Bob moved to block her from getting past. She spun around then stopped as a security guard approached.

"Everyone, stay where you are!" Tim said, then spoke to the guard.

"Macy! Macy!" A young woman pushed through the crowd.

"Mommy!" the girl yelled and started kicking and squirming again. Fake Momma seemed to realize she was screwed. She lowered the child to the floor and let her go.

The young woman dropped to her knees and hugged Macy, who clenched her arms tightly around her mother's neck and pressed her face into her blouse. The security guard grabbed Fake Momma by the arm.

"All of you need to come with me."

Chapter 2

Saturday night

Bob slid the pepperoni and sausage pizza into the oven and set the timer for twenty minutes. The Costco store manager had insisted Bob accept a free basket of groceries as a gesture of gratitude for preventing little Macy's kidnapping. Bob politely rejected the offer, but after more badgering by the manager in full view of a local news camera crew, he reluctantly agreed to take home a couple of their "homemade" ready-to-bake pizzas. Bob also picked up a single piece of chocolate cake for his birthday treat and the manager insisted on swapping it for an entire sheet cake large enough to feed an office party.

He poured two fingers of Macallan into a tumbler, added one ice cube and went out to the patio. It was "scotch-and-sofa" time, another favorite pleasure.

Beverages and furniture, two great things that go great together! Sometimes he cracked himself up.

What a day! His mind kept reliving the drama in the tire aisle and the crazy, time-shifting flashback thing. Somehow, he had kept his cool while the police interviewed him and the store manager did his publicity act for the cameras, but once he was free to leave Bob sat in his car for nearly a half-hour before feeling calm enough to drive home.

What the fuck happened? He sipped the scotch and his mind freewheeled through it all again, flipping back and forth between the confrontation with Fake Momma and the all-too-real experience of getting his junk caught in his zipper just a few hours earlier.

It wasn't just an old memory that inexplicably popped up in the middle of a stressful situation. It was the real deal, an embarrassing situation complete with intense, live pain. His mind—and maybe his body?—was displaced or transported or whatever, and he relived the entire awful experience exactly as it originally happened way back in third grade. And now, Saturday night at 6:42 pm, he recalled every detail and sensation as if—no, *because* it actually happened to him just a few hours earlier. The smell of the bathroom, the color of the tiles on the floor, his classmates laughing in the hall while he tried to zip up. The terrifically sharp pain causing his young mind to immediately shift into panic mode: *I NEED TO GET HELP RIGHT NOW* his only thought, completely overriding the fear of embarrassment from what he had done to himself. Running through the hall in agony, the girl stepping out in front of him. Dodging to avoid knocking her down and instantly feeling tremendous relief as the pain diminished. Looking back at the girl, her dark, brown eyes wide with fear—

Her eyes were exactly like Macy's.

The oven timer buzzed. Tossing back the scotch on the way to the kitchen, he scooped the pizza onto a cutting board and let it cool on the counter.

By design, Bob's life had been quiet for many years now, even boring. The last time he had experienced any excitement was ten years ago, when the news of his "condition" was made public. For a brief time, he was known as The Most Intriguing Man on the Planet.

The Reversal apparently started with his incredible recovery from terminal cancer, but it was four years later when Bob made the amazing discovery he was actually growing younger with time. One morning he nicked himself shaving, and his face in the mirror seemed different yet familiar, and jogged a memory.

He rummaged through a nightstand drawer until he found a photograph taken on his seventieth birthday. His nephew, Jonathan, had treated him to dinner at a Mexican restaurant and for some reason let the staff know it was Bob's special day. A flock of singing servers attacked and insisted Bob wear a goofy, over-sized sombrero while the hostess snapped a souvenir pic with an instant-photo camera. In the picture Bob was clearly unhappy to be wearing the stupid hat.

He returned to the bathroom to compare the image with his reflection in the mirror. His seventy-eight-year-old face looked remarkably like it did at seventy. His hair was still gray but thicker, and his crow's feet seemed less wrinkly, too.

During the next two years, Bob paid careful attention and discovered additional evidence indicating his mind and body had stopped aging and started...something. He wasn't sure what to call it. If the opposite of age was youth, had he started *youthing*? *Younging*? He had no proof, but he was absolutely convinced that whatever it was, it likely started that day in the hospice bed when he almost died.

His stomach growled so he pushed the memories aside, refilled his scotch and grabbed a couple of slices of pizza. He dropped into his recliner in the living room and started the DVD player where he left off the previous night, a *Seinfeld* show from the middle of season five. George was pretending to be a marine biologist to impress a woman. Bob was sure hilarity was about to ensue, especially since he had watched the episode several times before.

His cell phone rang: KILMORE FOUNDATION. It was probably a robocall to remind him of his upcoming appointment. He let it roll to voice mail. Seconds later the phone rang again just as he took a bite: JACK. He paused *Seinfeld* and accepted the call.

"Hrrrho?"

"Bob? Sounds like your mouth is full. Is she cute?"

Bob swallowed and took a drink, taking his time before answering his best friend. "You're not as funny as you think you are."

"I know. Hey, I just saw the news, you saved that little girl in Costco! They didn't say your name but I could tell it was you. Way to go! How are you doing after all the excitement?"

Bob heard a door slam and looked through the front window. Kids were piling out of a car parked across the street. "I'm okay, thanks. Yeah, it was quite a scene. I talked the news people into leaving my name out of it. I didn't want any attention. The Costco manager did give me a free pizza though."

"Score! I'll let you get back to your dinner, but I want to hear all about it. How about meeting at Mooncups tomorrow? I want to talk to you about another thing too."

"Sounds good. Around noon?"

"Perfect. And happy birthday, buddy! How old are you now? A hundred and three? Forty-two? I can't keep straight whether you are coming or going."

"Thanks. I'm ninety-one today and will turn fifty-seven on Monday if my math is right."

"Man, you're going to catch up to me in another year or so." Jack was fifty-five. "And in another three decades your wrinkles should fade enough for you to find yourself a companion. Someone to canoodle and share your birthday pizza. Maybe even at the same time."

"You should be so lucky, Jack."

"Hey, it's not about me. I know it has literally been a geologic era since you had any action, but I haven't given up on you yet. See you tomorrow."

Bob munched the pizza and watched George get in way over his head trying to impress his girl. He had trouble enjoying the show, his mind kept flipping back to the flashback experience.

He now had two, distinct zipper memories stored in his mind. They did not coalesce, they existed side by side. One was old, short, and fuzzy—*just like my pecker*—from long ago when it first happened. He was running down the hall in pain, yelling for his teacher to help, then somehow it shook itself free. In that version he did not remember the girl stepping out in front of him.

The second memory was only a few hours old, still raw and fresh. Every detail, sound, and smell was vivid, recalled in high-definition clarity. The girl in the hall, standing still, frozen with fear. How did he manage to avoid running her over? Why didn't he remember her in the old, original memory?

Bob jumped as several bottle-rockets exploded in the sky in front of his house. He stood and went to the window, clenching his fists, a knot forming in his gut. Dozens of cars lined the street left and right, and more were arriving.

The Anderson brothers were hosting a backyard pool party across the street. Again.

Chapter 3

Saturday night

Bob had known Todd and Ellen Anderson for several years, a nice couple who made valiant efforts to control their teenagers, Ryan and Jay. They failed miserably and eventually gave up, concluding the best way to protect the people of the community and minimize property damage was to let most of it occur at home. The boys cooperated fully and hosted well-attended parties every weekend and more than a few weeknights, especially during the summer.

This week the exhausted parents were away on a much-needed vacation, an anniversary cruise in the Caribbean. By Bob's count, tonight's party would be a record-setting six in a row starting last Monday. The parties were noisy and disruptive. It was unsettling to see the neighborhood choked with cars and crowds of kids hanging around and drinking. Todd spent much of his free time apologizing to irritated neighbors and picking up party trash from the street and nearby yards. Ellen mostly stayed indoors, presumably embarrassed.

The house vibrated from the pounding bass of the music

blaring from the Anderson's back yard. There had been too many nights like this. Bob knew exactly how the rest of the evening would go: he would set up his one-man neighborhood watch program in the living room. He'd read or watch television but mostly keep an eye on the street. He hated spending hours sitting by the window with his cell phone, ready to record shenanigans and hold the troublemakers accountable for any property damage.

A car full of kids pulled away from the curb in front of his house, probably making a beer or taco run. Bob watched as a large black pickup truck pulled in and parked in the same spot facing the opposite direction.

The truck came in fast and the front wheel jumped the curb, the tire digging a trench in the grass as the driver managed to skid to a stop just short of crunching into Bob's brick mailbox.

Dammit all to hell! Bob grabbed his phone and started recording video. A boy got out on the passenger side and immediately crossed the street to join the party. The driver took his time getting out, then raised a bottle high and chugged his beer. He was big, tall and wide, wearing blue jeans and a purple T-shirt. The kid tossed the bottle on the grass, unzipped his pants and took a leak on the mailbox, oblivious to Bob recording from the window.

Bob stood nearly paralyzed as he quickly ran through his options. He could go outside and confront the jerk kid with a too-classic case of "get off my lawn" old-manitude. That would probably not end well. Call the police? Maybe they would shut down the party, but it might inspire later revenge by the Anderson boys on the cranky neighbor across the street. He could complain to Todd and Ellen when they returned from their trip. No doubt they would apologize with sincerity and do whatever it took to make it right.

Purple Tee shook, zipped and headed to the party. Bob pounded his fist on the top of his chair. The punk had trenched his lawn and pissed on his mailbox, and Bob had done nothing. Disgusted, he went out the front door and across the yard. He took pictures of the truck and the damaged grass, then walked around to get a shot of the license plate. A pair of chrome "truck nuts" hung by a chain from the trailer hitch.

Of course, the kid decorates his truck with testicles. He clicked a picture, went back inside and restarted *Seinfeld*. He turned up the volume to compensate for the thumping party music and reached for his scotch. He'd figure out what to do later, maybe in the morning.

* * *

Despite getting only a couple of hours of sleep, Bob woke early and went right outside to see if anything else had happened. The Anderson house was quiet, no one in sight. Several cars were still parked haphazardly up and down the street. Bob thought the kids were a bit too old for a sleepover, but he had to admire the accidental wisdom of passing out in place rather than driving home drunk or stoned. The black truck was still parked next to his mailbox, the scar of damaged turf trailing behind the front tire. Beer cans and bottles were everywhere. Purple Tee apparently wasn't too concerned about his truck. He had left it parked all night with the windows down. Bob went inside and started the coffee brewing.

The asshole kid had trenched the lawn and pissed on the mailbox without fear or hesitation. *What a fidiot!* Bob scrolled through the pictures on his phone, an idea percolating alongside the coffee.

He went to the garage and opened the automatic sprinkler control box mounted on the wall. He selected station two, increased the watering time from ten to forty-five minutes, and initiated a manual start.

Bob took his "coffee and couch" in the living room and enjoyed the dancing waters as the rotating sprinklers soaked the inside of Purple Tee's truck.

* * *

A couple of hours later kids started trickling out of the Anderson's house and driving off. Bob kept watch until Purple Tee and his companion came through the side yard gate and ambled toward the truck. The big kid opened the driver's door, yelled and stumbled back as water poured out of the cab. He recovered, slammed the door shut and set off a series of F-bombs loud enough to wake the rest of the neighborhood.

Purple Tee turned toward the house, and he and Bob stared at each other through the window, twenty-five feet apart. Bob's heart raced. The kid took a step toward the front door but stopped when his buddy yelled at him.

"Hey, come on! It's your own fault for leaving the windows down. Let's just go."

Purple Tee hesitated, then climbed into the truck and roared off, the spinning tires adding more damage to Bob's lawn.

Bob let out a breath and started laughing. He hadn't known what to expect, the situation could easily have gone nuclear. He thought he might have to play the "old man" card, act feeble and confused. He'd say he was sorry about the truck getting soaked, but the sprinklers had an automatic timer and the kid shouldn't have left the windows down.

With a start, Bob realized he had a mild, emotional buzz. He still had a messed-up yard to repair but enjoyed getting revenge, however minor. He'd gone against his usual instincts, and things turned out okay. With a rare sense of satisfaction, he walked to the kitchen to make breakfast.

Chapter 4

Sunday noon

Bob glanced around the coffee shop as two young girls ahead of him ordered seriously customized cappuccinos. Jack waved from a corner table, their usual spot.

"Welcome to Mooncups! What may I prepare for you?" Lydia cheerfully greeted Bob, knowing full well what he would order: a bold coffee with a shot of hazelnut. She picked up a large cup and a marker.

"Yes sir, and can I get a name for the order, please?"

"Sure," Bob said. "Ramma-lamma ding dong, that's with two g's in ding."

"You got it, Mr. Dong."

Bob met Jack two years earlier during his first visit to Mooncups. He had talked himself into getting out of the house for a while, to do something new and different. First up: a cup of coffee in one of those trendy shops popping up all over Springburg. Mooncups had a distinctly youthful, new-age vibe, a place he normally would have skipped. But Bob 2.0 was boldly going where Bob 1.0 had never gone before.

Steve Moore

He was searching for the word "coffee" somewhere on the monster wall menu as a middle-aged man ahead placed his order. The girl working the counter had fastened two Mooncups name tags together to accommodate the full, all-caps spelling of her name: CHANDRALABRA. She took the order and asked for the man's name.

"Jack," he answered. The man turned and Bob broke into a grin; the guy only had one eye. Instead of a patch or blanked-off eyeglasses, the man had opted for a skin graft. It was a perfect job, the skin that replaced the eye socket and eyebrow was completely smooth and seamless, as though the eye had never existed.

Jack winked at Bob and stepped aside. When Chandralabra called his name, Bob picked up his coffee and Jack waved him over.

"Hi there, I'm Earl," he said, shaking hands.

"I'm Bob. Nice to meet you, Earl. But—"

"Yeah, I'm also 'Jack.' Just a joke, I try to have a little fun with the staff here, but they are too young to get the one-eyed jack thing. Looked like you got it, right?"

Bob nodded. "I like the ironic irony, very clever. I think I'll call you Jack, though, if you don't mind. Earl was my grandfather's name and I don't want to confuse myself."

Jack chuckled and they got to know each other. Earl "Jack" Lancaster had lost his wife several years earlier to a heart problem: she broke his by running off with another guy. He eventually bounced back and was cheerfully going forward, determined to enjoy life, have some fun and perhaps someday find another companion. Bob told Jack how he had lost his wife Linda to cancer many years earlier and understood what it meant to be alone after losing someone special.

20

A Fortune of Reversal

When he told Jack his last name was Dodd, a light bulb winked on. Jack stared at him and raised his eyebrow. Bob nodded and confirmed he was indeed briefly famous in the news many years ago. He glossed over the Reversal story and explained he had become really bored over the last few years and decided to try new places like Mooncups. The two men chatted for two hours and quickly became friends. They met a couple of times each week at Mooncups and occasionally elsewhere for breakfast or lunch.

"Coffee for Mr. Ding Dong!" Lydia announced, louder than necessary. Bob dropped a couple of dollars in Lydia's tip jar and joined Jack at the table.

"You're a sight for a sore eye," Jack said.

"Give it up, Jack, we've done them all." After two years of clever jokes about Jack's optically singular condition they were now down to lame puns and weak, twisted clichés.

"You've had quite a weekend, huh?" Jack asked. "That was a crazy scene in Costco, glad the kid is okay. Way to go."

"Thanks, but I really didn't do anything."

"Not what the news said. They called you a hero for preventing a kidnapping, could have been a really sad thing if not for you."

"I didn't watch the news, but all I did was get the store security to check out the woman's story. Glad it worked out okay."

"How did you know she wasn't the real mother?"

Bob shrugged. "I didn't. The girl kept screaming and trying to get away with a terrified look in her eyes. It just didn't feel right." He had already decided not to mention the freaky memory thing to Jack until he figured out for himself what exactly happened, and why.

"Did anyone find out the witch's plan if she had managed to

leave with the kid?"

"The police found her car parked outside the automotive service entrance. They think she was going to slip out through the garage, just a typical mother taking her screaming child to the car for a timeout, then drive off."

"That's a bold move," Jack said.

"Here's another bold move, if I say so myself." Bob told Jack about the black truck tearing up the grass in his front yard and running the sprinklers to teach the jerk a lesson.

"Impressive! Creative use of lawn irrigation equipment for home defense, truly inspired. What were you going to do if the guy came at you?"

"I failed to consider that, until he threw a fit after he opened the door and water poured out. Maybe hide inside the house and pretend I wasn't home? His buddy talked him into leaving, so I got lucky."

"Better watch your back, Bob. And your front. The kid will probably show up again sometime."

"If the Anderson boys keep throwing parties, I'm sure he will."

Jack tossed back the last of his coffee. "Got a proposition for you. How would you like to get out of town for a week or two?"

"What do you have in mind?"

"A couple of days ago I got a call from my uncle Mike in California. He and his wife run a bed and breakfast in a nice little town not far from Sequoia National Park and a small lake where people camp, hike, and pretend they want to see bears. Mike and Donna are semi-retired and they need to drive up to Washington state next week to help out her mother who's not doing well. They asked me to keep my eye on the place while they're gone. I'm flying out next weekend, why don't you come along? We can visit Vegas for a couple of days on the way back."

Bob thought for a moment then shook his head. "It sounds like fun, actually, but I've got my six-month checkup in Albuquerque next week." Bob had a binding agreement with the Kilmore Medical Foundation for a week of residency twice a year at their medical facility in New Mexico. In their quest to learn how and why Bob was continually growing younger, the KMF staff conducted physical and psychological examinations, took dozens of fluid and bone samples, and ran numerous crazy experiments dreamed up between visits.

"Okay, well how about this," Jack said. "I'll do the B&B thing until Mike gets back, then rent a car and drive to Vegas. You can fly in after you're done playing doctor with those sexy lab technicians. I'll make all the arrangements. Consider it a birthday gift."

Bob agreed to think about it, and they tossed their cups in the trash. Bob went back to the order station and purchased a bag of pastries from Lydia. He had one stop to make on his way home.

Chapter 5

Sunday afternoon

Bob parked the SUV at the curb beside the small neighborhood park, just a few blocks from his house. He admired the handmade signs stuck in the ground near the street: REVERSE THE REVERSAL! DODD IS THE DEVIL! And his personal favorite, a nod to Frank Capra: YOUTH IS WASTED ON THE WRONG PEOPLE!

A group of about twenty adults and children mingled around lawn chairs and coolers under the shade of a few trees. Bob tapped his horn and waved. A tall man walked over and stooped to see inside as Bob lowered the passenger side window.

"Hello Bob, you smelly sonuvabitch! Eat any babies today?" The man's white beard bobbed up and down with his words.

"Hi Frank, you slimy lizard-brained monkey molester. How they hanging?"

"Low and pitiful, like your reputation, you obsequious sycophant." Frank grinned broadly and reached in to shake Bob's hand.

"Nice day to be outside since you clearly have nothing else in life to occupy your time," Bob said.

"You know we have to be here, Bob. It's Sunday."

"Yeah, I know."

Frank was the leader of the group. He and his family and a few other congregants gathered in the park every Sunday afternoon, weather permitting. They were the last hold-out members of a quasi-religious crackpot organization, the Church of the Modern Peoples, more commonly and derisively known as CHUMPs.

The CHUMPs were a big deal a decade earlier, rising to overblown prominence after the public announcement by the Kilmore Foundation of Bob's condition and the fantastic Reversal. The CHUMP leadership immediately launched a noisy publicity campaign and denounced Bob. They claimed he was an abomination, a satanic demon cleverly taking the form of a senior citizen who must not be allowed to roam free and endanger the good people of Earth.

The publicity program was effective, and CHUMP membership expanded over the next few months, peaking at nearly a half-million souls. There was a brief setback when a particularly zealous CHUMP parishioner in Akron, Ohio held a press conference to proclaim a piece of wheat toast he was served in a greasy-spoon diner was clearly marked with the likeness of Bob Dodd. When a reporter pointed out the image seared into the bread didn't resemble Mr. Dodd all, the CHUMP explained with exasperation that it was the image of Bob as he *would* look in twenty years, at the age of forty-nine. The Church's credibility took a hit for a while, then somewhat recovered.

Many Church members were sincerely disturbed by the mystery of Bob's Reversal, it went against the normal, natural order of Life as They Knew It. The Church leaders played to their doubts and fears and continued to pound their message. Anti-

Bob sentiment ran high among the CHUMPs, but not so much outside the Church. Bob had his fifteen minutes of fame spread out over a few months before the news faded, people yawned and moved on.

In a desperate attempt to stay relevant—and financially comfortable—a particularly deranged high priest and a small group of CHUMP directors came up with a bold plan. They would kidnap Bob and quietly hold him captive somewhere far away. The Church would then claim Bob's sudden disappearance was proof their battle against Evil was successful and they had vanquished the Devil himself.

Franklin Weaker was the laity leader of the CHUMP parish in Springburg and was requested to assist with the abduction. While personally troubled by Bob's unholy reverse-aging "power," Frank was appalled by the unlawful plans of the Church leadership, which had clearly lost its collective mind. He alerted local police, the conspirators were arrested and prosecuted, and the Church became widely despised and soon collapsed.

Bob met Frank personally to thank him for intervening and over time they became friends. Frank continued to believe the Reversal was a freakish, horrific thing, but viewed Bob as a victim of evil circumstance and not the cause. Frank and a handful of other CHUMPs attempted to carry on the public awareness campaign, staging small protest events and warning citizens to be alert for signs of the coming Judgment/Apocalypse/Really Bad Day. They were ignored by the public and local press, and the residual CHUMPS eventually dropped their official animosity toward Bob. They soon morphed into a goofy cult just large enough to support a party planning committee that organized Sunday afternoon picnics at the park in Bob's neighborhood.

Bob handed over the sack of pastries. "You have plenty of

drinks for everyone Frank? Supposed to get really hot today." It occurred to Bob that he and Frank had at least one thing in common: they had both prevented a kidnapping.

"We're good, thanks. Mollie over there is sitting on a full cooler. We'll probably knock off a bit early today for the heat. Thanks for the pastries. So, what evil do you have planned for today?"

Bob tapped his chin and pretended to think. "Let's see, I'm going downtown in a few minutes to reverse the flow of the river and change the water to Diet Dr. Pepper. Otherwise, I'm free. Do you have any suggestions for me?"

Frank grinned, gave Bob a flip-you-a-dead-fish gesture and walked back to his group. Bob tooted his horn and waved at the CHUMPs as he drove off.

Chapter 6

Sunday afternoon

Denton Rafter needed cigarettes. The easiest thing to do was send Junior on a run so he went to his son's room. He figured the boy would be sprawled on his bed, smoking weed and listening to music, his usual routine before another night of partying, but the kid was gone. Denton was still foggy from last night's drugs and couldn't remember if DJ had told him he was leaving.

Denton looked through the living room window and was surprised to see DJ's truck in the driveway next to his own, a pair of matching black Fords. Except they didn't really match. Denton's truck was filthy, and the side panel was crumpled from banging into a light pole at Smitty's Bar a few weeks back. DJ's truck was clean and neat, except for those stupid truck balls hanging off the hitch. The kid had a few problems—he was kind of slow, actually—but he had a freaky passion for that damn truck. He'd worked as a bagger at the food mart for three years to buy it, then continued burning through his paychecks to trick it out. Denton had to admit it looked pretty sharp, especially compared to his POS. Denton had bigger things to handle than maintaining his truck, he was running an interstate commercial enterprise, for fuck's sake. He needed to get where he was going and do what needed doing. *Maybe I should have Junior clean up my truck. The boy owes me everything, right?*

The back door slammed, and a slobbering bulldog trotted into the front room, wagging his tail. DJ followed, dropping the dog's leash onto the floor as he dropped into a chair.

"Where the hell have you been?" Denton saw the leash but jumped on his son anyway out of habit.

"Had to clean my truck, then took Buster for a walk," DJ said.

Kid likes that damn dog almost as much as his fuckin' truck. "I need some cigarettes, go get me a couple of cartons."

"Money?"

"Didn't you get paid yesterday?"

"Haven't cashed the check yet."

"You little shit, you know you need cash for your share of the bills! You live in my house, you have to pay!" Denton glared at his son, who kept his head down.

"Yes, sir."

Denton fished his wallet out of his pocket. All he had was a handful of one-hundred-dollar bills, and he'd need them later.

"Shit. Stay right there." Denton went to his bedroom, opened the nightstand drawer and pulled out a black long-handled flashlight. He unscrewed the top and dropped a single, D-cell battery onto the bed, then shook out two bundles from the bottom of the cylinder. The high-quality LED flashlight normally used four batteries, but Denton had modified it to use only one. It would still provide light for a short time. The remaining three-battery space contained a thick plastic bag of cocaine and a tight roll of rubber-banded cash. He peeled off three fifties, repacked the flashlight and returned it to the nightstand drawer.

DJ was waiting, Buster in his lap. Denton handed him one of the fifties. "Get me two cartons and a case of beer. Hurry up and come straight back. Understand?"

DJ looked at the fifty, then up at his father. "It's gonna cost more than that to get beer too."

"Shit." Denton gave DJ another fifty. "Go on. And bring me the change."

DJ put the dog down and went out the front door. Denton headed to the kitchen to get something to eat. Buster trotted behind, probably for the same reason.

There was nothing in the cabinets. Denton opened the refrigerator and found a package of bologna. He leaned against the sink and ate the top slice. Buster sat motionless a few feet away, staring at him. Denton peeled off another slice from the package and put it in his mouth, watching Buster watching him. He swallowed and peeled off the next-to-last slice from the package, but it slipped out of his hand and fell to the floor. Buster made his move, but Denton was in position for the block, kicked out a foot and yelled "NO!" Buster relied on some relevant recent experience and froze, apparently understanding it was a bad idea to go for it. Denton slowly reached down and picked up the bologna, keeping his eyes on the dog. Buster laser-tracked the bologna all the way up, drool dripping to the floor. Denton looked at the slice, then back at the dog as he pushed it into his mouth. Buster remained frozen, a tremendous display of canine optimism. Denton swallowed and pulled the last slice from the package. He held it for a couple of seconds, then flipped it to the dog. Buster caught it in the air and swallowed it whole in one quick motion, tail wagging furiously.

Denton tossed the empty package onto a stack of dirty dishes in the sink. He'd have to remind Junior to clean the kitchen. The kid was stupid sometimes, but Denton was okay with that. It made him easier to control.

The electricity flickered, then went off. *Shit. Forgot to pay the utility bill again.* There were probably a couple of shut-off notices in the pile of unopened mail on the kitchen table. Denton had plenty of money, but his line of business required him to avoid banks, checking accounts, credit cards, anything that would generate a significant paper or digital trail. Living a cash-only life was inconvenient but necessary. Fortunately, all of his clients paid in cash, some of which he stored in the flashlight he had converted into a private ATM. He'd make a trip downtown on Monday and pay the electric bill. If they let him pay in advance, he'd give them enough to cover several months of service.

Denton took the last two beers out of the refrigerator while they were still cold, took a seat on one of the faded Adirondack chairs on the front porch, and waited for Junior to return with the cigarettes. He heard his cell phone ringing inside the house, but he wasn't in the mood to get back up.

* * *

DJ drove to Zippy Mart, shifting uncomfortably on the wet seat. He'd done his best to dry out the cab, but the seats had soaked up a lot of water from those fucking sprinklers. The raw, red rage still filled his mind, but he had things under control. He'd mentally placed a twenty-five-pound weight on top of it, keeping it pressed down just like Dr. Andrea had taught him. It was okay for now, but later…

Inside the store he pulled two twelve-packs of beer from the cooler and asked the clerk for two cartons of cigarettes. He put the cigarettes and one case of beer in the cab, the other case he put inside the toolbox in the bed. He'd take it to the Anderson's later, a rare Sunday night party while their parents were away. Dad wouldn't notice he used some of the cash for extra beer. His father wasn't very bright sometimes—in fact, sometimes he was kind of slow. DJ had learned if he did everything his dad told him to do, the asshole would leave him alone most of the time.

His butt squished in the seat again when he got back in the truck. DJ squeezed his eyes shut and pounded the steering wheel, remembering the water pouring out of the cab onto his boots. He mentally adjusted the weight, centering it directly on top of the rage, and immediately felt better. He wished he could talk to Dr. Andrea again, she had helped him a lot. His weekly sessions with her back in middle school provided him tools for controlling his emotions and kept DJ from seriously hurting dozens of kids who irritated the shit out of him.

But the old fart across from the Andersons had soaked his truck, no way he could let that go. DJ knew what happened when the rage was kept under the weight for too long. He'd have to do something soon. After a few seconds his mood improved with a new idea. He'd need to buy one more thing. DJ locked his truck and walked across the street to the liquor store, whistling as he went.

Awesome plan, dude. One of your best ever.

Chapter 7

Sunday afternoon

"Denton! Pay attention, shithead, I need you to do something for me, right now! I'm in County and need you to talk to Larry so he can bail me out. He'll need to get with the judge or whoever and find out how much it's gonna take. You need to call him and find out how much to get, the little shit won't do anything unless he gets a payment on my account and enough to get the bond. Get him the money and he'll know what to do. You need to do this now, you hear me? Tonight, I have to get out of this crap-hole tonight. This is the only phone call I get, so make sure you do what I'm telling you. CALL LARRY RIGHT THE FUCK NOW!"

Megan Jensen hung up the phone and returned to the cell. The guard locked the door from the desk console on the other side of the Plexiglass window. She slumped onto a bench, leaned back against the wall and closed her eyes. The woman sleeping on the other bench snored steadily, not all that loud but still irritating.

That fucker in Costco really screwed up her plans. She had the kid corralled in the tire section, the mom oblivious and way off in the other end of the store. All she had to do was lead the kid to the garage, past the customer service desk and out to her car in the parking lot. They would have been in Fayetteville in plenty of time for the hand-off to the broker. Three days later little "Jasmine" would have a new mommy and daddy and Megan would have an extra fifty grand.

But the little twerp panicked and pulled out of her grip, and Megan dropped her bag. By the time she picked it up the kid had run around to the next aisle and right into that old fart who blew up the whole deal. *Why did he butt in? It was none of his business!*

She remembered the guy's face when he froze, looking right *into* her. He knew what was going down, maybe not the details, but he knew Megan wasn't "Momma." Then it all went to shit.

Larry would get her out, assuming Denton came through with the money. Denton could be a little slow sometimes. She owned him, but her cousin liked to pretend he was a free man. He thought he was some kind of kingpin with his three-county drug operation, but he was just one of the larger toads in a small, scummy pond.

Megan and Denton were friendly cousins as kids, they were nearly the same age and both had the usual teenage problems with their parents. Her father and Denton's mother were brother and sister and lived in the same neighborhood. Growing up, the two spent a fair amount of time together, and their relationship became much more complicated in high school. When the opportunity presented itself, Megan seized control of Denton. It was surprisingly easy.

In her sophomore year Megan became pregnant by the starting linebacker for the football team at a party, a one-night thing. She knew she didn't want the baby, but the idiot immediately told his parents and they got involved, making plans for the kids to get married and live with them.

Megan didn't really have any plans yet but living with the dip shit and his parents wasn't going to happen. She asked Denton to drive her to a clinic upstate. When it was over, Megan was surprised to feel mostly okay. Those made-for-TV movies made it seem like she should be racked with emotional trauma or something. She was fine, it was time to move on. She swore Denton to secrecy, telling him she owed him a big favor. There was only one more thing to take care of.

Megan told Mr. Football she lost the baby, and instead of being relieved he surprised her by getting upset. He told her his parents were already making room in the house for their new family and he was ready to marry Megan and get her pregnant again. When she refused, they fought and things turned violent. Megan was able to leave before it went too far, but Justin was clearly crazy. She decided to permanently solve her problem.

Megan knew Cousin Denny had a thing for her, not because of any real quality she had but because she was pretty much the only girl he knew. He was socially dysfunctional and naturally became emotionally attached to Megan. It was amusing and a little bit irritating at first but eventually she began to see the advantages of having him wrapped and ready to serve.

When she told him she needed his help to "take care of Justin" he still believed he had free will and refused to take part in her plan, then immediately caved when she slipped out of her top. They kissed and groped for less than a minute before Denton ended things prematurely. He was embarrassed and Megan assured him it was okay. As long as he helped her out, she would never tell anyone and promised him the next time would be much better. He not only agreed to help but also to keep their "cousin thing" a secret. No one else could know.

Megan called Justin, told him she was reconsidering, and they should meet to discuss their future family plans. She picked him up after football practice and drove to a secluded wooded area outside of town. They walked through the trees for a quarter-mile, then Megan used her favorite trick again and peeled off her shirt. While Justin was distracted Denton quietly approached and whacked him on the head with an iron pry-bar. Megan ordered Denton to hit him several times until there was no doubt. She got dressed while Denton struggled to stuff the body inside a thick vinyl bag, then helped him drag it to a dark spot surrounded by dense trees. They covered the bag with leaves and branches, and Megan made sure to avoid touching the pry-bar. She instructed Denton to take the bar into the woods, walk 200 steps, then throw it as far as he could in the same direction. Using a digital camera she had borrowed from her dad, Megan took a picture of Denton walking off with the pry-bar in his hand. When he was out of sight, she uncovered the body bag, peeled it back to expose Justin's mangled head and took several more pictures. She replaced the bag and waited for her cousin to return. Denton was excited as they walked back to the car, anticipating the surprise Megan had promised if he helped her out with "the Justin thing."

In the back seat of the car they got things started. Megan knew Denton would need additional programming to keep things firmly in control. With perfect timing she stopped and explained softly that he had to swear he would never tell anyone what they had done. He readily agreed. She reminded him it was Denton, not Megan, who had killed Justin, and he would get in a lifetime of trouble if Megan told the police what happened. Denton tried to think things through but she made it extremely difficult for him to concentrate. Megan assured him everything would be fine, and he was about to get something really special, it was going to blow his mind. But he had to swear to do everything Megan told him to do, not just now but forever. Crazed and pumped with lust, Denton swore his agreement to anything and everything, and Megan gave him the experience she had promised.

Over the years she stayed connected to Denton often enough to keep him primed and ready in her toolbox, just in case. Justin's body was eventually found but the murder was never solved. Megan had the pictures and owned Denton; he would do whatever she wanted for the rest of his life.

Megan leaned back against the cinder block wall and stared at the small window in the cell door. Denton would get the money to Larry, she was certain. He'd probably try to ignore her call, tell himself he didn't have to do it. Maybe even pretend he never got the voice message. Then he'd remember, the fear would take over, and he would take the money to the lawyer and she'd get the fuck out of this cage.

Then she'd use Denton one more time to take care of that asshole in Costco who fucked everything up.

Chapter 8

Monday morning

Bob was on his knees at the chain link fence, cutting weeds the old-fashioned way with a set of hand clippers. It reminded him of middle-school summers when he mowed neighborhood lawns for spending money. It was hard work in the summer heat. Back then, everyone bagged the grass clippings which took forever. Edging the sidewalks and driveways with his dad's electric edger required constant wrestling with a tangled hundred-foot extension cord. And about every other week he'd use hand clippers and trim the grass around the bushes, trees and, worst of all, the chain link fences which were common in his neighborhood. All for five dollars a yard, not even enough to buy a new record album.

There was an electric weed wacker in his garage, but Bob only had about twenty feet of fence to clear and he didn't feel like fooling with the extension cord. As an engineer, he owed a huge thank you to the genius team that invented the cord trimmer, a tremendous improvement and time saver. But today he wanted a throw-back experience, down and dirty, assuming his knees held up for a few more minutes. He liked the swicking sound of the shears and the smell of fresh-cut grass.

"I'm clippin' it old school," he said out loud. Sometimes he cracked himself up.

A screen door slid open and shut. Through the fence Bob saw Betty walking toward him with a tall glass of iced tea in each hand. She wore a sleeveless blouse, tight white shorts, and a sly smile. Bob thought there was a little extra hip motion in her walk. *Uh-oh. Ray's away, Betty wants to play.*

"Hi Bob, how about some iced tea?"

"Hello, Betty." Bob accepted the cold drink. "Thanks very much." Every time he said hello to Betty, he remembered a chewing gum commercial years ago on television. A teenage boy teaches his kid brother the value of fresh breath by quickly chewing a stick of cinnamon gum, then greeting a cute girl with a long, sly "Helloooo Betty."

Betty was forty-something and attractive. She always dressed in flattering styles and loved to flirt. During warm weather she frequently sun-bathed in the back yard like a starlet in a classic art-deco movie poster, wearing a colorful swimsuit, floppy hat and oversize sunglasses.

Soon after moving into their new house, Betty and Ray were pleasantly surprised to learn their next-door neighbor was the famous Reversal guy. They quizzed him about his "condition" and Bob gave his usual answers. Betty seemed particularly intrigued and asked Bob a series of questions, each one more intimate than the last, until her husband intervened. It was obvious Ray had a challenge with his vivacious, super-friendly wife, and her behavior caused problems in their marriage. Bob was determined not to become one of them and tried to avoid being alone with her. Betty, however, engaged with Bob at every opportunity.

She's just being friendly, offering the old man next door a cold drink on a hot day. What could possibly go wrong?

The tea was sweet, cold, and hit the spot. As Bob lowered his glass, he saw the top two buttons of Betty's blouse were open. He quickly raised his head but it was too late. Betty seemed pleased he had noticed.

"I'm impressed you're able to work so hard at your age, how do you stay so fit and spry?" She knew all about the Reversal, but this was how it always went between them.

"Good clean living, I guess." He took another swig of tea. "And I try to stay out of trouble." Bob never missed a chance to remind Betty of this.

"Right. Hey, isn't it your birthday? Happy birthday!" She touched his arm, beaming.

She really is cute. "Thank you. Actually, it was Saturday." He shifted on his feet, knowing what was next.

"I'm sorry, Bob, but I can't remember. How old are you now?"

"I turned ninety-one," Bob said. *Wait for it, here it comes…*

"Wow, that's great! And how old are you really? I mean, with the new thing, how does that work?"

"I am also fifty-seven years old." *Today, as a matter of fact.*

Betty nodded as though she now remembered, her eyes bright. "That's terrific, congratulations. How do you feel? I mean, physically?"

Bob's Internal Warning System engaged. "Great, actually. Better every day." It was true, he did.

Betty glanced down at the grass for a couple of seconds, a clear invitation for Bob to enjoy her open blouse. He declined the offer, looked over her shoulder and studied the roof of Betty's house. After she raised her head, Bob dropped his to meet her gaze. Her smile thinned a little. *She's going to raise the stakes now.*

"Bob, I was wondering. Does everything, you know, work right? I mean, still…work? I mean…you know what I mean?"

Helloooo Betty! Okay, that's enough. "Betty, are you asking me if I can still get it up?"

She flushed, then recovered. Standing straight, she needlessly brushed hair back from her face. "Yes, I want to know if you can still get it up. I'm guessing there aren't too many ninety-one-year-old men who can still enjoy raising their flag. And maybe that's okay, since they might not know what to do if they did, you know?" Betty's smile returned.

Bob decided it was time to end the dance. "Yes, it works fine. One of the perks of my condition, I guess." He handed her the glass. "Thanks for the birthday wishes, and thanks for the iced tea. I've got to get back to my weeds. Say hello to Ray for me when he calls."

Goodbyyyye Betty! Bob walked back to the fence and picked up the clippers. He was a little juiced by the conversation but overall thought he handled it pretty well. Maybe mentioning Ray would remind Betty of her priorities.

Bob dropped to his knees and picked up the clippers, his mind circling back to Betty's remark about "knowing what to do with it." The last time he had sex with Linda—Bob allowed himself to round off the math this time—was more than twenty years ago, before she got sick. A long time. It wasn't like he never thought about sex—of course he did—but it was just a pleasant mental diversion and not a physical thing at all. Apparently, his body had not yet grown young enough to trigger those urges: he simply wasn't horny. He knew that sooner or later, assuming the Reversal trends continued, the idea of re-engaging in sex was going to come up—so to speak.

As he resumed clipping the grass, Bob allowed himself a brief moment of fantasy triggered by the image of Betty's open blouse, then pushed it out of his mind. Betty was a mature, sexy woman with a dangerously fun personality. She had flirted with him before and Bob now expected it, but nothing was ever going to happen. Another man's wife was definitely off limits. Privately he might occasionally enjoy the view, otherwise he took great care not to encourage Betty in any way. He was determined to remain a friend and a gentleman.

Bob pulled a clump of long grass away from the fence with one hand. His vision shifted dark, then cleared—

—*Bobby clipped the grass and tossed it behind him. He was kneeling next to the chain-link fence, the Bermuda grass etching crisscross patterns on his bare knees. A door slammed shut, and he turned toward the neighbor's back yard, sweat dripping from his nose.*

Mrs. Lindon walked from the garage door to the flower boxes that surrounded the patio, carrying a small caddy of garden tools. Bobby watched as she set the caddy down and dropped a folded beach towel on the ground. Facing away from Bobby she knelt on the towel, picked up a hand rake and bent over the flowers.

Bobby froze, mesmerized. Mrs. Lindon's butt bounced as she worked, her green shorts stretched tight. He couldn't look away and felt a stirring in his crotch. He stayed in grass-clipping position, ready to quickly pretend to be working if she turned around, but she kept digging in the flowers. She was humming a tune and seemed oblivious to Bobby, only ten yards behind her and staring intently.

Finishing with the first box, Mrs. Lindon stood and moved the towel to the left to work on the next. She dropped again to her knees, providing Bobby with a perfect side view. He was flabbergasted to see most of her breast jiggling as she moved, exposed through the loose arm hole of her blouse. She wasn't wearing a bra! He must have made some kind of sound as she turned her head towards him and raised up, still on her knees. He quickly dropped his head and started clipping, his heart pounding.

"Hi, Bobby. Whatcha up to?"

He looked up as if he just saw her. "Hi, Mrs. Lindon. Dad wants me to trim and cut the back yard today." Had she seen him looking at her?

Mrs. Linden smiled. "Does he pay you for helping with the yard work? I see you cut the grass every week, it can't be much fun."

He wanted to stand up to relieve the stress on his knees and in his groin but didn't dare. "Yeah, I get an allowance." Bobby wiped his face with his sleeve, keeping his other hand with the clippers down, covering his crotch.

Mrs. Linden shifted around to face him. Her yellow top was low-cut and Bobby could see the line between her breasts. "You cut grass for some of the neighbors too, right?"

He could see her nipples through her shirt! "Uh, yeah, I cut Mr. Taliaferro's lawn, and the one next to his, for Mrs. Wicker. Dad lets me use our mower." He could barely speak.

"Well, that's great! I get tired of doing all the yard chores, Charlie works all the time and he's never in the mood to do the grass. Maybe you could mow our lawn too? I'll pay you, of course. How much do you charge?"

"They pay me five dollars, and that includes edging the sidewalks. Sometimes I clip the grass along the house and fences, too."

Mrs. Lindon wiped her forehead with her wrist, her breasts swaying with the motion. "Sounds like a bargain if you ask me. Can you start next week?"

"Sure," Bobby said.

"Great! Thank you," Mrs. Linden said and turned back to the flower box. Bobby dropped the clippers, stood, and hurried to the patio door. He needed to get to the bathroom fast. As he slid the door closed, he turned *for one more look. Mrs. Lindon stretched, reaching for a weed—*

—his vision blurred, then cleared and Bob stared at Betty's ass as she picked up the nozzle end of a garden hose. Feeling woozy, Bob kept his focus on Betty, who glanced at him with a satisfied expression before turning and dragging the hose to the shrubs on the far side of the yard. The dizziness faded, replaced with an intense feeling of sadness. Bob realized Betty was a damaged soul, she'd been deeply affected by something that happened a long time ago. He was sad for her, for what happened then and for how she felt about herself now. He wanted to help. Betty needed attention, to feel worthy. She needed...something. He couldn't quite get it.

The emotions faded and Bob was weak and disoriented. He dropped the clippers and screwed his palms into his eyes, trying to adjust his head back to a sense of normal. He got to his feet, grabbed the bucket of grass clippings and the shears, and walked slowly to the far side of his house and the garage door.

"Bye, Bob!" Betty waved. "Talk to you later!"

Bob half-waved back and kept moving. As soon as he was out of sight, he dropped everything and collapsed on the grass. He leaned back against the house, a confusing mix of memories, images and emotions swirling for his attention.

Betty. He had great empathy for her. There was a reason for the way she acted. Bob was certain she knew Ray loved her and hated to leave her alone. But when Ray was gone, Betty slipped into another place. She changed...she needed...it nagged at Bob but he was overwhelmed and had to let it go.

It happened again! He'd had another flashback, second time in three days. He was clipping grass *here*, then in a flash he was *there*, as a kid, clipping grass in the yard next to...

Ho-ly cow. Mrs. Lindon!

At thirteen, Bob had only recently discovered girls were different and interesting. He developed a crush on his next-door neighbor just from watching her get in and out of her car and working around the yard. Gena Lindon was the first woman Bobby liked. She was pretty, had really great curves, and made him feel all screwy inside.

Bobby's encounter with Mrs. Lindon that day stuck in his mind for a quite a while. Eventually his crush faded as he grew older and became interested in other girls. The last time Bob thought of Mrs. Lindon and that special morning was several years earlier, when he read in the newspaper she had died.

Like the flashback in Costco, he now had two separate memories of the same event. The distant, original version when he was a teenager, alongside the fresh emotions and images from the incredibly vivid experience of a few minutes earlier. Bob was flushed and excited, like a thirteen-year-old boy dazzled by an erotic experience.

After a few minutes Bob was able to force his thoughts away from today's sexy, high-def encounter and focus on the original, pubescent memory of seeing Mrs. Lindon that hot summer day. He recalled three specific images from the old memory, the only mental snapshots one would expect a boy of thirteen to retain: Mrs. Lindon's butt bouncing as she worked, her half-naked breast, and her nipples showing through her blouse. All three images were permanently etched, as the cliché went, still retrievable from his mental filing cabinet.

Until today, Bob had no recollection of his conversation with Mrs. Lindon. As he cycled through both memory versions, he remembered he had cut the Lindon's grass every week for the rest of the summer. Each time he mowed their lawn he had taken his time and lingered, hoping for another Close Encounter but it never happened again.

"This is fucking nuts!" he said to himself, wondering if he was cracking up. Two weird flashbacks, two days apart. If they were going to continue, he'd like to make a request: *Let's have more like the Gena Lindon experience and skip the pecker-caught-in-zipper episodes. Okay?*

Feeling almost normal even though he was talking to himself, Bob put the shears away, dumped the grass clippings and got a glass of ice water. He rested on the wicker couch on the patio and let his mind drift through it all again. Betty was still outside, watering bushes on the far side of the yard. Bob had a feeling something ugly was going to happen if she didn't keep herself under control until Ray returned home.

Chapter 9

Monday evening

Bob was on deck in the only open checkout lane, patiently waiting behind a slow, elderly woman who was patiently waiting for a slower, more elderly clerk to finish scanning and bagging her groceries.

To his right, two young Target employees hovered near the self-check stations, primed to quickly assist anyone who needed help doing the thing they were supposed to do by themselves. Bob never used self-check, reasoning he often *shopped* at the store, but he didn't *work* at the store. Plus, he had tons of free time. Decades, really. Still, waiting in line at the grocery store was a massive waste of TELs, his Time-Energy-Life units.

Bob loaded a couple of items onto the conveyor belt and noticed Fred, Valued Target Associate, was struggling with the scanner. He slowly rotated each item back and forth on the sensor, seeking the Holy Beep before dropping it into the flimsy plastic bag.

Since he had time, Bob's analytical mind quickly tackled the problem and at least three solutions came to him immediately.

The two chatty Katy's occupying space at the Self-Check Monitoring Control Center remained oblivious to the bottleneck at Checkout Station Number Two.

Bob remembered his first real job as salesclerk and stock boy at a large drug store during his sophomore year of high school, seventy-something years ago. Mr. Hall, the store manager, drilled a single, simple message into the mush-minds of all the young employees: the customer comes first.

"Happy and satisfied customers mean sales and profits and paychecks for everyone. If you insist on whistling while you work, you better make sure it's a popular tune that will improve the customer's mood and increase the number of items they purchase."

An empty bag slipped out of Fred's hands and floated to the floor a few feet away. Bob watched as the nice old guy got down on both knees, snagged the bag, then started a slow and apparently painful process of getting back on his feet. Bob was about to thumb the calendar app on his phone to time how many days it would take to pay for his groceries and get home when he received a call: JONATHAN. His nephew-in-law.

Bob sent the call to voice mail as the Ancient One loaded the last bag into the lady's cart. This was the signal for the woman to initiate the payment process. She slipped her purse from her shoulder, unsnapped it, and pulled out a clutch. She put the purse back on her shoulder, unsnapped the clutch and pulled out a checkbook.

She started to unsling her purse again to get a pen, so Bob tapped open the calendar app and noted both the time and the day. Fred sprang into action, and proudly pulled a pen from his apron pocket and handed it to the woman.

Bob watched her write the check using big, loopy cursive letters, then carefully tear it off and hand it to Fred who, somehow, knew just what to do. Fred ran the check through a different scanner, was rewarded with a Beep, then handed the check back to the lady along with her receipt. Naturally this surprised and confused her, and Fred patiently explained things were different now, checks weren't handled like they were back in the good old days. Bob checked his phone: still Monday.

In an impressive display of perfect slacker timing, Katy Number One rushed over, took the cart from Mrs. Elderly and offered to walk her to the parking lot. Bob shook his head and continued transferring items to the belt. Fred greeted him with a raspy and hearty, "Hello there, young fella! Sorry for the wait."

Bob, probably twenty years senior to the nice old guy, chuckled and said, "Hello, Fred. Didn't mind at all. Take your time."

Chapter 10

Tuesday morning

Bob woke to the smell of something burning and the sound of the doorbell ringing incessantly. Someone was yelling and violently pounding at the door.

The digital clock on the nightstand displayed 1:13 am. His room wasn't filled with run-for-your-life smoke, so he put on a pair of shorts and tennis shoes—he was already wearing a T-shirt—and hurried to open the front door. Betty stood on the porch in pajamas and a robe, gasping and upset.

"Thank God! I thought I was going to have to break in—your house is on fire!" She pointed toward the driveway and Bob stepped out into the front yard.

The garage door was on fire near the upper right corner, flames licking up toward the roof and spreading to the side wall. Pieces of glass lay scattered on the driveway near the door.

"Holy shit!" Bob ran to the opposite side of the house. He grabbed the nozzle of the garden hose and cranked the faucet full open. Betty caught up with him.

"Call nine-one-one!" Bob yelled, and Betty rushed back toward her house.

Bob frantically yanked the hose across the front yard to the driveway. Glancing up the street, he saw a black pickup truck parked at the curb, facing his way. It looked familiar but he couldn't tell if anyone was inside.

Lights came on across the street, and Terry Garcia stepped out holding a phone to his ear. "I'm calling the fire department!" Betty stopped going for her door and rushed to the near side of her house for her own garden hose.

Bob sprayed water at the flames, which had consumed the upper half of the garage door and spread to the gable and roof. The smoke and steam made it impossible to see if they were making any real impact with the hoses, and Bob was relieved to hear sirens and feel the rumble of a fire truck. The first firefighter who jumped out immediately ran to Bob and Betty and ushered them across the street to Garcia's driveway. Bob looked up the street as two more fire engines arrived.

The pickup truck was gone.

* * *

Bob's heart was pounding. He was fully charged, adrenaline spiking from the excitement. Flames of anger crackled in his mind as he realized he could have lost his home. The two emotions somehow seemed to cancel each other, and he remained calm, surveying the damage to his house and the fire hoses snaking across his lawn and driveway. A familiar engineering response kicked in, and Bob began mentally organizing the logistics and details of the restoration project that loomed ahead.

Standing nearby, Betty was no longer crying and mostly calm. They stood in his yard near the street while the fire crews finished up, making sure the flames were out, opening up windows and setting up fans to clear the smoky air from the inside of the house and the garage. Several neighbors clustered nearby, many had already offered their sympathies and support.

A white SUV with Springburg Fire Department markings pulled up, followed by a police cruiser. Bob recognized the police officer from the Costco incident, Detective Marco Bent.

"Detective, how awful to see you again," Bob said.

"Hello, Mr. Dodd. Sorry to see you again too." They shook hands, and Bob introduced Betty.

The detective introduced Fire Marshal Jim Martinez, who was all business. "Mr. Dodd, I'm sorry this happened but glad no one was hurt, or worse. The engine crew notified me when they found the broken bottle in the driveway. It looks like someone threw a Molotov at your home. We'll be here for a while gathering evidence, but it's safe now, you all can wait inside or outside as you like." Martinez walked off toward the driveway.

"Let's talk out back on the patio," Bob suggested, feeling an urge to get out of sight from his neighbors. He led Betty and Detective Bent around the far side of the house and through the screen door to his patio. Despite the heat and muggy air Betty started shivering and Bob went inside to get her a light blanket. She wrapped herself up on the wicker couch and Detective Bent asked her to describe what had happened.

"I was asleep on the couch in the living room, and some kind of noise woke me up. I looked outside and saw flames at the front of Bob's house. I put on my robe and shoes and ran to wake him up."

"Did you see anyone?" Bent asked.

Betty shook her head. "No."

Bent turned to Bob. "Mr. Dodd, can you think of anyone who

might have reason to cause you trouble? I mean, besides the woman from Costco, obviously. She's still in custody. Her name is Megan Jensen, and we'll check out her friends and relatives, but anyone else come to mind?"

"Maybe," Bob said. "There was a party Saturday night, across the street."

Detective Bent nodded. "I'm familiar with the Anderson boys, we've been called to their house several times over the last few years."

Bob described the black truck damaging his lawn, still parked there the next morning. How the sprinklers had soaked the cab through the open window and how angry the driver became. Knowing his small-minded act of revenge might have led to the fire, Bob admitted he intentionally started the sprinklers as payback for trenching his yard.

Bent grinned as he wrote in his notebook. "I'd have done the same if I was you, Mr. Dodd. But if I was me and not you, I would have impounded his truck and arrested him for reckless endangerment and damage to private property. Good for you."

Bob told Bent about seeing a black truck parked up the street before the fire department arrived. "I can't say for sure it's the same truck, but I can give you the license number of the one that parked on my lawn."

Bent was impressed with the cell phone pictures and Bob explained the one-man neighborhood watch program he started after his mailbox had been damaged twice before during Anderson parties. The detective thanked them both and left to confer with Fire Marshal Martinez.

"Betty, thank you for waking me up. I might have lost the whole house, or not been able to get out. I owe you, big time! Are you feeling better?"

Betty nodded and shrugged off the blanket. She was wearing dark blue satin pajamas and slippers, now wet and dirty.

"I'm glad you're okay, and that the damage wasn't worse. When Ray is gone I don't like to sleep in bed alone, I watch TV and usually fall asleep on the couch. Guess that was lucky tonight, I might not have heard the noise back in the bedroom. Will you make me a cup of tea please?"

"Sure, it's the least I can do."

He handed her the mug and she thanked him. Bob sat in the deck chair across from the couch and watched Betty remove her slippers, fold her legs up on the couch and lean back against the corner cushions. Her satin pajamas rustled as she tucked her bare feet under the blanket. She sipped her tea and peered over the cup at Bob.

"You know, Betty, it occurs to me that for a fearless early-morning fire-fighter, you are not wearing appropriate flame-retardant clothing."

"You say the sexiest things, Bob. How are you still single?" She shifted, more rustling, impossible for him not to notice.

"Are you worried about the driver of the black truck coming back and doing something else?" she asked.

He was but didn't think anything would happen right away. It seemed certain it had been Purple Tee in the truck, watching the fire he had started. The Andersons had not returned from vacation yet, and since it was all quiet at their house, Bob assumed the boys were partying elsewhere for a change. Although, if there had been a party with the street full of cars and kids, maybe no one would have started the fire.

Fire Marshal Martinez approached from the side yard and stepped into the patio. "Mr. Dodd, we're wrapping things up. It's kind of interesting, someone tossed a modified Molotov cocktail at your house."

Bob stood up. "Modified?"

"Yes, sir, but in a good way, maybe by accident. It looks like the bottle was mostly empty, very little alcohol. My guess is the firebug drank it all first and then was too inebriated to know what he or she was doing, or maybe they just weren't too bright. They stuffed a rag in the bottle, lit it on fire and launched it. We think there was only a small amount of high-proof rum remaining, so the initial flames didn't spread far. I know you have enough damage as it is, but it would have been much worse if the person had thrown the usual version, a full bottle or one filled with gasoline. It's possible he or she wasn't intent on doing maximum damage, but that would be really unusual. People who set fires this way usually enjoy the flames, the bigger the better."

He noticed Martinez was careful to say he or she, but Bob was sure the driver of the black pickup started the fire. Using an empty bottle seemed to fit Purple Tee's profile. *What a fidiot!*

"It's okay to stay in the house now," Martinez said, "although I recommend you keep the windows open and the fans going to let it air out. And we tore out what's left of the garage door and cleared the driveway so you can back your vehicle out. It wasn't damaged, just dirty. We'll be in touch, let us know if you have any questions." He shook hands with Bob and tipped his helmet to Betty.

"I'm going to thank the fire crews, be right back," Bob said.

"I'll be right here," Betty said. More rustling of satin as she stretched out her legs. "Waiting for you."

Bob walked around to the front yard, Betty's words echoing in his mind. Maybe he could borrow an extinguisher from one of the firefighters.

Chapter 11

Tuesday morning

It was nearly 3:30 when Bob thanked the last of the first responders and went back inside the house. Betty was in the kitchen, putting her mug in the dishwasher. His Internal Warning System lit up: the top two buttons of Betty's pajama top were unfastened.

She must be clothing-challenged or something. No smile this time, she looks worried.

"What's wrong?" he asked.

"I'm scared. What if the black truck comes back?"

Bob shook his head. "Doubt it. Too much activity around this place. Plus, he knows I'll be watching for him."

She moved close to him, her hands clasped together at her chest, a clear signal she wanted his arms around her. The IWS fired off another alert and shifted to Level Two, but his instinct to comply was strong and seemed legitimate given all they had been through. He put one arm around her in a side hug and she snuggled tight against him. Her hair smelled of citrus tinged with smoke. Physically holding Betty sparked a cluster of awkward sensations and memories, and the image of Gena Lindon bending over her flowers flashed in his mind.

Betty wrapped her arms around his waist and pulled him closer. "May I stay here the rest of the night?"

Bob initiated Defense Protocol 2-B, gently pushed her to arm's length, and said nothing.

"Ray," she said with a sigh. "I know you two have talked. He loves me so much, and I haven't made it easy for him. He probably asked you to keep an eye on me, right?"

"Yes."

"When he's away I always have trouble sleeping. It's so late now—I mean early, there's no way I can be alone, knowing someone tried to burn down your house."

Someone tried to burn down my house. It was a slap of reality, a reminder the situation had actually been quite dangerous. He had already shifted into "Handle It" mode, identifying problems, sorting options, and compiling a mental list of stuff to do. There would be hassles with insurance, the tear-out and reconstruction project, and living in Contractor Hell over the next several weeks. But Betty was right: someone tried to burn down his house, maybe even kill him. He'd have to get a better grip on things.

"May I sleep here?" Betty asked. "On your couch? I promise not to…do anything."

Did she just push out her lower lip? Bob remembered the deep, emotional damage he sensed in Betty after the weird flashback at the fence yesterday. Something ugly happened to her a long time ago. He resisted the urge to figure out what, how, and why. Now was not the time. Betty gazed at him with pretty brown eyes, waiting for his answer.

"You're right, Ray and I have talked," Bob said. "He knows what a lucky man he is, and he worries about leaving you alone too many times, for too long. He loves you, and I know he wants to find another job and spend more time at home.

"But you need to know, right up front, now and forever: there's no way I would ever do anything with another man's wife. Not going to happen. Do you understand?"

Betty let go and took a step back. One hand fidgeted with a button on her pajama top, automatically drawing his attention there. Bob wondered if she even realized she was doing it.

"Ray thinks very highly of you, Bob. I do too." She sounded serious now, and sad. "And I admit I have a problem, have for a long time now. There were…things, a long time ago, and I know I haven't really been right since. Ray is sweet, and I love him, and love being married to him. But when he's gone, I start feeling…you know, that I need something. I get lonely, and scared, and I need to be with someone."

Bob turned to get a glass of water from the tap, stalling for time. He could feel Betty watching him. He took a long drink, then another. *Bob, you old fool. What have you gotten yourself into?*

He was standing in his kitchen, somewhat sleep-deprived but still jacked up from fighting the fire. Three feet away, his attractive next-door neighbor, in sexy satin pajamas with cleavage on display, had just asked if she could sleep over so she wouldn't be scared, pretty please?

It was another Molotov cocktail, this one loaded with high-octane rocket fuel. Bob sucked in a deep breath. The air smelled of toasted roof shingles. *Stay strong, be firm.*

"Betty, you can stay for a while, you can use the guest room, the bed is already made up. But it's been a long night, we both need some sleep. And only sleep, understand?"

Betty nodded with a tight-lipped smile, as though she knew all along nothing physical was going to happen but had to make her play anyway. "Goodnight hug?" she opened her arms.

"Uh, sure." Bob counted one-Mississippi, two-Mississippi and stepped back. "Thank you again, Betty. You saved me, and my home." He led her to the guest room, then went back to the kitchen to start a pot of coffee. There was no way he was going to fall asleep with Betty in the house.

He might, however, go over that flashback thing with Mrs. Lindon again. Slowly, and in great detail.

Chapter 12

Wednesday afternoon

Jack was just about to call to check on Bob when he spotted him walking through the door of the restaurant. "Good morning, sunshine!" Jack said, reaching out to shake hands as Bob slid into the opposite side of the red leather booth. "Glad you could make it."

"Sorry I'm late," Bob said. He looked tired and Jack noticed a slight, musky odor.

"You take up cigarettes, Bob? Smoke some weed? You smell."

Bob shook his head. "Had a fire at the house early yesterday morning."

"Holy crap!" Jack stared at Bob, his eye wide. "What happened? How bad was it?"

"Actually, not too bad, thanks to Betty," Bob said. "She heard noise, saw the flames and ran over to wake me up. I did some good with a garden hose until the fire department showed up."

Both men looked up as a girl approached wearing a dark red apron over black shirt and pants. "Welcome to Hell!" she said, slightly too cheerful. "My name is Esmeralda, and I'll be tormenting you today. What can I get you to drink? And are you ready to order?"

Hell's Grill and Bar was one of their favorite lunch spots, specializing in gourmet cheeseburgers flame-broiled over the Eternal Fires of Damnation. Bob ordered the Brimstone Guacamole burger and Jack chose a Diablo Double with jalapenos. All burgers came with a side of crispy fries and a small packet of two chewable antacid tablets.

"So, what in hell happened?" Jack asked. "Pun intended, by the way."

Bob described the broken bottle on the driveway and the black pickup truck parked up the street.

"You think it was the same truck you irrigated last weekend?"

Bob shrugged. "Seems likely. It looked the same, but it was too dark to tell for sure. I couldn't see anyone inside."

Jack took a slug of iced tea and thought of all the questions he wanted to ask. *How did it feel watching your house burn? Why did you go for the garden hose instead of running inside to save something valuable? What happens after the fire is out? Do the fire crews leave, or do they stay and help clean up? What did the police say?*

"What was Betty wearing?" Jack asked. He'd met her and Ray at Bob's Super Bowl party a year and a half earlier. Betty was stunning and a tremendous flirt.

"The fire marshal said things could have been worse. I'm just glad my SUV wasn't damaged. Thanks for asking," Bob said.

"Yeah, sorry, you said the garage and roof are burned, right? Glad it's not too bad. Seriously, what was she wearing? Lingerie? What color? It must have been a huge distraction, having a super-hot woman watch you wrangle your hose while your house goes up in flames. How'd you pull it off?"

Bob grinned. "Karl is at the house now starting the tear-out and figuring out the restoration plan." Bob made an exaggerated show of reaching for his tea and taking a long, slow drink. "He says he'll give me a cost estimate by the end of the day."

Jack kept still and waited.

Bob laughed. "All right! She was wearing a white robe over blue satin pajamas."

"Pajamas? What, like a onesie? With footies?"

"Your mind does not work in mysterious ways, Jack. No footies. Adult, satin pajamas. And soft leather slippers, which were ruined. I plan to buy her a new pair."

"Satin, huh?" Jack conjured the image. Betty was a fine-looking woman no matter what she was wearing. He shook his head to reboot. "What did you say about the garage?"

"The garage door is a large piece of toast. The fire guys tore most of it away so I could back my SUV out. Inside the garage there's damage to the ceiling near the front, and quite a lot to the roof above."

"Seriously, that sucks. You must have really pissed off that kid."

"I don't really know if it was him. But get this." He told Jack the fire marshal's theory about the half-assed Molotov cocktail.

"What a fidiot!" Jack said. He had adopted Bob's favorite abbreviation soon after they became friends. "Lucky for you, though. What happens next?"

"I'm waiting to hear from the police and fire department about the investigation. They are tracking down the owner of the truck from the license tag picture I took, and trying to get fingerprints from the bottle glass too. Hopefully, he was too shit-faced to wear gloves and they can identify him."

Jack leaned forward. "Let's get back to business, eh buddy? How did you thank Betty for saving your life? I mean, you owe her big time. Right?" He grinned, knowing this would make his friend uncomfortable.

Bob took his time chewing his burger. "Well, after the police and fire left, I invited her in and made her a cup of tea. I thanked her, gave her a big hug and slipped her robe off. I picked her up— almost dropped her, that satin is slippery—threw her on the bed and ravaged her the only way an old fossil can: poorly, but with great enthusiasm."

Jack's eyebrow shot up. "Really!"

Bob laughed. "No, you ass! You know me better than that. I thanked her and let her sleep in the guest room. Betty and Ray are my friends, I would never do anything with a married woman, much less one who lives next door, and much, much less with the wife of a friend. Ray has a real challenge living with her and he handles it pretty well, I think. Better than I would."

Jack agreed with everything Bob had said. He liked to joke around but both men mostly shared the same values. Jack was more interested in eventually finding a companion and having some adult fun, but he figured as time went on and Bob got younger, he'd eventually do the same.

Bob frowned. "There's something else I wanted to tell—" He glanced at his phone. "This might be someone calling about the fire. Hello? Sure, just a second."

Bob nodded to Jack and left to talk outside. Jack munched on a french fry and imagined Betty in satin lingerie, aiming a giant water hose at a raging fire.

Chapter 13

Wednesday afternoon

"Okay, Detective Bent, go ahead."

"Mr. Dodd, we've been working closely with the fire department investigating what happened at your home. We were unable to obtain any useful fingerprints from the glass bottle fragments, but the official cause of the fire will be listed as arson for your insurance claim. You'll be notified by email when the final report is available.

"From the license tag you provided we determined the owner of the pickup truck is Denton Rafter, forty-six. He lives in the Flatwater neighborhood, north of town. My partner, Detective Robinson, met with Mr. Rafter this morning at MetalWorks, a machine shop of which he is co-owner. He confirmed the truck is registered in his name but is used by his son, Denton Junior. Rafter said the kid didn't come home last night and he didn't know where he was. He said his son frequently stays out all night, partying with his friends."

"Big surprise," Bob said dryly.

"Mr. Rafter told us where Denton Junior works, and had

nothing else to say, even got a little hostile when pressed for more information. Robinson headed straight to the grocery store where the kid bags groceries and spoke with him about twenty minutes ago. Junior said he was out all night by himself, driving his truck around, and didn't feel like going home. Said he slept in his truck in a parking lot downtown but couldn't remember which one. Robinson asked for permission to look inside the truck and the kid refused. We'll try to get a search warrant, but it's doubtful we'll find anything now. It's pretty clear Junior had been tipped off by his father. The kid seemed to know what not to say."

"Sounds like a scene from *Law and Order*," Bob said.

"Excuse me?"

"Nothing, sorry. Go on, Detective."

"Okay. Well, here's the thing. Both Rafters are well known to the PD. Denton Senior has a record of a dozen incidents and crimes over the last decade, domestic disturbances, violent altercations in bars, destroyed a guy's car with a baseball bat, that kind of thing. He's been linked to others suspected of being involved in small-time drug operations in counties down south, but nothing definitive has popped yet. He's actually stayed out of trouble the last couple of years. Denton Junior has a teenager's version of his old man's record, lots of fights, some vandalism, two shoplifting charges, behavior problems in school."

"Setting my house on fire kind of fits, doesn't it?" Bob asked.

"Correct. My partner also said Junior seemed a little off, sort of mentally slow or something, he wasn't sure. The kid said all the right things in an automatic manner, like he was used to receiving and carrying out specific instructions, but he didn't come across as very bright."

Bent paused before continuing. "Off the record, my guess is there's not a lot of hugs and tickle fights at the Rafter house.

Junior's father probably keeps him in line when he's home. Denton Senior told our detective his wife ran off when the boy was little, the kid has never known his mother. We're checking into her but haven't found anything yet."

"Okay," Bob said. "Anything else?"

"Yeah, get this: The woman trying to grab the little girl in Costco, Megan Jensen? She and Denton Rafter are cousins. Her father and his mother were brother and sister."

Bob stared at the cars in the parking lot. Two separate, nasty encounters with fidiots who turn out to be related? What were the odds?

"Still there Mr. Dodd?"

"Still here. That's pretty interesting, Detective."

"Watch your ass, Mr. Dodd. Stay sharp, keep your head on a swivel, and toss in your own favorite cliché about staying safe. The Rafters are not high-quality individuals, and you know all about Megan Jensen. There may be more trouble. I'll let you know if we learn anything else, feel free to call me if you have any questions or something else happens."

"Will do. Thank you." As Bob ended the call, he noticed the icon for an unplayed voice message: JONATHAN. He ignored it again and headed back inside. Jack had finished his burger and upgraded his iced tea to a beer.

"That was the police with an update," Bob said. Just to irritate Jack, he took a bite of his burger.

"So? What did you find out?" Jack asked.

"You said I should watch my back with Purple Tee. You were right."

"Yeah? Well, if an old fart had soaked the front seat of my truck when I was that age, I would have been pretty motivated to get some payback. Wouldn't burn his house down though. What

66

else?"

Bob summarized what he learned from Detective Bent.

Jack whistled. "So, the mother-faking witch who shops for kids at Costco and the incompetent, purple firebug are second cousins? Hope they're not romantically involved too."

"Not second cousins," Bob said. "First cousins, once removed."

"You're such an engineer. Bet you have to fight the ladies off with your slide rule."

"I need to talk to you about something else, too." Bob gestured to their server to order himself a beer.

Chapter 14

Wednesday afternoon

Megan knew the drill. She placed her hands high against the cement wall and spread her feet wide as the guards came into the cell, weapons drawn. She grunted as the first cop slammed her flat against the wall, keeping his hand firmly around the back of her throat while his partner examined the unconscious woman lying twisted and bleeding on the floor.

Megan hissed like an angry Siamese cat and gritted her teeth. This would make things worse, but not by much. Her cellmate had slept off the drugs that landed her in jail and woke up grumpy and chatty, an annoying combination. Megan warned her to shut up, but the bitch started hassling her, asking where she got her pretty clothes and touching her hair. Megan violently knocked her arm away and ducked when Grumpy took a swing at her. Megan dropped her to the floor with one punch in the mouth, then kicked her in the head and put her back to sleep.

From past experience, she knew the security cameras would prove Megan finished the fight but hadn't started it. It might complicate her situation, but things could still work out okay. If, that is, her idiot cousin had followed her instructions. And if Larry the lawyer showed up and posted bail. After three days, though, it looked like Denton had blown her off, a huge mistake. When she got out of this shithole she was going to enjoy reminding him who actually had possession of his balls.

She would have to call Larry herself, but the guards at the jail couldn't care less. She had her one call to Denton on Sunday, but it was unlikely they would let her use the phone again, especially after today. Megan knew she had rights and was supposed to be able to make additional phone calls and contact her attorney, but she also knew the shit-for-brains jail cops weren't going to be diligent about following the rules for a prisoner charged with attempted child snatching. The cops might get annoyed if her crack legal team filed a lawsuit alleging prisoner mistreatment, but everyone involved would know Megan would never win in court.

Paramedics arrived and stopped the bleeding, then loaded the sleepy crack whore onto a gurney and wheeled her away. The guard gave Megan a violent shove and she fell to the floor, banging her back painfully on the metal bench attached to the wall. She glared as the guard showed her his teeth while backing out of the cell. The steel door clanged shut, upgrading Megan's room from a double to a single.

To get the fuck out she would have to come up with another plan. In the meantime, she would entertain herself by dreaming up something special for that pair of assholes, Cousin Denny and the Costco buttinski.

Chapter 15

Wednesday afternoon

Even though it was ninety degrees and felt warmer, DJ took his afternoon break sitting in his truck at the far end of the lot where Mr. Jezek insisted the employees park. He had eaten his lunch and had another ten minutes before going back on the clock. The rest of his shift would be spent bagging and loading groceries into big-ass Cadillacs and Town Cars parked crookedly in the blue spots close to the store by wrinkled geezers who could barely see over the steering wheel.

He tossed the flashlight back and forth in his hands, wondering when his father would discover it was missing. He'd be royally pissed, might even punch another hole in the wall, especially if DJ wasn't around. Then again, his dad might not come home for a while. Sometimes he'd be gone for two or three days "on business." DJ loved being at home when his father was away. He'd drink beer and play video games for hours, Buster sleeping on his lap. But after taking the flashlight he couldn't chance going home tonight. He'd have to find somewhere to sleep until he figured out exactly what he wanted to do.

A Fortune of Reversal

Hope Dadhole won't take it out on Buster. DJ studied his face in the rearview mirror and rubbed his cheek. It was still purple but the swelling had gone down. His father, the fuck-wad chicken shit, had beat him awake that morning. *For eating his leftover fucking pizza.*

* * *

DJ got home Tuesday morning sometime after three am, seriously buzzed and pissed the fire hadn't been larger. He didn't understand. He'd poked the rag into the rum bottle and lit it with a match just like the Internet video. He threw it at the house and ran back to his truck. DJ laughed at the old guy and some woman scrambling around with a water hose, but the flames should have been a lot bigger. When the sirens sounded close, he got the hell out of there.

Starving when he got home, DJ ate the leftover pizza he found on the kitchen table and crashed on the couch in the living room. The next thing he knew his father was screaming and pounding on his head with one of DJ's boots, cussing him out for eating his breakfast. Buster barked constantly during the attack but stayed across the room, knowing not to get too close. DJ curled up and covered his head with his arms until his father wore himself out. He didn't move until the door slammed and he heard his dad's truck spin out of the driveway. He sat on the couch for a moment, hating himself.

His father kept beating on him because DJ never fought back. Until he figured out another place where he and Buster could stay, he'd just have to take it. But the day was coming soon...

Payback's a bitch, old man. You'll see. DJ cleaned himself up and hustled to work. When he got home late after his shift, his father was already asleep in his bedroom.

When he woke this morning, DJ was relieved he and Buster had the house to themselves. His father was probably already at work. He showered, careful to keep the streaming water from hitting his bruised face, then dressed for work. Passing by the door to his father's bedroom he paused, then turned the knob and stepped inside. Buster whimpered but stayed in the hallway.

DJ hadn't been in his dad's room since the beating he received several years ago for snooping around. Now, he didn't give a shit. After rifling through the closet and the dresser, DJ found the flashlight in the top drawer of the nightstand. He balanced it on his palm for a moment, then stuffed it into his back pocket and headed off to work.

* * *

DJ looked across the parking lot and watched a green POS El Dorado creep into one of the handicapped parking spots. He turned on the flashlight, aiming it at the floor mats. The light was not very bright. He flicked it off and on, wondering why it was so special. Sometimes Dad carried it around the house, occasionally out to his truck, but DJ never saw him turn it on and use it for light, even when the electricity was off.

I don't get it. He beats the shit out of me with my own boot one morning, then calls to tell me the cops are coming the next. What the fuck?

DJ jumped at the sound of a car horn. Danny had parked two spots over and got out wearing his store apron. He waved to DJ and pointed at his watch. DJ nodded and put the flashlight in the glove compartment.

He took his time walking across the lot. He thought he'd

handled the cop's questions pretty well, but how did they know so quick to talk to him? Someone must have seen his truck, maybe got the tag number. He should have left after starting the fire, but he'd wanted to watch the house burn. He didn't have much of an alibi, but the cop didn't arrest him, they probably didn't know too much yet.

On his way to work he'd made a quick side trip to the old fart's house to check out the damage. He hoped it had burned to the ground, but only part of the garage and the roof above was damaged. It could probably be fixed in just a couple of weeks. Some construction guy was already there working on it. The sprinkler asshole deserved a lot more pain than that.

I'm gonna have to fuck him up.

Chapter 16

Wednesday afternoon

Jack waited patiently as Bob ordered a beer and then pretended to be engrossed with something on his phone. He knew his friend was playing with him, drawing it out to get his goat dander up. It's what two old men did when they each had under-performing senses of humor and too much time on their hands. Jack wouldn't give Bob the satisfaction. He had his own beer to drink and nothing else to do the entire afternoon. He'd wait him out.

He lasted twenty seconds before leaning forward and opening his eye as wide as possible. "Well? We're waiting!" Jack bellowed, overacting enough to turn a dozen heads their way.

Bob cringed, then apologetically shrugged to the other diners. "Okay! Well played, sir. Let's see: Ted Knight, at the end of Caddyshack, right?"

Jack grinned, enjoying the moment. "Judge Smails, actually."

"Right," Bob said. "Well, speaking of blasts from the past, I haven't told you everything that happened at Costco."

"Really? Shoot."

Jack listened intently as Bob described his weird flashback

experience during the confrontation with Megan Jensen. He interrupted only once, laughing at the image of Bob as a third grader running through the hall with his willy caught in his zipper. After an irritated glare from Bob, Jack pulled it together and urged his friend to continue. Bob told him how juking around the girl in the hall solved the problem, and when he turned around he was back in Costco, watching "Jasmine" trying to squirm away from Megan.

"The eyes of the Costco kid were some kind of trigger? Made you flash back to grade school where you saw the eyes of the girl in the hallway?"

"Yeah, but it didn't really match, not at the start," Bob said. "I've gone over this a lot. Here's how it went: Jasmine—I mean Macy—was struggling, and her eyes got big and scared, then I was in the boy's room at school and, you know, had my little accident. When I looked back at the girl's eyes in the hallway I zapped back to Costco and was looking at Macy's eyes again."

Jack thought for a moment. He had nothing. "What do you think this was?"

"I don't know. But get this: it happened again on Monday."

"What?"

"This one was a little different. You'll find it a little more, uh, interesting."

"More interesting than snagging your dongle in your zipper?" Jack asked.

"Yeah. I'll tell you, but keep quiet until I'm done, okay?"

Jack nodded. "Sure, go ahead."

Bob described the incident in the backyard. Jack did his best not to react to Betty offering Bob a cold drink with an open blouse. Bob continued with full details. Clipping the grass along the fence, then flashing back to his youth. The encounter with Mrs.

Lindon, then returning to the present and realizing he was staring at Betty's backside as she watered the shrubs.

Bob finished and reached for his beer.

"That's incredible!" Jack said, not knowing what else to say. Bob nodded and excused himself to the men's room.

Jack's first thought was Bob might be experiencing some form of dementia. That wouldn't be unusual for a ninety-one-year-old man, but what about a ninety-one-year-old man who was biologically fifty-seven? Was it some kind of twisted Jedi mind-trick brought on by stress? That fit the scene at Costco for sure, but flirty talk with Betty over iced tea didn't sound stressful at all, just titillating.

Bob slid into the booth. "Well, what do you think? Am I a crazy old man?"

"Yes," Jack answered without hesitation. "You're old and definitely crazy. But let's try to stay on topic, okay? Let me get this straight: you were using the grass shears at the chain link fence, and that was the first thing you saw in the flashback?"

"Yes."

"And at the end you were watching Mrs. Lindon bend over, and when you flashed back—I mean forward—to the present you were staring at Betty's, uh, asset?"

"Yes." Both men grinned. Jack surprised himself by quickly getting back on point.

"And in the Costco incident, you were looking at the eyes of the girl in school, and when you returned to Costco you were locked onto Macy's eyes?"

"I see what you're getting at," Bob said. "The flashback exit and return images matched during both incidents."

"Yeah, but I don't have any idea what it means."

Bob was quiet for a moment, then said, "Just before the first flashback I did see the girl's eyes, but back in school the first thing I saw was the boy's restroom. Matching images at the end but not at the beginning. In the backyard episode, the images matched both going and coming back: first, clipping grass along the fence, then at the end, similar views of Mrs. Lindon and Betty." Bob's face turned slightly pink.

Jack ignored his friend's embarrassment. "So, similar but different between the two experiences," Jack said. "I got nothing, have to noodle on this some more. Anything else?"

Bob nodded. "One more thing. I now have two distinct memories of each flashback experience. The original, fuzzy old memory without all the detail, and a new, high-def memory where I can still feel and remember the entire full-body experience. Right now, it is easy for me to recall either memory, old or new, of each flashback. They both seem accurate and real, but the recent ones are much easier to process and relive."

"I've never heard of anything like this, Bob."

"Me neither. But thanks for listening, it was good to talk it out."

They both sat still for a moment, pondering. Jack tossed back the last of his beer. "I'm assuming with the fire and all that's happened, there's no way you're going to join me on the trip to California?"

"I'd like to go, Jack, but I need to be around while the house is getting repaired. I'll have to postpone my trip next week to KMF in Albuquerque too. They won't be happy. Plus, I promised Ray I'd look after Betty."

"Be careful with that last one, buddy, but I understand. No worries." Jack picked up the tab and waved off Bob. "I'll get lunch this time since you provided the entertainment. But we're not done with this. Next time I expect a full report on what happened next between you and the fabulous Mrs. Lindon."

* * *

Before getting into his SUV, Bob fished his phone out of his pocket and selected a number from the favorites list. As expected, it rolled straight to voice mail.

"Hi Marley, it's Bob. Oh, right, your phone already told you it's me. Sorry, old habit by an old hobbit. And now I'm wasting your time apologizing. Anyway, I need you and your wizard skills for a new project."

Chapter 17

Wednesday afternoon

Marley leaned back against the soft vinyl couch in Mooncups, her feet on the edge of a coffee table, her knees up and supporting a tablet. She held a mug of chai latte with both hands, and her eyes were closed. She was wearing wireless ear buds painted a bright royal blue to match her hair. A casual observer might think she was napping or meditating and would never suspect she was actually absorbing two independent streams of audio simultaneously: an MIT lecture on single-pulse packet transfer protocols played in one ear and electronic trance music pulsed in the other.

She glanced at her vibrating phone and let the call roll to voice mail. She'd finish her tea and the lecture before listening to Mimp's message.

Marlena Carducci developed a formidable set of life skills at a young age. The daughter of three mothers and two fathers in a successful, rare, and under-the-radar group marriage, she was raised with eight siblings in the complete opposite of a broken home. Smothered continuously with love and attention from her family, around the time she turned twelve it began to feel like too much. She craved private time and immersed herself in video games and technology and discovered she had natural abilities in mathematics, science and logic. Years later Marley came to think of herself as having been born with superlative intellectual software preinstalled at the factory.

Middle school was without challenge and boring. She applied critical thinking to her dissatisfaction with teachers and classmates and realized that learning *how* to learn was all one needed to be successful. She aced all her classes and began competing in on-line gaming contests during evenings and weekends with the full support of her parents. After winning a national gaming title at fifteen, she grew bored and began designing her own games, discovering joy in creative world-building.

Instead of starting college, she launched her own gaming company, EmCee Simulations. Two years later she sold it to a major competitor for a modest price, retaining a mammoth royalty with a ten-year, do-nothing consulting contract.

At twenty-one she learned a valuable life lesson watching an older brother recover from the loss of a leg in a construction accident. However strong your intellect and talents, you had to have an adequate supply of human resources. Perhaps even a handful of actual *friends* to deploy during a crisis, or maybe just to help you move your rack of servers from one apartment to another. This logically led to the next irritating conclusion: occasionally, Marley would have to appear to others to be a functioning and pleasant member of society even if she had to fake it nearly 100% of the time. She taught herself how to act charming, cold, helpful, indifferent, and, if necessary, evil. Whatever the situation called for.

The one person she not only tolerated but had the tiniest whiff of fondness for was Bob Dodd. *People* magazine named him the "Most Intriguing Man on the Planet" shortly after the news of his Reversal. Marley preferred the abbreviated version, Mimp.

She met him four years earlier when she was working part-time at The Electron Emporium. She didn't need the money, but it was a good opportunity to practice her social skills and she liked the employee discount for her tech supplies. Bob was shopping for a new laptop, his first in many years, and she was showing him an overwhelming variety of models and options. He asked decent questions, she gave excellent answers and they were having a flawless commercial interaction until Bob's phone rang.

It was not only too loud, it was an obnoxious ring tone. It sounded exactly like the kitchen wall telephones in those old black-and-white movies her mothers liked to watch. Marley stared as the nice old guy fished the phone out of his pocket and tried to muffle the sound with both hands, waiting for the ringing to stop. She choked back a laugh and then froze, staring at him.

"Something wrong?" he asked.

"I, uh, recognize you. You're Robert Dodd," she said, not asking.

He nodded. "Call me Bob. And you are?"

"Marley."

"Nice to meet you, Marley."

"I knew you lived around here," she said. "I was only about ten years old when you..."

"When I was the news," he said. "A long while back."

"Do you mind if I ask? How old are you? Now, I mean."

"It's fine, I'm used to it. Chronologically I'm eighty-seven, but best estimate is I am biologically about sixty-one."

Marley nodded. He was correct, she had already done the

math in her head. She remembered her whole family watching the live press conferences and television interviews when the Reversal was first made public. Her parents said it reminded them of watching the Apollo 11 moon landing in 1969. And now she was about to sell this Most Intriguing Man a laptop. First things first, though.

"You know you can send a call to voice mail immediately without letting it ring on like that, right?" Marley forced a smile. Bob shook his head. She showed him what to tap to silence the phone.

"Thank you," he said.

"Sure. And one more thing: you really need to change the ring tone. It is extraordinarily irritating. I mean, it probably is. To some people."

"Yeah, I know there are options but I don't get many calls and I just didn't care." Bob said. "But I take your point. Why don't you set me up with something else?" He handed over his phone and watched in amazement as her fingers tapped furiously.

Three seconds later Marley asked, "How's this?" The theme song for *The Twilight Zone* played at low volume.

Bob grinned. "Perfect. I'm not surprised you picked that one." He purchased the computer Marley recommended.

The next day he returned with a proposal. Bob apparently was going to be around for a long time, but knew he was technologically out of touch. He wanted to hire Marley for technical support, to be his mentor as he re-engaged with modern life. She thought it could be an interesting experience and they negotiated a deal. Bob would pay Marley a monthly retainer fee for a maximum of eight hours of anything-goes tech support, with an astronomical bonus rate for overtime. Over the next few years Marley not only taught Bob how to use his laptop, explore the Internet and update his software, she programmed his universal remote and even changed the batteries in his smoke alarms. Occasionally Bob asked her to do Internet research on various topics and she would prepare documents and presentations for his review.

The MIT lecture ended and she thumbed her phone to play Mimp's message. She tapped DELETE and picked up her tablet. Bob wanted her to check out a couple of guys named Rafter and a woman named Jensen. It shouldn't take long. Marley opened an app and tapped the client icon MIMP to initiate a work log. She started another music track and got to work.

Chapter 18

Wednesday evening

Time for another scotch and sofa on the patio. Bob sipped the single-malt and paused, holding his drink at eye level. He liked the way the beveled glass split the setting sunlight into kaleidoscopic pinks and blues.

The last several days had been an unusual mix of excitement, confusion, and stress. Toss in a couple of encounters rife with sexual tension and it was easily the most interesting week he had experienced since withdrawing from public view a few months after the Reversal. And it was only Wednesday.

Fake Momma grabbing the little girl in Costco. Reliving the painful pecker-pinching incident back in third grade. Watering Purple Tee's truck. Hello Betty flirting over the fence and sexy Mrs. Lindon weeding her flowers—Bob allowed himself to linger for a moment on that one. An asshole setting his house on fire at one o'clock in the morning, and less than two hours later Betty tempting him in his own kitchen. And according to Detective Bent of the Springburg PD, Fake Momma and Purple Tee's father were cousins.

I'll be a monkey's uncle...

Jonathan. He never listened to his nephew's voice message. He tapped his phone.

"Uh, hi, Uncle Bob. It's Jonathan. Just calling to check on you, hope all is well. Been quite a while since we talked. I think I may be heading your way in the next week or two and would love to pay you a visit. Not exactly sure when, things are kind of crazy now, but next week or the week after, I think. I'll try you again in a day or two, or call me back at your convenience. Talk to you soon."

Typical Jonathan. Kind of introverted but not crippled by it. The son of his wife's long-dead younger brother, Jonathan was Linda's only living relative and now, by extension, Bob's. He always thought of Jonathan as sort of floating through life, moving along with the current. Not in a river or even a stream, just a small pond where light breezes made tiny ripples.

Before Linda died, Bob was mostly neutral in his feelings for his nephew-in-law. Jonathan was pleasant enough, a guy who had a knack for finding jobs but never able to hold one for long. Linda maintained a distant relationship with him, exchanging calls once or twice a year, a visit every two or three, but there was no depth to it. They stayed in contact like relatives were supposed to, but there was no real affection between them.

Things changed when Linda passed. Jonathan arrived quickly and said all the right things. He helped with the arrangements and did Bob a tremendous service by taking the lead in greeting and hosting the friends and neighbors who dropped by the house after the funeral. Bob's opinion of—and affection for—Jonathan rose quite a bit that day. He had been far too devastated to act properly social and was grateful Jonathan stepped up.

Over the years Bob developed another emotion toward

Jonathan: sympathy, bordering on pity. For a unique and interesting reason.

The Reversal had a huge impact on both of their lives. When he told Jonathan he was terminally ill, it was clear that, as Bob's only living relative, Jonathan would inherit a small but life-enhancing bit of wealth: a furnished house, a vehicle, and a modest set of financial assets. Bob not only survived the cancer, but a few years later Jonathan and the entire world heard the fantastic news that he was growing younger each day. Bob knew Jonathan had never wished for him to die but human nature being what it was, he must have anticipated the windfall of inheriting Bob's estate. There was no way to fully appreciate the emotions and thoughts Jonathan must have worked through. To the younger man's credit, he continued to maintain a positive, though limited, relationship with his uncle, and Bob appreciated that Jonathan consistently tried to always do the right thing.

There also loomed a huge, ironic possibility: if current life trends continued, someday Bob was likely to be the only heir to Jonathan's estate, a complete reversal. They were probably the only two humans in history forced to deal with this unusual and emotional dynamic in their relationship.

Bob regretted ignoring Jonathan's voice message for two days, but he wasn't up to calling him back tonight. He opened the messages app on his phone.

JONATHAN THX FOR THE CALL SORRY I MISSED YOU. WILL CALL YOU BACK IN A DAY OR TWO.

Marley had taught him not to use all caps in his messages, wizard-splaining it was the texting equivalent of obnoxious loud-talking. Bob didn't care, it was easier to read. He was reasonably certain his nephew would not interpret his choice of font style as new-age digital shouting.

Chapter 19

Thursday evening

Denton stood in the doorway, gawking at the mess in his bedroom. The contents of his closet and dresser were strewn around the room. Magazines, ancient VHS cassettes, beer bottles, shoes, socks and underwear—some clean, some dirty—littered the floor, the bed, and the furniture. Even his favorite (and only) book, *Scarface,* had been flung across the room to the floor, the paperback cover partially ripped and folded over, now a scar itself. Nothing else in the house was disturbed, but someone had tossed his room.

Junior. Son of a bitch!

Denton opened the drawer of the nightstand. Empty. He swore and kicked the nightstand, gashing a large hole in the wall behind. He picked up a beer bottle and hurled it across the room. It missed the window by inches but left another dent in the wall. Denton sat on the bed, stared at the floor and waited for his mind to clear. He had to think this out, the kid had lost his fucking mind.

DJ knew better. Three years earlier he had caught his son

checking out several porn magazines from the adult (and only) section of Denton's library in the closet. Denton made sure the kid knew the bedroom was off limits; Junior missed two days of school recovering from his father's "lecture," and never set foot in the bedroom again.

Until now. Something had changed. *What the hell was happening?* Denton's gut was tight. He went to the kitchen and pulled a beer from the fridge. He'd planned to get the cash from the flashlight and meet with Larry about posting Megan's bail. Thinking about her made him tense up again. He went outside and walked around the backyard, trying not to panic.

Megan's normal state was "pissed" when everything was running smoothly, by now she'd be at a record high level of ape-shit furious. She'd consider Denton's failure to immediately post bail a colossal fuck-up. The truth was he didn't even know she was in jail until Monday afternoon, when he stopped for lunch halfway to Casstown and noticed the unplayed voice message. His balls got small and tight as he listened to Megan yelling her instructions. It was too late by then to drive back and get the cash to Larry, so he continued on to Casstown. Megan would be maxed-out angry, but one more day in jail wasn't going to change that. Unfortunately, one day turned into three.

Denton got home Monday night sometime after eleven, ate most of a pizza, and decided to field test a sample he brought back with him from Casstown. The next two days were the usual fuzzy mix of screwy memories and large gaps in time. He knew he'd had a fight with Junior—yesterday? the day before?—over something stupid, he couldn't remember what but it was the kid's fault. Then a cop showed up at work—yesterday?—wanting to talk to him. Denton thought he really screwed the pooch this time, but he held it together and was relieved the cop only asked about DJ and his stupid truck. Denton was still pissed at Junior for…something, and he almost blew off letting him know the police were on their way. Eventually a tiny, irreducible amount of parental instinct sparked and Denton sent his son a text, warning him not to say anything to the cop.

Father of the Fucking Year!

Denton chugged the rest of the beer and threw the can into the neighbor's yard. He had to get the flashlight back and teach his dumb-ass son another lesson. This time the hard way.

Chapter 20

Thursday evening

Betty pulled the last two bags of groceries from the back seat of her car and hip-checked the door closed. She jumped as a royal blue Mini Cooper zipped into Bob's driveway and parked at an angle to avoid the pile of reconstruction debris.

A slender young woman with short hair matching the color of her car got out carrying a pizza box and dangling a six-pack of soda. The girl noticed Betty and tossed her head back in greeting.

"Sup?" Without waiting for a reply, the girl went to Bob's front door and banged on it with her elbow. Bob let her in and waved at Betty before going back inside.

Betty carried the bags to the kitchen, leaned over the sink and peered outside, trying to see inside Bob's house through his living room window. She'd seen the girl before, some kind of techie support person Bob had hired to teach him how to use his computer or DVR or something. Her name was Marty, or Mac, some kind of stupid nickname.

It had been a while since Betty had seen the little blue car in Bob's driveway. What was she doing here now, bringing pizza in those tight, shredded blue jeans? And her hideous blue hair? That was something new, and irritating.

Bob must have purchased the deluxe extended-service option with his tech support plan. She frowned, uncomfortable with her thoughts, and started putting the groceries away. After dumping a can of stew into a pan to heat, she poured a glass of white wine and carried it to the full-length mirror at the end of the hallway. She twisted around, taking inventory.

The thin green top hung perfectly over her white stretch pants. Betty worked hard to look good and it paid off. Ray often told her how hot she was. No doubt, every guy she met enjoyed the view. Like the kid at the store with the ugly bruise on his face. He was definitely checking her out as he bagged her groceries. She'd flashed him a sexy smile as she left, knowing it would make his day. Betty turned heads everywhere she went. She even caught Bob, the most decent man she had ever known, staring at her ass the other morning while she was watering the bushes. He seemed mesmerized, with a strange, turned-on expression on his face. She'd seen that look on other men but never Bob. From the way he rushed off he must have been embarrassed, but she hadn't minded at all. It proved Bob thought she was attractive, even though he turned her down the next morning after the fire.

So why was he having dinner with the blue pixie? Betty would have been more than happy to be his companion for the evening. All he had to do was ask.

Chapter 21

Thursday evening

"What's with the pile of burned trash on the driveway? Did you lose control of your weenie roast?" Marley poured two glasses of soda.

Bob pulled plates from a cabinet. "Did you say, 'weenie roast'? I didn't think your kind used language like that."

"What do you mean, 'your kind'?"

"You know, high-functioning geek-nerds. Or is it nerd-geeks? Have you ever been to a weenie roast? Or anything at all involving an actual weenie?"

"Careful, Mimp, or I'll roast yours." It would have been an unusual conversation for any other ninety-one-year-old man and twenty-four-year-old woman, but for Bob and Marley it was perfectly normal. They carried their dinner into the living room and Bob sat carefully in his recliner. Marley plopped down cross-legged on the couch without spilling her drink as only a young, fit person could. "Seriously, Bob, what happened?"

"Let's watch the show and eat first, then I'll fill you in," Bob said.

Marley took a bite of pepperoni pizza and gestured at the frozen television picture of four people sitting in a booth in a restaurant.

"*Seinfeld* again? Seems like you're watching that every time I come over. Don't you ever get tired of that show?"

Bob shook his head and swallowed a bite. "Nope, love this show. Lots of life lessons wrapped up in goofiness. What's not to like?"

"What episode is this? The one where they sit in a diner and talk?"

"Funny." Bob picked up the DVD case and read the back. "This is episode twenty-two of season five, *The Opposite*. George tries doing the opposite of his normal instincts to improve his luck and his life."

"Cool."

They watched half of the show while they ate, then Bob paused the video. Marley listened intently as Bob told her about the incident at Costco, his encounter with Purple Tee, and the fire. He didn't mention the flashbacks.

"The police are still investigating but get this: Detective Bent told me the Rafter kid and Megan Jensen are related. I called you to get the rest of the story."

Marley nodded. "Yeah, I can confirm that. Denton Rafter, Senior, is first-cousin to outstanding citizen Megan Jensen." Marley handed Bob her phone showing pictures of both when they were teenagers. Megan had a bold, almost cocky expression. Denton's face suggested a complete lack of confidence despite his rugged good looks, a striking combination. "Their adventures go all the way back to high school, where creepy rumors floated around that they were a bit more than kissing cousins."

Bob handed back the phone. "You mean—"

"No, Megan is not Junior's mother. More on that in a minute. OK, first, in order of appearance, Megan. She was extremely social in high school but quite a disruptive force: drinking on campus, vandalism, lots of fighting. As a sophomore she became involved with a football stud named Justin, and records indicate she became a little bit pregnant soon after. She took care of it, then—"

"Wait," Bob interrupted. "What records? How did you get all this stuff from, what, twenty-five years ago?"

Marley gave him a sly grin and shrugged. "I'm good at what I do. There are tons of juicy digital bits of information on everyone if you know how and where to search. And I have, uh, let's call it 'special access' to sources that are mostly off the normal grid."

"You mean like the black web?" Bob asked.

Marley laughed. "Dark web. Yeah, like that. There's another level too, sometimes called the invisible web, but I'd have to terminate your 'live forever' plan if I told you more."

"Okay, please continue. Megan got pregnant?"

"Yeah, but she took advantage of a free clinic and moved on. Around this same time Justin goes missing for several months, then is discovered decomposing in the woods outside of town. Blunt-force trauma. The murder was never solved."

"Holy cow!" Bob said. "Was Megan considered a suspect?"

"No, she was questioned but not implicated. Her history goes mostly quiet for a while, but I'll come back to her. Next up is Denton Rafter, Senior, same school and class as Megan. As mentioned, they were very close, and Megan was the dominant personality of the pair. Denton was less than a remarkable student, school records indicate he passed all his classes but he doesn't show up anywhere else, he's not even in the yearbooks except for one standard student picture his freshman year."

Bob nodded. "In my day we called guys like that 'nons'. No personality."

"That fits," Marley said. "Anyway, both cousins graduate from high school but neither goes to college. Megan vanishes and Denton gets married a couple of years later to Anna Bellamy, who grew up in Casstown. Denton Junior is born just three months later. The marriage didn't last long as Anna literally disappears shortly after Little Denny turns two. Big Denny files a missing person report, police investigate and can't find her. There is no further reference to Anna Bellamy Rafter anywhere, ever. A judge grants Denton a divorce three years later. Denton raises Junior by himself and doesn't become romantically involved with anyone else, except for occasional one-night parties with strippers. He does become criminally involved with other unsavory characters."

Marley summarized Denton's criminal record, matching the information Detective Bent provided to Bob the day before.

"Where's Megan during all that?" Bob asked.

"Unclear. There's a big gap in her history, then eight years ago she pops up in Oregon, charged with reckless endangerment as an employee of a child day-care center. Charges for her were dropped, but the owners of the day care were convicted of child molestation and are guests of the federal penitentiary now and forever. Megan probably flipped and cut a deal, but those records are sealed, quite effectively too. She moved back to this area soon after, then there's nothing else officially on Miss Megan, until you two bonded over snow tires in Costco last weekend."

"Nothing official. Unofficially?" Bob knew there had to be more.

Marley took a drink of soda and continued. "Megan is connected to some really nasty assholes involved in drugs and human trafficking. I don't think she is directly involved, at least not yet. My theory is she'd like to be a player and was trying to work her way in. Grabbing that kid in Costco might have been her ticket to the show, Bob. You did a good thing."

It was Bob's turn to shrug. "Right time, right place."

Marley went on. "Phone records indicate since she moved back from Oregon, Megan and Denton talk and text frequently, but they both avoid social media completely."

Bob frowned. "You have access to phone records too?" He didn't want Marley to get into trouble.

"Relax, it's all good. Remember I told you I have other clients?"

Over the last few years Marley had hinted her 'other clients' likely included high-level government agencies. She was an impressive and talented young woman. Bob realized he should not be surprised by the extensive information she had compiled.

"At least tell me this," Bob said. "Is it legal for you to access all of this information?"

Marley made a point of picking up a piece of pizza crust from her plate and pretended to answer with her mouth full, garbling her response.

Okay, I get it. "Marley, you use your skills for good and never evil, right?"

"Of course," she said flatly. "Assuming, that is, your requests for my services are for good and never evil, right?"

"Touché," Bob said. "What about Junior?"

She finished off her soda and showed Bob her phone again. Denton Junior was a larger, meaner version of his father. "He was the easiest to dig into, thanks to the web and social media. Even if a kid never logs on to the Internet, there's nothing you can't find out about him. Denton Junior—he goes by DJ—graduated last year. Barely, like his teachers gave him passing grades in core subjects just to avoid having him in their class again. He ran with a bunch of delinquent kids and got in a lot of trouble. The notes from his high school counselor indicate she believed DJ had a serious learning disability, a sociopathic personality disorder, or both. The word 'slow' pops up a lot, also 'not bright.' He was well below the norm in every category. Sports wasn't a good fit either; he was kicked off the football team after crippling the back-up quarterback in a practice scrimmage. If you're tangling with him, Mimp, you may want to have a couple of contingency plans. He might tear you apart and solve your 'going to live forever' problem."

"Right," Bob agreed. "Solid advice. Anything else?"

"Yes. Detective Bent probably mentioned Denton the Elder's ties to drug operations? He's correct, but I doubt the local PD knows the whole story. Even Denton may not know exactly what he's mixed up in. He coordinates a lot of small and medium-size drug deliveries, collects money, takes his cut, and passes it up the chain. His primary supply source is a large organization headquartered in the town of Edgar, up north. Denton's distribution operation is a lot smaller, centered in Casstown to the south and includes the surrounding three counties. I checked out the Edgar gang. They're the real deal, connected all the way up the chain to a huge and nasty South American cartel. Serious, big-boy stuff. So far, Denton's managed to stay mostly under the radar of both the law and the cartel, but I wonder if he really knows who he's dancing with."

Bob nodded and let that soak in. He carried their plates to the kitchen, refilled their drinks and returned to the living room.

"Marley, great work, as always. I really appreciate all the info, helps me understand who I'm dealing with. Thank you."

"Sure, Mimp, that's what you pay me for, right?" Marley

grinned. "You still have a couple of hours credit for this month, anything else you need?"

Bob thought for a second. "Yes, you can replace the ink cartridges in the printer in my office, but let's watch the rest of *Seinfeld* first. I want to see how the 'opposite' thing works out for George."

Chapter 22

Thursday evening

Betty was pouring a second glass of wine when her phone rang: RAY. He had already called early that morning to say he loved her and ask about her plans for the day. No doubt this time he was checking up on her. What time was it in Germany, the middle of the night? Early the next morning? He must have set an alarm to wake up and call her now. *He doesn't trust me at all.* Of course, she'd given Ray many reasons why he shouldn't. It was her own fault. She stared at the phone, not wanting to answer, then reached for it just as it rolled to voice mail.

Let him worry. Serves him right for being half a world away.

She looked through the kitchen window again, the little blue car was still parked in Bob's driveway. What kind of sleazy 'tech support' took an hour and a half? The kid must be giving Bob what he paid for. Where were they doing it? His bedroom? The couch in the living room? The kitchen? Maybe the exact spot where Bob rejected her after the fire?

He prefers the techie chick over me? She walked around the kitchen island three times, then forced herself to stop and calm

99

down.

Her cell phone dinged; Ray had left a voice message. Her husband was a good man, she had put him through a lot and he still loved and cared for her. She remembered the agreement they had reached in the therapist's office: if she ever decided to physically stray from the marriage, she had to tell Ray first. There were a handful of times when she had considered it, but the challenge of admitting what she wanted to do always made her back down, ashamed. The shame frequently made her feel miserable but kept their marriage intact for several years now.

She realized she forgot her promise to talk to Ray before trying to seduce Bob in his kitchen. She told herself it was okay, she'd been distracted, stressed out by the fire. No harm, no foul. Betty knew she was lucky to be married to a great guy and living next door to another. Bob was a good friend and a high-quality person. It was a delicious challenge, trying to entice such an ethical man.

The truth was she wasn't as good as Ray or Bob. She needed more. In a private session with her therapist years ago, they discussed the old mantra "just be yourself." The therapist explained that approach usually failed because most people don't know themselves well enough to understand who they truly are.

Betty knew who she was: a bad person, morally flawed and defective. Admitting it meant she had courage, right? Acknowledging the worst about yourself—wasn't that a good thing? She reached for the bottle of Pinot Grigio to pour another glass, then put it in the refrigerator instead. It wasn't too late to go out and have a drink someplace where a girl could get a little attention. She promised herself she would be good, just some harmless flirting for fun. Nothing more.

She walked to the bedroom and into the giant closet. She needed to change into the perfect outfit.

Chapter 23

Thursday evening

George Costanza's opposite strategy actually worked. By taking Jerry's advice and ignoring his natural instincts, he started dating an attractive woman, stood up to a couple of loudmouths in a movie theater, and by the end of the episode had scored a dream job working for the New York Yankees.

Bob loaded the plates into the dishwasher while Marley headed to his office to update the laptop software and replace the ink cartridges in the printer. Light flashed across the living room window and Bob looked outside. A black pickup truck had stopped in the street, angled toward his house. Daylight was fading and he couldn't see anyone in the truck, but Bob knew it was DJ Rafter.

"Marley? I'm going out front for a minute. Stay inside, please."

He stepped outside and was not at all surprised to hear Marley following a few steps behind. She stopped on the porch as Bob walked across the yard and stood near the sidewalk. He stuck his hands in his pockets and stared at the truck parked twenty yards away, engine idling.

A half-minute passed. Bob raised one arm, gesturing *your move, asshole.* Five seconds passed before the truck lurched and accelerated, heading straight for Bob.

Bob tensed but stood his ground, ready to jump. The truck reached the edge of the driveway and skidded to a stop a few feet short of the brick mailbox. Bob still could not see through the tinted windshield but could feel the driver staring at him. His mind flashed to Dennis Weaver doing battle with a maniacal semi-truck driver in *Duel,* an early Spielberg movie from decades earlier.

The engine revved twice, the truck slammed into gear and lurched forward into the mailbox, broken bricks flying into the yard and street. Bob flinched at the impact but willed his feet to stay planted.

"What the fuck?" Marley yelled. Bob turned to tell her to call nine-one-one, but she was already on it. He spun back to face the truck, idling deep and loud over the demolished mailbox, the chrome balls swinging wildly from the rear trailer hitch.

Bob's heart was pounding. It was time to settle this. He was afraid but he controlled the fear, a child ordered to stay inside while the grownups dealt with the situation. He waited, arms at his side.

The engine shut off and Junior got out. Bob almost laughed; the kid was wearing the same purple T-shirt. He was just as large as he was on Sunday morning, too. Junior walked forward and stopped a few yards away. Bob hoped Marley had called for backup or at least dialed a nine and a one and was ready to tap another.

Okay, whatever this is, let's get on with it.

"Hello, Denton. What are you doing here?" Bob was impressed how calm he sounded, the fear still contained for the moment.

If Junior was surprised Bob knew his name, he gave no sign. He stared at Bob without expression, fists clenching and unclenching at his side, then turned to admire the damaged garage and roof with a satisfied smirk.

Bob noticed a large bruise on the side of the kid's face. It nearly matched the color of his shirt. "Why are you here?" he asked.

No response.

"You threw the fire bottle at my house, didn't you?"

Junior spoke slowly, his voice deep. "You...got my...truck...wet."

He sounds just like Lurch. Bob wondered why his brain wanted to play around with old movie and television memories at a time like this. "You tore up my grass! Look," Bob said, pointing.

DJ looked and said nothing.

"You set fire to my house, and now you've destroyed my mailbox." Bob's voice wavered on the last word. He was suddenly aware he was confronting a huge, angry young man and completely overmatched. Confused, he tried to take a step back but somehow moved forward instead.

Junior looked surprised and quickly stepped back, then seemed to remember who he was and stopped, drawing himself up to his full height of six-feet two large. Bob held his ground, feeling more like ninety-one than fifty-seven.

Junior frowned, squinted, and raised a hand to rub his bruised face. Bob's vision fogged, turned gray—*Not now!*—then cleared—

—*and Troy towered over him, running a huge hand through his greasy hair. With his other hand the giant bully held Bobby a foot off the ground by his jacket collar. Hot tears ran down Bobby's face as he looked past Troy's huge head and spotted his kite, rapidly shrinking as it sailed away, the broken white string trailing behind like a second tail, long and useless.*

It was the first time he'd been able to get his kite launched by himself without help from Mom or Dad. He was proud and excited, he decided to go for it and let out nearly the entire reel of string. The kite flew higher than ever, tugging so fiercely on the line Bobby had to hold the reel with both hands.

He was concentrating hard and didn't hear Troy walking on the sidewalk. Troy was big, bad, and seventeen, with a long history of terrifying kids and adults in the neighborhood. Troy walked right in front of Bobby and into the kite string. It broke with a twang and Bobby's arms slammed down against his legs as the tension disappeared. Bobby yelled in frustration and glared up at Troy, more angry than afraid. Without thinking he threw the empty reel and it bounced off the bully's stomach. Troy laughed and grabbed Bobby's jacket with one hand and hoisted him up in the air.

Troy brushed his hair back with his other hand before grabbing more of Bobby's jacket and using both hands to raise him up to eye level. He laughed again, his face breaking into a wide, scary clown smile. The pain of losing his high-flying kite was larger than his fear, and Bobby's anger bloomed into full-blown fury. He jerked and squirmed and managed to kick Troy in the knee, and with a violent twist he fell free. He scrambled to his feet and screamed.

"You asshole!" It was the first time he had used that word.

On impulse Bobby sprinted off, not just to get away from Troy but to try to catch the kite string. He heard Troy yelling and chasing after him. He ran as fast as he could and kept running even after he realized he would never catch the string, he couldn't even see the kite now, it was gone. Bobby ran until his legs burned and he was out of breath. He tripped and threw his arms out in front of him —

—and Bob swung his fist and punched Junior hard in the throat. Junior staggered back, coughing and holding his neck, trying to breathe. Bob was dizzy. He bent over and put his hands on his knees, trying to catch his breath while keeping his eyes on Junior.

Bob's mind reeled as it was suddenly processing input from multiple data streams. Raw, fresh emotions of fear and anger from tangling with Troy and the loss of his kite. His legs wobbled with exhaustion from running. A voice behind him, Marley, telling someone Bob's house number and street. His face hurt, and he realized he was bleeding from the knuckles on his right hand. He must have been fighting with Junior, but he didn't remember anything except connecting with the throat punch.

The swirl of thoughts and feelings were suddenly displaced by a new rush of intense emotions, not his own. They surged into his brain, flooding his mind with sensations too violent and quick to comprehend. He was forced to drink from an emotional fire hose, an overwhelming stream of unfamiliar consciousness. Gradually Bob was able to focus all his mental energy on the task of simply absorbing the huge flow of information. After a few seconds of great effort, he realized he could throttle back the rate and more easily process the rushing inputs. His mind parsed the data into myriad small packets until some critical threshold was reached and the swirling mix neatly coalesced into a complete sense of understanding and perfect clarity.

The kid's name was DJ, he hated being called Denton or Denny or Junior. He was mad, the old guy had punched him in the throat, and it hurt. How the hell did that happen? DJ was confused, and...damaged. Depressed. Angry, but in a sad way. His father hit him too, way worse than the old man just did. DJ loved and hated his father, who attacked him while he was asleep, hitting him in the face with his own boot. He curled up and his father kept pounding on him—

Steve Moore

Bob staggered back until Marley caught him and steadied him on his feet. Another source flow began, not as intense but thick with emotion. Marley. She was shaken, upset. Pissed at Bob for being an idiot and confronting the giant asshole. He could have been seriously injured, or…worse. She was ashamed, she should have helped during the fight but had been paralyzed, transfixed. Mimp just jumped right into it, taking several punches and landing a few of his own. Especially the last one, very impressive. And all she did was call for help. Totally pathetic...

The external wave of information began to fade and Bob's own thoughts bubbled up through the thick slurry of Marley's and DJ's emotions. His face was sore, and his hand hurt like hell. DJ was staring at Bob with wild eyes.

Bob's mind cleared and he knew exactly what to do. "DJ, I'm sorry I hit you. I'm sorry about your dad hitting you, too. That sucks. It shouldn't happen, ever."

DJ blinked but didn't move. *He's an abused boy in a man's body.*

"It's okay, now. I understand." Bob stuck both hands in his pockets, there would be no more fighting. "Your dad is a shithead, DJ, but you're going to be okay. You know that, right?"

DJ's eyes teared up and he quickly wiped them with his hands, then turned away toward the street. Bob and Marley watched as the boy worked to figure things out. It took less than a minute. DJ turned and walked to his truck, the driver's door still open. He leaned into the cab as police sirens sounded in the distance. Bob and Marley shared a glance. Now what?

DJ pulled out of the truck, approached Bob and held out his hand. "Do you…know what this is?" he asked.

"Flashlight," Bob said.

He thrust it forward. "Here. I'm sorry I burned down your house."

106

"It's okay, DJ. You didn't burn it down, it can be fixed." Bob reached out and took the light, knowing it was important to the boy. "I'm sorry I soaked your truck. It won't happen again."

"Okay," DJ said.

"You'd better leave now, the police will be here soon."

DJ climbed into his truck and started the engine. He backed slowly over the rubble of bricks, then spun away.

Bob's legs gave out and he collapsed. Marley half-caught him and they both sat down hard on the grass. Marley put her hand on Bob's shoulder.

"Hey, Mimp? You didn't have to go to all that trouble, you know. I have a flashlight in my car you could have borrowed."

Chapter 24

Thursday evening

Betty checked her hair and makeup in the visor mirror and liked what she saw. The dark red lipstick was definitely a grabber. She locked the car and scanned the parking lot, then twisted around to see her backside in the window. She had squeezed into a pair of black jeans and wore a clingy, long-sleeved mock turtleneck the same shade of red as her lipstick. Tonight she was counting on her hair, her face, and her figure, but not her cleavage. It was ridiculously easy to get a man's attention with a low-cut top, but she wanted something different this time. Maybe a couple of drinks and conversation with an interesting guy who wouldn't be staring down her shirt the entire time.

With a start she realized she didn't need sexual attention and validation, not tonight. She was lonely and needed company.

Betty stepped through the front entrance into Hell. The bar was to the left, the dining room to the right. In between was a long hallway marked with a sign that read PURGATORY and an arrow pointing the way to the restrooms in the back.

Betty veered left into the bar and realized her black and red outfit perfectly matched the decor. She might be mistaken for one of the service staff. She headed towards the bar, picking her way through scattered tables. The walls were plastered with dozens of autographed photos of local celebrities and three movie stars who had grown up in the area. Each face had been disfigured with horns and a sharp goatee added with a fat red marker.

Three people were sitting at the bar, an old man watching a baseball game on television at the far left and a couple sharing an appetizer at the opposite end. Betty put her purse on a stool in the middle, ordered a glass of white wine and turned to survey the crowd. A handful of people gyrated to the electronic dance music in one corner, and four guys were throwing darts nearby. The rest of the people sitting at the tables seemed bored, spending their Thursday night dutifully working to create empty beer bottles.

Betty swayed on her feet and bobbed her head to the music, occasionally sipping wine and watching the crowd. One of the dart guys threw her a grin and then leaned to his friend to point out the hot new chick at the bar. She flashed a smile then coyly looked away.

A decent-looking man with rough features and thick eyebrows sat alone at a table near the wall. He was scoping her out, holding a beer near his mouth, elbow on the table. The man kept his eyes on her as he tipped the bottle just enough for a swig.

Betty fished her phone out of her purse and pretended to read a text. She sipped her wine and casually glanced around the room until the man at the table came back into view, still gazing at her over his beer. They locked eyes for a brief second, then the man dropped his head in a slight nod, drained his beer and got up from the table.

It's about time, Betty thought, tingling with excitement. She watched the dart game as the man walked up and put his hands on the bar, standing to her right between the next two barstools. Betty wondered what opening line he would use. The man ordered a beer, then turned toward her with a slightly smug expression. He said nothing, apparently waiting for her to speak first.

What kind of move is this? Betty shifted on her feet and tried to stay calm. She took a sip of wine to hide her sudden apprehension. After several uncomfortable seconds she made her decision and turned to the man with a practiced smile.

"Hi there, my name is Betty."

"Hello, Betty. I'm Denton."

Chapter 25

Friday morning

Bob slept until almost ten o'clock before being rousted by his bladder protesting vigorously. He quickly solved the problem and realized it was likely to be the easiest of the challenges he faced in the day ahead. Coffee could only help.

He dropped into his chair on the patio, already warm from the August sun. His hand hurt and his face was still tender and sore. He wished he remembered more of the fight, by all rights it should have been a massive beatdown by Kid Rafter. Marley told him he was amazingly quick, dodging punches with a speed she couldn't believe, as though Bob knew exactly what DJ was going to do right before it happened. DJ did connect with a few glancing blows to his face, and Marley said Bob managed to hit DJ in the head at least twice before the "death punch" to the throat ended the fight in less than two minutes.

The police arrived as Marley helped Bob to his feet. He was grateful she took the lead in describing the incident to the officers. He was still shaky from being somewhere and somewhen else during most of it. Bob hoped the police caught up to DJ soon, the boy needed help and to be safely away from his father.

Bob reached over and flipped on a small table fan, aiming it so the breeze would cool his face. The flashback was unsettling, but even more disturbing was the swirling mind-fuck that followed, all those images and emotions from DJ and Marley ripping through his mind. His head still didn't feel quite right, the mental shitstorm had left an impression like a thumb pressed into soft clay.

By the end of his second cup of coffee Bob felt marginally better. He chuckled, remembering telling Jack two days ago about his interesting week: Costco, flashbacks, crazy Betty. Toss in a fist fight with a kid seventy years younger, another time-bending flashback starring Troy the Bully, and a psycho-emotional mind-trip and the week had been upgraded to a full-blown clusterschtup. *The gods must be angry. Or maybe they're just jerking me around.* It was too much to process, and Bob's engineering instincts kicked in.

Define the problem. Break it down into small, manageable parts. Gather and analyze the data. Interpret and respond.

He drained his coffee and grabbed a bottle of water from the fridge. "Water on a Walk" didn't really sync with his usual "Fluids and Furniture" theme, but today it was close enough. He left his phone on the kitchen table. He didn't want any distractions as he strolled through the neighborhood.

Time for *Bob's Week in Review*. In honor of the Reversal he would tackle last things first: the kite flashback and the twisted phantasmagoria. He had been fully focused on DJ, expecting violence, then his vision went screwy and he was suspended in the air, watching Troy brush the hair back from his eyes. Just like...DJ, when he raised his hand to rub his bruised face. The match point in the two realities was the arm rising to the head.

Bobby was maybe eight years old and small enough for Troy to pick up with one humongous hand. Bob concentrated, trying to reconcile the two kite-flying memories retrieved from his mental archives. In the classic version he remembered the kite flying extra-high in the sky, then Troy walked right through the string. Bobby yelled something at Troy and raced after the kite even though he knew there was no way he would catch it.

The new memory filled in the gaps: He had thrown the reel at Troy. He managed to kick him and wriggle free. He screamed "asshole" and ran after the kite, and the big bully had chased after him. Bobby tripped but before he hit the ground, Bob was back in his front yard taking a big swing at DJ. The punch landed and DJ staggered back, gasping for air. And then, as the kids say, *shit got real*.

Almost instantly he was receiving multiple streams of overwhelming input. A kind of psychic portal had opened and for a brief time he had access to the authentic, personal essence of first DJ, then Marley. Not their thoughts, exactly, but their emotions, impressions and images had mixed with his own, creating confusion and displacing his situational awareness.

Then, as though invisible hands had silently clapped, a light blinked on and Bob knew what to do, and exactly what to say to DJ to end the confrontation. That was a new twist.

Or was it? He went over the Costco flashback again. After he returned to the present time from his nostalgic field trip back to third grade, he'd known something wasn't right. And sure enough, Megan Jensen was a mother-faking kidnapper. Bob didn't realize it at the time, but it must have been his first experience with post-flashback insight.

Let's call it PFI for short, as it was Pretty Freaking Incredible.

So, what was the PFI after the Gena Lindon episode? (Big grin.

He liked that flavor of flashback way better than the others. *Okay, Bob, back to work.)* When he returned from the titillating time-trip he was staring at Betty's backside. A short moment later he felt a great, settled sadness, a stagnant pool of dark emotion sourced from something ugly that happened to Betty a long time ago. The sensation faded quickly as Bob struggled to clear his head and comprehend what had just happened.

The PFI that morning was all emotion, feelings without substance. As he considered it now Bob realized Betty's flirtatious, risky nature, her need to be admired and desired by men, was a psychological response to emotional injuries she had suffered many years earlier.

He arrived home but kept walking, taking a second lap around the neighborhood. He was sweating from the heat but thought he was making some progress. Something strange was happening to him; three weird flashbacks in less than a week, each followed by enhanced abilities of insight relevant to the present-time situation. Somehow, he'd become a bizarre character in a spooky summer-carnival story by Rad Bradbury.

Why did he think he could stand up to DJ like that? What had possessed him? Bob realized the question might be too on-the-nose and not just a cliché. It was way out of his character to act so boldly. Hell, soaking the kid's truck Sunday morning was a radical departure from his norm. *One small step for geezers everywhere, one giant leap for Bob Dodd.*

Trying to help the little girl in Costco? That wasn't out of line, any decent person would have done the same.

He turned a corner and walked past the park near the neighborhood entrance. One of the CHUMP yard signs had been left behind on the grass near the sidewalk. DODD IS THE DEVIL. Bob knew at one time many CHUMPS believed this was true, he wondered if any still did. Frank and the others had always treated him with respect; they did not hold him responsible for his evil "condition," and even saved him from his own abduction. Quite the opposite of what one would expect from a group that once officially proclaimed Bob shouldn't even exist.

He returned home and checked his phone. Stella from the Kilmore Foundation had called to confirm his arrival on Monday for his biannual week of evaluations and tests. He'd call her back and reschedule, he needed to stay home until his house was repaired. Plus, he was worried about Betty and had promised to keep an eye on her until Ray returned. Extrapolating from the recent pattern, it seemed certain he'd be having more of those pesky time-traveling mind-seizures too. All things considered, definitely best to stay home for a while.

He heard Karl pull into the driveway with a truckload of roofing materials for the next phase of repairs. Bob decided to give him a hand and as he passed through the living room he noticed the *Seinfeld* DVD case on the coffee table. He picked it up and stared at the list of episodes on the back. He tapped a finger on the DVD case and stared out the window at nothing.

Sunday morning he'd surprised himself by turning the sprinklers on DJ's truck and enjoying a brief moment of revenge and satisfaction. Of course, this led to his house being set on fire, but still. He had stepped out of his comfort zone.

Tuesday, he went against all instincts and let Betty sleep at his house for a few hours. Nothing bad happened.

And last night he stood up to DJ, ended up exchanging punches, and arguably won the fight. He talked to the kid and defused the situation. He even scored an extra flashlight, somehow. It was the exact opposite of Bob's normal behavior, and somehow it worked out mostly all right.

Just as it had for George Costanza.

Holy cow, that's just crazy enough to work.

Grinning, Bob pulled his cell phone from his pocket, opened the email app and fired off a short note to Stella at the Foundation. He switched to the phone app and dialed a number. It went straight to voice mail.

"Jonathan? Hi, it's Uncle Bob. Sorry it took me so long to get back to you, it's been a hell of a week..."

One more call.

"Hey Jack? If the invitation to join you on your trip is still good, I have an idea..."

Chapter 26

Friday afternoon

The agent returned to his office and spread several paper towels across his desk before pulling the Reuben sandwich out of the white paper bag. He pulled a can of soda from the mini-fridge and unlocked his computer screen. He scrolled through the data and clicked on a new item, received seven minutes earlier. He read the message, took a swig of Diet Coke, and dialed a number on his phone. At the tone he recorded his message.

"This is Agent Jonesmith, access code Bravo Football one-two-two. Subject has confirmed plans for travel to New Mexico, arriving Monday, three days from now." He hung up the phone and chomped down on the Reuben.

Chapter 27

Saturday morning

Denton woke at the crack of 11:22 am, his phone vibrating with a call. It rolled to voice mail before he could grab it. It took five minutes and a supreme effort to reactivate his brain and sit up on the edge of the bed. Buster was on the floor nearby, tail thumping in anticipation of finally being let outside.

There were seven voice messages and eleven text messages. Something was fucked for sure. Denton hit the bathroom, let the dog out and pulled a Red Bull from the refrigerator. He sat at the kitchen table, read the first text message and slammed his fist on the table. He listened to the voice messages in order. All were from Brutus, his crew boss in Casstown.

Two of his distributors got mixed up in a bar fight the previous night. The responding cops searched their cars, found three undelivered packages, and arrested both of his guys. Fortunately, Brutus arrived late, saw the men being hauled off, and immediately contacted the local attorney Denton kept on retainer for exactly this kind of situation. Within an hour of being arrested Chaco and Jimmy were both reminded of the serious consequences of cooperating with law enforcement.

It had a decent chance of turning out okay for the business in the long run. Denton was fully aware of the limitations and morals of the staff when he hired them. He set up contingency plans to handle all legal and financial issues and safeguards to insure no one would talk if apprehended. In the short run it was going to be a challenge to stay on schedule with the deliveries. Denton ran a lean operation and being short two distribution "specialists" meant he and Brutus would have to run the routes themselves until they could vet and hire a couple of replacements. If not a full-blown disaster, it was definitely a giant pain in the ass.

It had been a fucked-up week. Meeting that hot chick in Hell was the only highlight, other than his solo product sampling party Tuesday night. Or was it Wednesday? He'd already been to Casstown once this week, and last night's cluster meant he'd be heading back this afternoon and probably be there several days. To top it the fuck off, his idiot son and the flashlight were still missing. DJ refused to answer or return Denton's calls on Friday, and the store manager told him DJ had called in sick. What else could happen?

Megan.

"Aw crap!" He pounded the table again. Denton forgot to call Larry and deliver the bail money. He got sidetracked trying to find DJ and get his flashlight back. Megan left the voice message on his phone last weekend, why hadn't she called again? If she'd been released, she'd be way up his ass right now. They must have her locked up nice and tight. Denton realized he didn't even know why she was in jail. He retrieved his tablet from the living room and searched the local arrest information. There she was, glaring at him from a scary mug shot.

"No fuckin' way," he muttered. He'd heard something about a woman trying to snatch a kid at Costco. That was Megan? What the hell? She'd been mixed up in nasty business before, and some of it was pretty freaky shit, but as far as he knew none of it had ever involved kids.

He scanned a local news report. A Costco customer butted in and stopped Megan from getting away with the girl. A bunch of witnesses saw Megan with the kid, pretending to be her mother. She was in the county jail with bail set, but it was a huge amount of dough. Denton took a slug of Red Bull and leaned back on the couch to think it through.

To raise enough cash for a bond he'd have to scramble and dip into two or even three different assets. It would be a major hassle getting it done on a Saturday, plus he needed to be in Casstown as soon as possible. Megan was going to have a tough time beating this rap, the authorities tended to take child kidnapping cases seriously.

Denton realized it might turn out to be a good thing he had blown her off. If he pretended he never got her message and did nothing, his crazy cousin was likely to stay locked up for a long time. He could focus on handling the Casstown bullshit, finding DJ, and getting his flashlight back.

Denton picked up his phone and deleted Megan's voice message. He found her call from Sunday in the RECENT list and deleted it too. Then he called his son and left a message.

"Listen you little shit-fucker, if you want to have any chance at all for a happy life you need to get your ass home and bring me my flashlight. Every hour I don't hear from you is going to make it so much worse. Bring it back now and maybe I'll take it easy on you, give you a chance to get your attitude back in order. We'll see. But you better call me soon, I'm running out of patience.

BRING ME MY FUCKING FLASHLIGHT!"

Denton ended the call and chugged the last of the Red Bull. Then he walked to his bedroom and started packing.

Chapter 28

Saturday afternoon

It had been a rough couple of days. The night before, DJ hung out with friends until the bars closed, then drove around town searching for a good place to park and sleep. He found a spot between two dumpsters behind a Target store.

He slept for a few hours scrunched awkwardly across the cab with his feet sticking out the window. Waking up stiff and tired of being in the truck, he decided to get out of the heat and kill a couple of hours in a movie theater. DJ was surprised to learn it was only five dollars for a ticket to the first matinee. He enjoyed the latest sequel in the *Fast and Furious* series and realized he was hungry.

DJ parked at Burger King but before going inside he opened an app on his phone. A few months earlier DJ activated the location feature on his father's mobile phone to allow "friends" to track his location. After he took his dad's flashlight, he made sure to deactivate the same feature on his own phone, even though he was pretty sure his father knew nothing about cellular device tracking.

DJ opened the app, which he had mentally renamed *Find the Asshole*. He was pleased to see Denton's phone was several miles outside of town and heading south at a fast clip. After a quick burger he'd be able to go home, check on Buster and maybe grab a shower and a nap before his father returned.

Buster was barking furiously as DJ parked on the driveway. Denton had left the dog outside without food or water, a real dick move. DJ gave his best friend fresh water and watched Buster slurp it up, making a mess on the kitchen floor.

He checked the app again, his father was close to Casstown, which meant he would be gone at least five or six hours. Time to make the call. It didn't even ring once before his father answered.

"It's about time, shithead. Where's the fucking flashlight?"

"I don't have it."

"What?"

"I had to give it to someone. I, uh, knocked down this guy's mailbox with my truck. By accident. I didn't have money to pay for it, so I gave him the light."

"You're shitting me! A flashlight for a busted mailbox? What the hell are you trying to pull?"

"Telling the truth," DJ said, not caring that his father didn't believe him. "I'll try to get it back later, when I get some money to fix the mailbox. I gave it to him so he'd know I was going to come back and make it right."

Denton was silent for a moment, then said, "I can't believe what an idiot you are. Where's this asshole live?"

"He lives across the street from the Anderson brothers. You picked me up there once, remember? When my truck wouldn't start?"

"I don't remember nothing like that. What part of town is it?"

"East side. Not too far from the store." Silence. "Dad, you still there?"

"Shut up, I'm thinking." It was almost a minute before Denton spoke.

"Okay, listen up. I'm going to be away for a few days, got some things to take care of with the business. You get that fucking light back as soon as you can, and stay home, don't go anywhere except work until I get back. When I get home we'll talk about consequences, work something out so you can make up for what you did. But if I get back and the flashlight is not there, I'm gonna make that dog of yours an orphan. Do you get what I'm telling you, son?"

"Yes, sir. I'll get the light and bring it back."

"You better. Call or text me as soon as you get it."

Denton ended the call and DJ collapsed on the couch. He had a little breathing room. His dad was at least a four-hour drive away and sounded like he might be gone for several days. He'd be able to get some rest, go back to work and figure out how to get the flashlight back. It was pretty stupid, really, giving it to the old guy after their fight. He'd been pretty fucked up and hadn't been thinking right.

DJ went to his room and lay down, then sat up again and reached for his phone. He didn't trust his dad. He set an alarm to go off every three and a half hours to remind him to check his father's location. With or without the flashlight, DJ planned to be far away by the time his father returned home.

Chapter 29

Monday afternoon

Bob walked up the short flight of steps and through the double doors of the Kilmore Medical Foundation administration building. Stella rushed over and gave Bob a hug.

"Mr. Dodd, nice to have you here again." Dr. Kilmore's assistant was beaming with affection. "I hope your trip went well?"

"You know I want you to call me Bob, Stella. Yes, trip was fine. Nice to be back."

Stella nodded. "Dr. K sends his apologies for not being here to greet you, but he's looking forward to seeing you at dinner tonight. It's planned for seven but please let me know if you would prefer a different time. Shall we?" She motioned toward the hallway where a private elevator waited, doors open.

"Seven is fine, Stella, thank you." They both knew the drill, it was his fifteenth visit to the facility. His luggage was already on the way to his room thanks to Nick, the driver who met Bob at the Albuquerque airport two hours earlier.

As he passed the reception desk, Bob gave into a small bit of vanity and glanced at the large portrait of himself on the wall. It touched off the usual mix of emotions. He hated being the center of attention in any circumstance, but fully recognized the significance of his special "condition" and the potential implications for all humans. The portrait was painted from photographs taken nearly ten years ago, and the oversized Robert S. Dodd who almost smiled down at him from the wall was clearly much older than how Bob looked today.

It struck Bob for the first time how similar his situation was to the legend of Dorian Gray. Each time he visited KMF he was younger, more vibrant, healthier. Unlike the portrait of Dorian, Bob's image inside the ornate wooden frame remained the same, frozen in time. And yet, the obvious difference between his current physical appearance and his picture on the wall sparked a mental illusion that Bob was staying the same while his portrait was actually growing older.

* * *

Shortly after the public announcement of the Reversal, Dr. Kilmore suggested Bob approve and participate in the creation of a medical research foundation, dedicated to understanding the cause of his incredible "younging" phenomenon and disseminating the findings to scientific communities and the public. The foundation would be funded by donations from thousands of investors, many of whom were philanthropic seniors seriously interested in speedy discoveries that could potentially arrest or reverse the aging process.

Bob seriously considered Kilmore's proposal. Prior to his cancer diagnosis he had managed his financial assets fairly well, but they had diminished naturally over the years. When he learned he had terminal cancer and his end-of-life care would deplete his savings, Bob realized with grim satisfaction that he might fulfill the old adage: your last check should be written to the undertaker, and it should bounce.

Then the Reversal occurred, and Bob faced the monumental challenge of potentially living another seven decades under unique and unusual circumstances, a huge life extension for which he had not planned. Eventually, Bob agreed to the foundation in principle, but the devil was in the details. He hired Harry LeRoy, a brilliant attorney specializing in estate planning, to help negotiate legal protections and financial arrangements with the founding directors of the new organization.

Details of the negotiations were leaked and published by the press. Religious groups (including the CHUMPs) filed a number of frivolous lawsuits trying to prevent the establishment of the foundation. At the same time government agencies filed lawsuits seeking to seize control of all medical research under the guise of serving the greater good. The lawsuits were consolidated and fast-tracked to the U.S. Supreme court, which promptly declined to hear the case. The ironically named Kilmore Medical Foundation—Bob was adamant his name not be used—was launched.

Harry LeRoy took excellent care of his famous client. Bob would receive an annual stipend of $500,000 (significantly reduced by taxes) and KMF agreed to pay Bob's legal expenses. In exchange Bob committed to biannual seven-day residencies at the KMF facility in New Mexico for tests and examinations. Every three years the two residencies would be combined into one extended period lasting six weeks. Arrangements were made for additional periodic tissue and fluid sampling through a local facility in Springburg; it was critical to monitor Bob's amazing physical and biological developments over time with as much data as possible. Every ten years the agreement renewed automatically unless either party requested new negotiations. These arrangements would continue until Bob "no longer existed."

(Terms such as *death* and *expiration* were avoided, as the ultimate fate of Mr. Dodd was entirely unclear. No one knew what would happen to a person who continually grew younger, but thousands of speculative fiction authors did their best to imagine a plethora of outcomes. The Reversal spawned a new literary genre: *Leaving of Age* stories.)

There was one complicated issue still to resolve: social security. Bob had been receiving monthly benefit checks since reaching his normal retirement age fifteen years earlier. The U.S. government naturally balked at the prospect of paying benefits for another seventy years. They insisted Bob's unusual circumstances meant he was not entitled to monthly benefit payments and in fact should reimburse the government for monies received since the Reversal. Harry successfully defended his client in Federal court, pointing out Bob had paid taxes into the system his entire life, and eventually a compromise agreement was reached. Bob continued to receive social security payments until he reached his "reverse" retirement age of sixty-five, then the payments stopped, forever. Harry also negotiated a special exemption: Bob would not have to pay social security taxes on future earnings as presumably he would never reach "retirement" age again. Since all of his future medical needs would be provided by KMF, Bob also agreed to withdraw permanently from the Medicare system.

* * *

Bob followed Stella into the elevator and she pushed the single blue button for the short ride to the fifth and top floor. The elevator traveled directly to his suite and the doors opened to an impressive view. Beyond floor-to-ceiling windows, low mountains sprawled under a giant blue sky dotted with clouds. The bright sunshine was muted through automatically tinted windows.

Per Bob's request the residence was designed much like a medium-priced hotel suite. The Foundation representatives had initially proposed incredibly luxurious accommodations for Bob's ultimate comfort. He quickly vetoed the plans and helped with the new design. His home away from home included a king-sized bedroom, a spacious bathroom wired for audio entertainment, a desk and computer workstation, two comfortable reading chairs, and a small kitchenette with cabinets full of snacks. There was also a wet bar stocked with Bob's favorite spirits. The walls were decorated with colorful works from local artists, a new collection installed before each visit. KMF staff treated Bob with regal respect, and it took him a while to accept the deferential service. Stella had gently explained Bob was the reason KMF existed, and all the staff were grateful to be part of such an important project, and for their employment.

Stella answered a polite knock on the hallway door. A woman and man entered, both wearing scrubs. Bob recognized Gwen, the phlebotomist.

"Mr. Dodd, how nice to see you again! This is Tony, a new member of our staff. He will also be drawing samples while you are here this week."

Bob shook hands with the young man. "Call me Bob, please. Shall we get right to it?"

A rigorous blood sampling protocol was followed when Bob was in residence. The first samples were taken soon after he arrived, and every four hours except for overnight sleeping periods. By examining the samples taken over short time periods during and between the various mental and physical testing regimens, researchers hoped to correlate variations in fluid chemistry with Bob's activities. If the research specialists had been granted their ultimate wish, Bob would never leave the facility and undergo round-the-clock monitoring and sampling. Fortunately, more humane and sympathetic philosophies had prevailed, thanks to the efforts of Bob, Harry LeRoy, and Roger Kilmore.

Tony hovered nearby as Gwen deftly took the samples. She thanked Bob and told him Tony would return in four hours to collect the last samples of the day. They would start again at six am the next morning. The technicians wished Bob a pleasant stay and left, along with Stella.

Tired from traveling, Bob took a nap. His phone buzzed him awake at 6:45 pm, and he congratulated himself for setting an alarm for dinner. He rinsed his face and changed into jeans, loafers, and a black and gold shirt left untucked in comfortable old-guy style. He studied the man in the mirror. Was that a new patch of dark hair sprouting on his head?

He left the suite and walked to the dining room at the opposite end of the hallway. Dr. Kilmore sat at their usual table, next to a large window which would soon provide an outstanding view of the sunset.

"Roger, how are you?" Bob asked, shaking his hand.

"Better than I deserve, Bob. Great to see you again." Bob knew his friend and physician was sincere. More than once, Roger reiterated how fortunate he was to be involved in the most exciting medical story of his lifetime, perhaps in all of history. When the reality of Bob's Reversal was initially confirmed, Kilmore instantly recognized the implications. He sold his medical practice and devoted the rest of his life to the Foundation's work and supporting his former patient. Still sharp at seventy-nine, Kilmore was highly motivated to unlock the secrets of Bob's reverse-aging phenomenon.

Drinks arrived, a cabernet sauvignon for the doctor and a scotch for Bob. They clinked glasses for their traditional toast.

"To extra-long life and good health!" Roger said.

"Prosper long and live!" Bob replied, reversing the classic Vulcan mantra.

After a few minutes of small talk, Kilmore initiated Bob's first official examination. "So, how's life? Everything going okay?"

"Things are mostly pretty well, considering."

"Has anything changed since your last visit?" Roger asked. "Any new behaviors or symptoms?"

Bob sipped his drink before responding. He knew Roger would ask and while he hadn't prepared a specific answer, he planned on being open and honest, as always. He nodded.

"Yes, something bizarre has been happening. You're going to find it interesting."

Bob summarized the events of the past week. He described in detail the three time-shifting flashbacks and how different they were from his original memories. Roger listened intently without interruption until Bob finished, then followed up with several questions, asking Bob to repeat various parts of his story.

Dinner arrived and both men were silent for a time, pondering what had been said. Roger spoke first.

"Please tell me your own ideas and interpretations of the enhanced insight—I think you called it PFI?—you experienced after each flashback episode."

"Sure, I've given it a lot of thought. It was like a series of *Twilight Zone* episodes. I had an unusually high level of clarity, as though I had somehow achieved a deeper level of understanding. I was a bit shook up from the dislocation of snapping back to the present, but not from the sudden insight. If anything, knowing the truth of what was happening had sort of a calming effect, especially after the altercation with the kid in my front yard. In that moment I understood exactly what was happening. I *knew* DJ, what he was doing, and the reasons why. It didn't feel like a direct telepathic connection or some kind of Spock mind-meld thing. It wasn't a glimpse of the future, either. Just an incredibly clear sense of in-the-moment understanding. It only lasted a few seconds, and then I knew what to do next, at least in Costco and after the fight with DJ. After the backyard thing I was confused and just wanted to walk away so I wouldn't have to talk to Betty right then."

Bob paused. "What do you think, Doc? Have I fallen off my cosmic rocker?"

The doctor leaned back in his chair and swirled the wine in his glass. "I don't have an answer for you, Bob, but it is fascinating. I know you will be here through Sunday. Any chance I could talk you into extending your visit?"

Bob shook his head. "I understand why you ask, but no. I have plans. I need to fly out on Monday as scheduled."

Roger nodded. "Understood. I had to ask. You don't need special super-power insight to know what I'm thinking. This is a fantastic development! We need to learn as much as possible while you're here. I'm going to discuss this with my team tonight and modify the schedule to include some additional scans and alternate evaluations. We'll skip the usual first-day tests tomorrow. Instead, I'd like you to meet with Dr. Barlow first thing in the morning. Please tell her everything you've told me and omit nothing, especially anything you might consider, uh, embarrassing. Don't hold back."

"Embarrassing? Like losing my kite and watching it fly away? Hiding a boner from the nice lady next door? Or maybe getting my willie caught in my zipper?"

"It's impressive you can joke about it after all you've experienced, Bob. Bravo!"

"I'm too young-old to care anymore," Bob said. "Don't worry, I'll tell the good doctor Barlow everything, right after breakfast."

Chapter 30

Tuesday morning

"If you don't mind, Bob, I'd like to go through the sequence again. You were running through the school hallway, trying to catch up to your class, and then...?" Dr. Karin Barlow focused on Bob, her eyebrows furrowed. She held a notebook in one hand and pen in the other, so far unused. They sat in a conference room furnished informally like a coffee shop, with comfortable easy chairs and small tables scattered around. The session was also being recorded by a technician named Mark, who reminded Bob of the audio-visual kids who ran the film projectors back in junior high school.

"Sure, Doc. A girl stepped into the hall just a few feet ahead of me. To avoid running her over I jumped to the left, almost clipped her anyway, and the motion somehow freed my...zipper. It popped loose and felt better instantly. I stopped to zip up the rest of the way and turned to look back at her. She was kind of frozen, staring at me with great big eyes. I think she realized how close she came to being knocked flat. Then my vision went gray for a microsecond and I was back in Costco, looking at the girl squirming on the floor."

Barlow nodded and wrote her first, quick note. She had asked Bob to describe his flashback experiences in great and slow detail, frequently interrupting and asking him to repeat various portions. After forty-five minutes they were still discussing the first of the three incidents.

When Bob described his trouble in the boy's room neither Dr. Barlow nor Mark laughed or even cracked a smile. Bob wondered about their apparent lack of humor, it wouldn't have bothered him if either had an amused reaction. They were both keen professionals, or perhaps Roger had tipped them off. If Bob had just returned from a flashback, he might be able to use the magic power of PFI to understand their curious lack of reaction. Talking to a nonagenarian about the time he snagged his junk in his zipper back in third grade wasn't something one did every day.

"I'd like to clarify one more point," Dr. Barlow said, "and then we'll move on. You stated when you returned to the present situation from your time in the school you sensed something was wrong, and later it became known the woman was not the child's real mother. In that moment, did you make an association between the flashback experience and feeling something wasn't right?"

Bob shook his head. "No, it was just a quick thought, didn't feel like anything special. I just sized up the situation and it seemed like baloney. Later, maybe after the second episode and definitely after the third, I figured out my sense of something wrong in Costco must have been connected to the time-trick memory thing, but I didn't at the time. I was kind of messed up, you know, having relived that stupid thing back in school, then jumping back to Costco. And before that, the woman accused me of being a child molester. It was all jacked up."

"Of course. Let's go on, please tell me about the second episode. You were in your backyard?"

Bob took a deep breath and nodded. While this was his favorite of the three flashbacks, it was the one he was most reluctant to discuss. Admitting having a problem with your zipper as a third grader was embarrassing, but it was an understandable accident. Telling a world-renowned psychiatrist how you got turned on watching the neighbor lady pulling weeds when you were thirteen—that was quite a bit more difficult.

As Bob now expected, Barlow and Mark both maintained their professionalism throughout the story. After asking a couple of follow-up questions, Barlow paused and gazed out the window. Bob didn't need Post-Flashback Insight to know what she was thinking.

"Dr. Barlow?"

"Yes?"

"Let's discuss the tiny elephant in the room. My pecker had a starring role in the first flashback, and, uh, figured prominently again in the second. Even though my *groinal* equipment was involved in both episodes, it doesn't feel to me like it is a significant correlation, more like a coincidence."

Dr. Barlow let slip the tiniest hint of a smile. "I tend to agree. We'll go into the details of the third incident next, but as I recall it did not include any 'groinal' activity. Correct?"

"That's right."

Bob described the confrontation with DJ and his retrospective encounter with the bully, Troy. Dr. Barlow was especially interested in the apparent match point between the present and the past: the movement of DJ's arm to touch his face and Troy brushing back his hair. They also discussed how the flashback ended: Bob tripping and throwing his arms out to catch himself, then flashing to the present in the act of throwing a punch at DJ.

After three hours of discussion with one bio-break, it seemed they had covered everything. Bob finished off a bottle of water. "So, Doc, what do you think?"

Barlow put her notebook and pen on the nearby table and stretched out her arms before answering. "There's a lot to unpack here. Your heightened sense of understanding, or telepathic insight, or — we may have to come up with some new terms to use — is obviously intriguing. The concept of people experiencing flashes of insight is not new, but the association with the temporal and spatial dislocations you described is new to me. I'm also struck by your description of now having multiple memories of the same event: one old and naturally ill-defined, the other fresh and highly detailed.

"Finally, I'm fascinated by the apparent stimulation imagery, the triggers and match points between the present and historical scenes. I want to review your descriptions again later from the recordings. There are a few inconsistencies I want to understand better."

Bob nodded but had nothing to add. He and Jack had gone over the same match points in Hell the week before.

Dr. Barlow continued. "I'm going to recommend to Dr. Kilmore that we completely revise your testing program for the rest of the week and focus on these new developments. There are a number of different scans and imaging techniques available to analyze your brain activity under various conditions and stimulations. I also have some ideas for specific memory testing and analysis. I'm not sure how this will all pan out, but by tomorrow morning we'll have a new schedule ready for you.

"One last thing, Bob. The optimum situation would be the opportunity to monitor your brain function and other physiological parameters during an actual flashback event. But clearly, it would not be practical to keep you wired to monitoring equipment for extended time periods on the off chance it happens again. It is absolutely imperative you notify us immediately if you experience another flashback episode during your time here at the facility. I will alert the entire staff at KMF. Just grab the nearest person, they will implement an emergency protocol and get you to an examination lab as soon as possible. If you're alone in your residence just use the call button, someone will be standing by day or night."

Bob understood. "Sure, Doc, will do."

"This is exciting!" Barlow said, shaking his hand. "Thank you for your time, and for your honesty."

Bob left the conference room and passed Tony in the hall walking in the opposite direction.

"Good afternoon, Mr. Dodd."

"Afternoon, Tony." Bob headed for the elevator.

* * *

Tony turned the corner and walked into a small, empty workroom. Turning his back to the open door he activated his phone, composed a short message, and pressed send.

PONCE W SHRINK ONGOING

He slipped the phone back in his pocket and continued on to the lab.

Chapter 31

Tuesday evening

Denton needs to die. Slowly.

More than a week had passed since Megan left the voice message for her cousin. She was light-years beyond pissed. No question about it, the shitfuck had blown her off.

The day after Megan taught the chatty crack whore a lesson in manners, she was moved to a small, one-person cell. The low sound of prime-time programming from the television at the guard's station down the hall bled through the narrow opening beneath the cell door. In one corner near the ceiling, a grimy frosted-glass window served no purpose other than to indicate whether it was day or night outside. In the opposite high corner was a security camera with a constantly blinking green indicator light. The guards were keeping an eye on her, but Megan seriously doubted they would rush in to save her if she braided a rope out of her own hair and tried to hang herself.

Megan passed the time humming and whistling. It helped her think, and what she thought about most were creative ways to inflict pain on Denton. She'd analyzed the situation a hundred times, and in every iteration she always reached the same conclusion: Denton believed Megan was going to stay permanently locked up for attempted kidnapping. Therefore, she was no longer a threat, and he could ignore her demand to bail her out. The only other possible explanation was Denton was dead, and Megan knew he was not that lucky.

"It's just you and me, kid," she said to herself.

She was going to have to contact Larry herself, which required access to a phone. That meant she was going to have to manipulate one of the guards, maybe two. Megan knew how the system worked; this was not her first prison rodeo.

She sat on the cot and twisted around to face up to the camera. Flashing her sweetest smile, Megan shrugged out of the top of her prison jumpsuit, pushing it down to her waist. She leaned back against the wall and waved a hand toward the camera: come see me.

This shouldn't take long at all.

Chapter 32

Wednesday evening

Betty finished her second glass of pinot and checked her watch. Denton was more than an hour late. He wasn't coming.

Well, shit. First time for everything.

"Another glass of wine, miss?"

"No, thank you." She put a twenty-dollar bill on the bar and slung her purse over her shoulder. She was aware every man in the place and probably one or two of the women tracked her as she crossed the room. She was surprised to realize she wasn't enjoying the attention. Denton blew her off without even a text message, and she was pissed.

She started her car but left it in park, trying to remember exactly how their initial encounter Thursday had ended. They had talked for nearly an hour. Denton offered more than once to buy her another drink, but she was being careful and declined. He looked a little rough but decent enough. She liked his eyes, dark and brown. Denton was clearly interested, very polite, but sort of quiet and not aggressive at all. She had played along patiently, waiting for him to make his move, give her a clever line, maybe touch her arm or put his hand on her knee. Instead he just sipped his beer, gazing at her, and maintained his side of the conversation. It was almost as if he was waiting on her to make a move on him, the exact opposite of what she wanted.

When it became obvious nothing was going to happen, she decided to leave and he didn't try to stop her. He simply said goodnight and that he had enjoyed their visit. Betty was flustered, it had not gone the way she expected. To reassure herself and confirm his interest, she told him there was a "very good chance" she'd return to Hell next Wednesday night around eight. Denton said there was a good chance he'd see her then, too.

Okay, that had been a little vague. Maybe technically he hadn't stood her up after all. She felt a little foolish, but her record was still intact. For the second time in a week she drove away from Hell and headed home, alone.

It was close to 9:30 when she pulled into the driveway. Two men were working at Bob's house, illuminated from a pair of portable tripod work lights. She recognized the man on the ladder. Cal, or Ken, a handyman who had worked for Bob before. She didn't recognize the other man but assumed it was Bob's nephew, house sitting while Bob did his medical thing in New Mexico. Betty applied a quick swipe of lip gloss before walking over to say hello.

"Hi guys! Kind of late to be working, isn't it?" She waved her hand around her face and took a step back to avoid the gnats swarming around the lights.

The man on the ladder looked down at Betty and grinned. She returned the favor, feeling a familiar tingle. The man apparently liked what he saw. From his high vantage point he must have a terrific view of her best assets. She turned to the other man standing nearby and held out her hand.

"You must be Jonathan. So glad to finally meet you."

"Hi Betty, nice to meet you. Uncle Bob told me how you saved him and the house from the fire last week. That must have been exciting."

"It was just lucky I was awake," Betty said. "How are the repairs going?"

"Great! Karl here really knows what he's doing. Have you two met? I'm sorry, Karl, please tell me your last name again?"

"Speckman," Karl said. "Hello, Betty. We met last year when I was here painting the house."

Betty remembered. She had teased him by sunbathing in her backyard while he painted the near side of Bob's house. It was fun watching him try to work and stare at her at the same time without getting caught.

"Are you boys going to work all night?" Betty asked.

"Nope, just about finished," Karl said. "Tomorrow—" A blast of rock music interrupted.

All three turned toward the street as a royal blue Mini Cooper parked at the curb. *Not again*, Betty thought. The blue-haired girl locked her car and walked over.

"Hi Jonathan, I'm Marley." Marley looked up. "Hey Karl! Achieved eternal consciousness yet?"

Karl grinned. "I hope not, that would mean I'm dying. How you doin', Marley?"

"I am excellent!" Marley turned to Betty and stuck out a hand. "Hi, I've seen you a couple of times but we haven't actually met. I'm an F.O.B."

Betty forced a smile and took her hand briefly. "F.O.B.?"

"Friend of Bob. I help him out with stuff."

"How nice," Betty said.

"Uncle Bob told me to call Marley if I had any problems with the computer, the home theater system, stuff like that," Jonathan said.

"So, you're some kind of techie support person?" Betty asked.

Marley shrugged. "Bob could handle everything himself if he wanted to, he's really smart. I try to teach him sometimes but usually he just wants things fixed, you know? That's what he pays me for, and I don't mind. Bob's a really nice guy."

Betty couldn't stop her face from making a small frown. Marley turned to Jonathan. "The universal remote is messed up?" Jonathan nodded. "Should be easy. Nice to meet you, Betty." Marley headed for the front door.

"Karl, let me know if you need a hand." Jonathan said, following Marley.

"I've got it, almost finished." Karl gave Betty one more admiring glance, then got back to work.

Apparently, she had been dismissed. "Goodnight, Karl." Betty walked to her house feeling awkward and unsettled. Jonathan had barely looked at her, although he hadn't seemed all that interested in Tech Girl either. Betty was much more comfortable with one-on-one situations. She knew how to handle herself with one guy. When there were others around, especially women, she felt small and not in control.

Still, it wasn't a total shutout. Karl had obviously enjoyed his view from above. He probably had no idea how hungry he looked, staring down at her. *He remembers me in my bikini.*

She still had it. So what kept Denton from going to Hell tonight?

Chapter 33

Wednesday evening

Jonathan leaned against the door and quietly watched Marley working at Bob's computer. The universal remote was on the desk, blinking patiently as it received a new set of instructions through a USB cable.

"You don't have to lurk in silence, Jon. I can handle multiple inputs," Marley said without looking up, her fingers flying over the keyboard.

"Sorry, didn't want to interrupt."

"It's fine. Talk to me."

"Wondering about what you said to Karl, something about external consciousness?"

Marley gave him a glance, then refocused on the monitor. "Eternal consciousness. It's a line from the movie *Caddyshack*."

"Yeah?"

"Karl's last name is Speckman, kind of like Carl Spackler, the name of the crazy groundskeeper played by Bill Murray."

Jonathan shook his head. "Haven't seen it."

"Not surprised. It's about as old as you are. Your uncle made me watch it, he considers it a classic. Hijinks at a golf country club, most of it is pretty lame. In one scene Carl talks about achieving eternal consciousness on his death bed, a gift from the Dalai Lama himself."

"Nice!"

"Our man Karl has lived with *Caddyshack* jokes his entire life. He just plays along." Marley picked up her phone. "I'm going to add you to my contacts. What's your last name?"

"Last."

"Yeah, your last name, please."

"Last."

"Your last name is Last?" Jonathan nodded. "That's a first." She entered it into her phone. "How do you like your E-Cube?"

"Love it!" Jonathan said, stepping around the desk to face her. "I started gaming about five years ago, and just upgraded to the latest model. Figured I'd use it during the next couple of weeks while I'm here. Thought it would be easy, just plug it in to the receiver amp and play my games and videos."

"Just plug and play," Marley muttered.

"Pardon?"

"Never mind. Another oldie."

"Anyway, I went to change the input on the universal remote and fried it somehow. Hated to bother you, but Uncle Bob was very specific, insisting I should call you if anything screwed up while I'm here. He said you were on retainer for tech support?"

"That's our deal. He pays, I fix. It's not a big thing, the remote was overdue for a software update anyway. Almost finished."

Marley typed for a few more seconds then paused, her right hand hovering in front of the keyboard with her index finger pointing up. Her hand rose in the air several inches before arcing over, her finger cliff-diving down.

"Ka-boooossshhh!" She blew out the sound of an explosion as her finger splashed onto the Enter key.

Jonathan chuckled. "That's pretty funny."

"My signature move. Task complete. You should be good to go." Marley handed him the remote. "Go plug in your game and then you can play."

They went to the living room and Jonathan activated the entertainment cube.

"Thank you! Now I can finish season three of *Silicon Valley* this weekend."

Marley flopped onto the couch and put her feet on the coffee table. "Gilfoyle is my favorite, a perfect level of snarkiness. Dinesh is way too whiny."

Jonathan brought two beers from the kitchen and sat at the other end of the couch. They clinked bottles and drank.

"How did you and Uncle Bob come to this arrangement?" Jonathan asked. "I mean it's terrific he has your help and all..."

"I'm working a scam on the old geezer. I'm after his money when he dies," Marley joked. "Looks like it's going to take a while. Even if I'm successful it'll be my great-grandchildren who will inherit the money. He's going to outlive all of us by a long shot."

Jonathan nodded. "Bob's pretty smart—you know he used to be an engineer?—and with fifty-plus years to go he's bound to accumulate some wealth as he grows younger. Sort of a fortune of reversal."

"Hey, that's good. I like it."

Jonathan shrugged. "I do some writing. I like wordplay."

Marley took a swig of beer. "Maybe you should write Mimp's biography, at least volume one. The rest of his life story is going to take a while."

"Mimp?"

"Short for Most Intriguing Man on the Planet, from the *People* magazine cover after the Reversal. What about you, what's your story?"

"Sure. You know about Linda, Bob's wife? My dad was Linda's younger brother, he died a long time ago. I'd already lost my mom when I was little, Aunt Linda was my only relative. After college I bounced around, trying to figure out life, I guess. Linda made sure I knew she was family, someone I could connect with. She was always reaching out, calling, sending cards and emails. I miss her. Bob loved her so much. He took great care of her during her illness.

"After her funeral, I helped him clean out her stuff. It was hard for him, I did most of it. Bob and I get along fine, but he wasn't really going to get close to anyone, at least not then. I was sort of between gigs when she died and had time to help. It became pretty clear he wanted to be alone, I understood and moved on. I did some freelance work on the east coast, mostly small stuff, writing ad copy for local businesses. I tried to stay in contact with Bob, and he always answered my emails and calls, but it didn't feel normal."

"Sounds like something else was going on, too." Marley said.

Jonathan stared at the wall for a few seconds, then took a drink. "Yeah, I needed some help and was angling for some kind of living arrangement or support from Bob. Thought maybe he'd figure I was his only family. You know about his kids, right?"

Marley stared. "Kids? Mimp has reproduced?"

Jonathan nodded. "Twice. A boy and girl with Janet, his first wife. The boy was killed, some kind of accident, I think. A couple of years later when their daughter, Lindsay, turned eighteen, she left home. Went overseas on some kind of peace mission, then disappeared, permanently. The marriage didn't survive the loss of both kids."

"What happened to the daughter?" Marley asked.

"No one knows. The organization she joined reported she arrived as expected, somewhere in Asia, I think, then the next morning she was gone. Bob and Janet tried to find her, of course, but she was never heard from again.

"Years later, Aunt Linda meets Bob and they're a good match. They'd been married almost twenty years when she got sick." Jonathan stared at the same spot on the wall again.

"Uncle Bob took it pretty hard. I was kind of lost myself at the time. I thought Bob might not want to live alone and hoped he might ask me to live with him." Jonathan turned back to Marley. "I'm not proud of this, but I'm not afraid to say it: I thought I could help him in his final years and maybe inherit his house and live here. Finally chase my dream and write novels.

"But Bob wasn't really right after Linda died. He never got hostile or anything, he was always polite and nice. It seemed like he didn't enjoy life anymore. I realized we weren't going to connect so I gave up. When he got sick, I offered to come back and help but he said no. I think he was ready for the end. After his remission—what turned out years later to be the Reversal—I realized famous Uncle Bob was probably going to live forever. We stayed friendly and in touch occasionally, and last week he asked me to stay here during the repairs while he was away. It was perfect timing for me."

Marley asked, "You want another beer?"

She returned from the kitchen with two bottles, kicked off her sandals and sat cross-legged on the couch facing Jonathan.

"So, you went for a rich uncle payoff, kind of icky but you were also willing to take care of Bob for better or worse going forward.

The Reversal smacked that plan out of whack and you reevaluated, did the right thing and moved on. Bob told me some of this, Jonathan. Pretty much the same story. He never described you as anything other than nice."

"Thanks for saying that," Jonathan said. "Tell me, what brought you and Uncle Bob together?"

Marley snickered and said, "The theme song of a 1960s sci-fi TV show."

Chapter 34

Thursday morning

After enjoying breakfast in his suite, Bob took the short walk to the psych lab. He greeted Dr. Barlow and Gwen and waved to Tony and a woman he didn't know standing on the far side of the room. The woman, wearing a buttoned-up lab coat, nodded.

"We have designed a series of interesting experiments for you this morning," Karin Barlow said. "After extensive discussions with Dr. Kilmore and a variety of specialists, we've developed a testing protocol to delve further into your recent flashback experiences. Please take a seat and I'll explain what we have in mind."

The KMF team planned to recreate many of the social stimuli and environmental conditions Bob had described in his previous three episodes. They hoped to induce either a new or repeat experience and monitor Bob's cranial activity and physiological parameters before, during and after the event.

"We know this is a long shot," Barlow said, "but we want to investigate the potential triggers and try to determine whether the flashbacks are related to specific situational conditions or environmental factors such as visual objects, sounds, or even smells. We can't match all the parameters, of course, but after studying the transcripts of your descriptions, we've selected a handful of criteria to test."

Bob had wondered if there was a way to experience the flashbacks again—one in particular—but he had to agree: the odds for success were probably low. *Still, it wouldn't be the craziest thing to happen to me this month.*

"Sure, Doc. Nothing to lose," he said. "I'm game. What do you want me to do?"

Barlow waved Tony over and directed Bob to a vinyl examination chair. After reclining the chair slightly, Tony and Gwen attached sensors to his arms, legs, and chest.

"Bob, you'll need to wear this headgear to allow us to monitor your brain during the experiment. It replaces the normal leads and wiring we used during your previous visits. We only need two connections, one on your neck, the other on your temple. The rest of the data is obtained by the electronics inside the headband itself. We realize wearing this equipment will likely be a distraction and perhaps reduce the chance of initiating a flashback, however..."

Bob nodded. "Ready when you are."

Tony approached and placed the electronic ring on Bob's head and adjusted the fit. After attaching leads to Bob's left temple and the back of his neck, Tony stepped back.

"And these," Dr. Barlow said, "are specially modified virtual reality goggles. The original technology was developed by the online gaming industry, but it has numerous applications in the medical fields as well. Our technical team has been scrambling since Tuesday morning writing the software code for our experiment today." Barlow nodded to Gwen, who handed the goggles to Bob. They were only slightly larger than a pair of sunglasses and incredibly light. They looked very cool. The frames were a blue color that reminded him of Marley's hair.

Barlow continued. "One hypothesis is that your flashbacks are tied to specific stimulation triggers. To test the theory, we're going to set up a handful of 'match' conditions based on your descriptions and determine whether they will initiate a similar episode. In the first incident, you described the eyes of the little girl in Costco matching the eyes of the little girl in the school hallway. Obviously, we can't set up the exact scenario, but our technicians have come up with half a dozen virtual reality scenes we hope will spark a new or repeat memory-experience. Okay?"

Bob nodded. *This should be interesting.*

"One more item. We are not set up to replicate the audio experience, and in fact too many variables can complicate the experiment. We will be using noise-canceling ear buds to provide a silent environment and allow you to focus only on visual input."

Bob took the buds from Tony and inserted the devices in his ears.

"You should be able to hear normally until we start the process. Okay, Bob, please relax and get as comfortable as possible, and when you are ready put the goggles on." Dr. Barlow sat at a large console equipped with several monitors. Gwen and Tony stood behind her. The woman in the white lab coat remained in the far corner of the room, standing patiently. Bob wondered who she was and why she was here. He settled himself in the chair and put the goggles on. A pleasant field of pale blue light filled his vision.

"All right, here we go," Barlow said. "No need to say anything unless you have some kind of negative experience and wish to stop. Speak up and we'll terminate the sequence."

Bob heard keyboard tapping, then total silence. The goggle-vision image transitioned smoothly to a wide aisle lined with tires displayed on shelves, similar to the aisle in Costco. As he moved his head slightly the perspective changed perfectly in an astonishingly realistic manner. Looking down, he saw a small girl with a curious expression. The image seemed slightly artificial but was a decent representation of an actual human face. Her eyes were dark brown. The scene was strange, both new and familiar at the same time. Bob recalled the great George Carlin joke about *vuja dé*, the weird feeling that nothing like this has happened before.

He heard Dr. Barlow through the ear buds. "Bob, we're going to cycle through several variations, no need to verbally respond."

Bob concentrated on the girl who steadily gazed back. Her expression changed from curious to puzzled as she frowned and scrunched her eyebrows as though she were trying to figure something out. A few seconds later her expression changed to surprised, brows arched, eyes wide and mouth open. Then frightened, her head and body shaking in agitation. Bob couldn't look away and guessed correctly what came next.

The girl stared intently as her expression went from fear to intense panic. Her eyes became huge and her body trembled. Bob was surprised to see her knees bend slightly and her head tilt back. His mind snapped into a frame of recognition: portions of the scene were close to the Costco experience. The angle of her head, the intensity of her eyes, the shape of her mouth. Bob's mind shifted, seating itself inside the memory. The image was not perfect, but Bob judged the simulation to have an extremely high "goodness of fit." The electronics might have indicated his reaction, as the scene remained constant.

Doc's giving me time to flash. Bob realized his focus had fractured, split into absorbing the imagery while pondering the fantastic technology behind it. His ancient engineering mind was interfering with the process and probably defeating the purpose of Dr. Barlow's experiment.

Bob refocused on the girl. The simulation wizards had programmed the girl's chest to heave as she gasped for air, shaking in fear. Emotions of sympathy and concern filled his mind and his stomach tightened. The scene continued for half a minute before fading, and Bob's thoughts returned to the experiment itself. It was an incredible experience, yet completely artificial.

The display reverted to the pale blue field of light, and Bob took off the goggles. Gwen and Tony assisted with removing the ear buds and headgear and adjusted the chair so Bob was sitting upright facing Dr. Barlow.

"That was impressive," Bob said.

"From the readings, I'm assuming we achieved a satisfactory resonance with the original Costco experience?" Barlow asked.

"Yes! Several elements seemed identical to what I remember. The eyes, her expression, the angle of her head. I felt some kind of...*comfort*, familiarity, a sense of rightness. Not really déjà vu, although that comes close. It's difficult to describe, we may need to develop some new language to communicate this stuff."

"I assume you did not experience a flashback?" Barlow asked.

"No. I did experience an emotion that seemed like an echo of what I felt that day in Costco," Bob said.

Barlow nodded thoughtfully. "We did detect some interesting variations in certain parameters, which we'll analyze in great detail. As I said, we knew the odds were against us."

"My compliments to your team, that was very well done."

"Thank you. They were highly motivated, and still are. We may tweak the scenarios and try again in a day or two."

Bob handed the goggles to Gwen, then stifled a laugh as his mind retrieved a standard, garden-variety memory from his archives. As a young boy he would sit on the living room floor in his pajamas, eating Cheerios from a plastic bowl and watching Saturday morning cartoons on TV. Bugs Bunny pops out of a hole in the ground, rips goggles from his head and looks around. He munches on a carrot and declares he made a wrong turn in Albuquerque.

Bob mentally swiped away the memory and swiveled in his chair to face Dr. Barlow.

"What's up next, Doc?"

Chapter 35

Thursday morning

"This next experiment will be a bit different," Dr. Barlow said. She and Bob sat at a conference table in the lab, sharing a small pitcher of orange juice.

On the other side of the room Gwen, Tony, and the lady in the lab coat were talking quietly. It looked like a staff smoke break, minus the cigarettes.

"Are we going to continue work on the first flashback or move on to the second?" Bob asked.

"The second. In our initial session Tuesday, we asked you to describe, in as much detail as possible, everything about the current, real-time situations as well as the past-time flashback experiences. We've studied the interview recordings multiple times, and Dr. Kilmore arranged consultations with several neuroscience experts and a few cognitive memory specialists. Everyone was excited to explore this new development."

"You brought in a bunch of experts here, to KMF?" Bob asked.

"No, all communication was done remotely: virtual meetings, sharing digital data, and so on. It was quite a scramble, but in the end we achieved a consensus in identifying certain aspects believed to be the most likely triggers for your flashback episodes."

Bob considered this. "The group thought the eyes of the little girl was the trigger in the first episode?"

Barlow nodded. "As you concluded yourself. The matching images of the eyes of the girls in Costco and the school hallway may have served as a transition bridge between the two experiences. It was interesting that the last image you describe in Costco before the flashback was her eyes, and the first thing you describe during the flashback is standing in the boy's restroom. Later, you turn back and see the eyes of the schoolgirl, then flash-return to the present and you're still looking at the Costco girl's eyes. In the instant before returning to the present you had a seriously traumatic event, getting your...that is, the pain you experienced in the restroom.

"In your description of your memory...sorry. You're right, the language is tricky. The second flashback occurred after you had a short visit with your neighbor over the backyard fence, and the transition match point was the sight of the clippers in your hand while trimming the grass at the bottom of the fence."

"That's right," Bob agreed.

"And right before you exited the flashback you were staring at...uh, let's just say the flashback exit and return images were similar. Correct?"

"That's also right." *Doc's quite the professional.*

"For the second test we plan to simulate the first match point, with the addition of social elements based on your conversation with the neighbor."

Uh-oh. "Social elements?" Bob asked, raising his eyebrows.

Barlow shifted in her seat before elaborating. "Another term might be 'psycho-sexual tension.' We realize the risk of including too many variables to control for meaningful results, but since we are limited in time the team concluded this would be the best approach. If we are able to initiate a flashback and obtain real-time neural data, it will be a tremendous success and facilitate our investigation going forward." Dr. Barlow gestured to the group across the lab and the woman in the white coat approached the table.

"Bob, this is 'Betty.' She works in HR and volunteered to help. Today she will literally be a human resource for this test. If you'll please return to the examination chair, we'll get started."

Bob nodded to Betty and tried to ignore the flock of butterflies in his upper GI. He had a pretty good idea what they had planned. He sat in the chair and Tony placed the monitoring gear on Bob's head as HR Betty waited a few yards away. Tony finished securing the connections as Gwen approached carrying two glasses of iced tea.

A swarm of moths joined the butterflies. *Easy, Bob. Maintain. Other than getting a boner in front of all these nice people, what's the worst that can happen?*

"As you can see," Barlow said, "we are going to simulate the, ah, circumstances preceding your second flashback. We don't feel it is necessary to duplicate every aspect, but we will focus on the emotional and sexual aspects of your encounter with your neighbor. Then Tony will show you a pair of shears as a potential visual trigger."

Bob glanced at Tony, standing by with a plastic bag and a strange expression. *He's trying not to grin.*

"We don't want to show you the shears until we have set the stage first. By the way, I forgot to mention — these tests are being recorded." She pointed around the lab at several cameras installed in the walls and ceiling, and another mounted on the console desk aimed at the examination chair. Bob hadn't noticed the cameras earlier, but recording the experiments made sense.

"All right, let's begin." Dr. Barlow took her seat at the console.

The woman from HR shrugged off the lab coat. Her hair had been styled like Betty's from Bob's description, and she wore a green sleeveless blouse and white, form-fitting shorts. Once again Bob stifled a laugh. *She's here to simulate Betty, and stimulate me.*

Gwen handed the glasses of tea to Betty 2.0 and stepped away. Betty approached with an engaging smile. Bob noticed how she swayed her hips, just as he remembered and described to Dr. Barlow.

"Good afternoon Bob, it's great to see you! Would you like some tea?"

"Sure, thanks Betty," Bob said. She leaned over to hand him the glass, exposing a terrific view down her blouse. *Helloooo Betty!* Bob kept his eyes up, avoiding temptation as he did that morning in the backyard. He felt his face flush. The cameras were probably auto-correcting for the deep crimson color.

"It's your birthday, isn't it?" Betty leaned down further and her lips brushed his cheek with a quick kiss. She whispered in his ear. "Happy Birthday, Bob."

Arousal was unavoidable. *This has to be a violation of KMF policy.* Betty stood over him, one hand holding her glass of tea, the other on her hip, her blouse stretched tightly across her chest. They held each other's gaze in silence for a few seconds. In Bob's peripheral vision Dr. Barlow gestured to Tony.

As Tony stepped forward, HR Betty flashed one last sexy smile and turned around. Bob gave in and admired her figure as she walked away. *I have to, for the experiment. For science...*

Tony moved in, blocking the view and holding dirty garden

shears in his hands. The green-stained blades smelled of fresh-cut grass. Bob gazed at the clippers for several seconds, replaying in his mind the close encounter of the second kind with alt-Betty.

Nothing. Bob was fully aware he was in a clinical environment conducting a scientific test. The engineering part of his brain admired the clever attempt to recreate the scene and initiate a flashback. As a standard-model *Homo sapiens* male, Bob also appreciated the willingness of the staff to delve into the more adult aspects of the situation to achieve success. But the experiment failed.

After a few moments he called it. "Nope. Nada." At her console, Dr. Barlow was clearly disappointed. Bob tried to lighten the mood.

"Perhaps we should try it again, only much slower?" Bob said. "And maybe just skip the thing with the clippers?"

Chapter 36

Thursday morning

"The team was particularly challenged trying to design a simulation plan for your third flashback," Dr. Barlow said. "You experienced apprehension and stress, and a physical altercation was imminent. Marley stood nearby. You were in your front yard, a familiar environment. These situational circumstances may or may not have been important in triggering your episode, and we debated the time and effort to include them in the scenario. In the end we decided on a small experiment of limited scope.

"The match point for your third episode was DJ raising his hand to his head. It might have been an involuntary nervous reaction, or a complimentary 'thinking' movement, touching his bruised face as he decided what to do next. The visual entry point of the flashback was the bully, Troy, running his hand through his hair as he loomed over you. In both scenes the motion of the arm and hand to the head are synchronized, the end of the present time-scene and the beginning of the past-time scene.

"In this third experiment, Tony is going to assume the posture of a hostile person. As he approaches, he will attempt to mimic

DJ and raise his arm and hand to his head in several variations. We admit to having the least confidence in this test but concluded there were too many variables involved to develop a realistic simulation. Still, we have nothing to lose. Please take your seat in the examination chair one more time, if you don't mind."

Bob sat in the chair and Gwen replaced the headgear and leads. Tony stood off to one side, perhaps getting into character. Dr. Barlow nodded and Tony approached Bob quickly. He looked angry, his hands balled into fists. Bob watched without reaction as Tony reached the chair and raised one fist high near his head with an expression of rage. Tony froze for a half-second, then relaxed and walked off a few steps.

A moment later he approached again slowly, as if to inflict harm in a controlled manner. He stopped close to Bob, then robotically raised his left arm to his face. Bob watched calmly and fought against the urge to grin as Tony was clearly overacting in his role as The Intimidator.

Tony diligently tried three more variations with the same null result. After the last attempt, Tony relaxed and briefly put his left hand on Bob's shoulder. Turning toward Dr. Barlow, Tony lifted his right hand and swept it through his hair, and Bob had a quick moment of déjà vu. The authentic movement by Tony to touch his hair in mild exasperation was the closest match to Bob's memory of Troy doing the same, but it did not trigger a flashback.

"Okay, thank you everybody," Dr. Barlow said. Bob sat upright in the chair and Tony removed the headgear with one hand and reached around to remove the sensor patch from the back of Bob's neck. Bob's vision faded gray, then cleared —

— and the sleep lab technician pulled the lead from Bob's neck and reached for another on his forehead. She was not very tall and as Bob sat motionless, waiting for the leads to be disconnected, he stared at the *name tag on her uniform: MONICA. He was groggy from Ambien-sleep but wanted to hear the results of his sleep apnea test. Monica removed the last lead. "Okay, Mr. Dodd —*

—you're all set," Tony said. There was a tiny shift in time-space and Bob looked up at Tony, who was enveloped by a light gray fog that echoed the shape and movement of the technician's body. Bob sensed a displacement, his mental construct of "Tony" subtly morphed into a slightly different form. Tony was a KMF lab technician, but there was a shadow of something else...

The sensation vanished after no more than a second. Gwen offered to show Tony where to store the gear. Dr. Barlow was thanking HR Betty for her assistance.

Bob remained in the chair while the others were occupied. The headgear had already been removed when he "saw" Monica from his sleep-study years ago, so no data had been recorded. It didn't feel at all like his previous flashbacks. The shift in his vision was fast, quick as a normal blinking of his eyes. There was no PFI either, he had not detected any extraneous sensory inputs from Tony or anyone else. Just the weird vision of Tony, outlined in light fog and backlit by the ceiling lights.

Just an illusion, a trick of the light. It wasn't a flashback, just a flash of normal memory from the sleep study, triggered by the wire leads being pulled from his head.

Dr. Barlow approached, taking off her glasses. "Thank you for indulging us, Bob. I'm disappointed we were not successful, but not really surprised."

"Sure, Doc, glad to. Sorry it didn't work out." As Bob exited through the lab door he passed by Tony, who advised him to enjoy the rest of the day.

Chapter 37

Thursday morning

Tony entered the break room and nodded to the man in scrubs casually spooning yogurt and reading a tablet at one of the tables. Tony sat on a couch behind the man near the wall. He typed a short text message on his phone, then paused before sending.

It had been an interesting morning. Dr. Barlow's attempts to induce Bob into a real-time flashback were brilliant, and creative. They also seemed foolish, with little chance of success. Still, why not? It was well-established that the ever-younging Bob Dodd was not a normal human. There was nothing to lose by trying anything and everything, no matter how improbable.

He had enjoyed watching the hot HR chick flirt with Bob. It was obvious the old guy was turned on. Tony admired how everyone maintained a professional manner throughout the experiment. Too bad it failed.

He wondered about Bob's quizzical expression when Tony removed the headgear for the last time. Probably from a mix of emotions, the aftereffects of sexual teasing in front of others, fatigue, maybe even relief the experiments were over. Bob had endured wearing the monitoring headgear through all of the tests with good-natured patience, cracking jokes and puns the whole time. Tony was actually starting to like Mr. Dodd.

Back to work. Tony glanced at yogurt guy, then sent the text message.

PONCE TESTS NEGATIVE.

Chapter 38

Sunday night

DJ parked his truck once again near the busted mailbox. The broken bricks had been gathered into a neat pile but the box had not yet been repaired. The burned-out section of the roof was rebuilt and ready for the installation of new shingles, stacked on the driveway. The damaged siding between the garage and the roof had also been replaced but not yet painted, and a new garage door had been installed.

He hadn't heard from his father, but the *Find the Asshole* app indicated he was on the move, heading back toward Springburg. He'd probably arrive in two or three hours. DJ needed to get the flashlight back from the old man.

He jumped as someone pounded on the passenger window. Ryan Anderson peered in, dripping wet and wearing only swim trunks.

"You coming to the party or what? Did you bring beer?"

"In a minute," DJ said. He hooked a thumb toward the back. "Take the beer." Ryan pulled the thirty-pack from the bed and headed back to his house. DJ looked at the geezer's front door and remembered the last time he was there.

The fucker had surprised him, rushing in with arms flailing. DJ wasn't ready, and geezer smacked him with a couple of wild swings. DJ got in a couple of licks but didn't do much damage before he took that lucky punch to his throat. It hurt like hell, and he had to stop fighting until he figured out how to breathe again.

Then the guy started talking about his father hitting him and DJ lost it. He couldn't think straight, his mind spinning and confused. It was totally fucked up, fighting some guy after setting his house on fire and busting up his mailbox. He didn't know why he gave the guy the flashlight, it just seemed like something he should do, to make up for the bad shit. It was stupid, he had to get it back or he'd never be able to go home again.

He got out of the truck and crossed the yard to the front door.

Chapter 39

Sunday night

"Jonathan? What's up?"

"Hi, Uncle Bob. There's a kid—I mean a very large young man at the front door who says he needs his flashlight back. Do you know what he's talking about?"

Ah, crap! The flashlight was here, in his travel case in the closet. Bob usually packed a small penlight when he traveled. DJ's flashlight was handy and he'd tossed it in his bag.

"Yeah, I do. I have it here, with me. The kid's name is DJ. Did he say why he wants it?"

"No. He's a man of few words. A big man."

Bob heard the fear in his voice. "Jonathan, tell him I'm sorry, I'll be home next weekend and he can have it then."

"All right, will do."

"Be careful, he might get a little excited, but it should be okay. Oh, and Jonathan?"

"Yes?"

"I just want to tell you good luck, we're all counting on you."

"Who's 'we'?"

"Never mind. It's a line from a movie. Call or text me if you have any trouble."

"Okay."

Bob ended the call and retrieved the flashlight from his bag. It had a sturdy, hefty feel in his hands. He flicked it on, the light wasn't as bright as he expected but good enough. Maybe the batteries were low. He sat on the bed and tried to figure out why DJ wanted it back. It had seemed important for Bob to accept it after their fight, like it was some kind of peace offering by DJ for the trouble he had caused.

His phone vibrated with a text message.

DJ GONE. DIDN'T SAY A WORD. LOOKED UNHAPPY

Chapter 40

Sunday night

DJ inserted the nozzle into the gas tank and locked the trigger open. He leaned against his truck and took deep, slow breaths. He was charged up, almost panicked. A block of energy was trapped in his chest, trying to pound its way out. He stayed calm and quiet until it faded. When he was little a doctor told him when he got too excited, he should pretend to be frozen and think about his breathing until he felt better. It still worked.

After the man at the door told him the guy with the flashlight wasn't going to be home until next weekend, DJ blew off the party and drove around until the low fuel light flashed red on the dashboard.

What the fuck now? Can't go home, Dad will be there in two hours. He heard tires crunching and looked over to the next pump island. A large SUV towing a boat on a trailer parked and a couple and three young kids spilled out. All were grungy and pink with sunburn, probably returning home from a weekend at the lake.

The cabin.

When DJ was five or six, his father purchased a cabin at a small lake, less than an hour's drive from town. It wasn't actually a cabin, and it wasn't all that close to the lake. It was a double-wide mobile home separated from the water's edge by a half-mile of dense woods. Denton and DJ used to stay there every summer weekend and several times during the rest of the year. DJ entertained himself exploring the woods and watching VCR movies while his father met with the men and women who would drop by for short visits. Most of the time the women would stay over, sleeping in the bedroom with his father. Sometimes Aunt Megan visited, but most of the time she slept by herself in Denton's room. Then DJ slept on the floor and his dad used his bed.

It had been over a year since DJ had last been to the cabin. He could stay there and keep track of his father's location with the app until he figured out what to do. He'd have to make a quick trip to the house to pick up Buster and grab a few things. Maybe he'd stay at the cabin for the whole week until the guy with the flashlight came back.

He finished gassing up, went inside Zippy Mart and purchased three cheap Styrofoam chests, ice, and plenty of beer and food. He loaded everything in the truck and started for home. DJ hoped the VCR at the cabin still worked, otherwise it would be a long, boring week. Maybe he and Buster would go fishing, do some hiking. *Buster's gonna love romping through the woods.*

Chapter 41

Monday morning

Denton Rafter winced from the sunlight spiking through the kitchen window. The coffee was still brewing but his first cigarette of the day was smoked. He ground the butt in the sink and slumped in a chair at the table, exhausted. The house was empty when he got home last night, DJ and Buster both gone. Denton briefly debated which of the two he missed the most before flopping into bed with his clothes on. He'd slept until his bladder alarm went off a few minutes before eleven.

The coffee machine beeped, he poured a mug and went to the front porch to sit.

He figured he had three problems. The cops who arrested the two morons in the bar also confiscated three large packages of product. The pissed-off customers Denton could handle, but the loss of giant chunks of cash revenue meant he'd be short in his payment to Management next week in Edgar. Denton called his boss, explained what happened and his plans for damage control and covering the scheduled deliveries. Denton promised he would make the rest of the payment within a week—with interest, natch—but Denton knew his boss was silently seething before the call was disconnected without another word. Problem Number One was a major fuckcluster for sure.

The obvious solution to Problem One created Problem Two: Denton needed the contents inside the flashlight to replace the lost funds. This led directly to Problem Three: he had to find DJ to get the flashlight.

Denton checked his phone, there were no new texts or emails. He wished there were some kind of magic technology that would let him keep track of DJ's location.

During his third cup of coffee he figured out the other thing nagging at him: he'd missed a date with Hot Betty. She'd made it clear she would be back in Hell Wednesday—Thursday?—night, but he was down in Casstown. Betty was *fine*, no doubt about it, and intriguing, too. The way she looked at him sometimes, like she was waiting for—no, she *needed* something. *Just tell me what to do, babe, and I'll do it.*

If she wasn't too pissed, maybe she'd meet him in Hell again and this time wave the green flag. His imagination danced with the possibilities until he remembered the Three Problems. Denton forced himself to concentrate. He sifted through options and tested various strategies step by step until he developed a workable action plan. He would tackle the problems in reverse order and do the third thing first.

Find DJ. Get flashlight. Pay Management.

He was proud of his analysis, but his head hurt from two and a half minutes of continuous thinking. He went inside for Tylenol and more coffee. He'd text Betty and feel her out. Maybe she'd cut him some slack and meet him tonight or tomorrow. That would be sweet. He was way overdue to catch a break.

Chapter 42

Monday afternoon

The view from the back seat of the town car was the perfect archetype of a southwest naturescape. The desert browns, dark green hills and crystal blue skies perfectly matched the stereotypical scenes painted on thousands of artsy-craftsy products sold in street festivals throughout the country. The vista conveyed a peaceful simplicity; clean curves and smooth color transitions interrupted only by roadside utility poles and power lines which, somehow, looked surprisingly natural. Bob understood why so many artists were drawn to the area. *I'd paint this too, if someone gave me a couple of lessons first.*

As they drew near Albuquerque the scenery changed, dominated by bland and boxy industry and warehouse districts that so often greeted highway travelers at the outskirts of sizable cities. *This would be easy to paint, but why would you?* Bob knew the rest of the trip to the airport would look pretty much the same.

His last few days at KMF were mostly normal, the usual mix of examinations, tests and fluid samples typical of his routine visits. The schedule was modified to include additional brain scans, and Bob had two more sessions with Dr. Barlow. Roger Kilmore joined the last one only two hours ago. Both doctors believed the flashbacks represented a new and exciting development in the mysterious times and life of Robert S. Dodd. Bob didn't need his special insight power to know Roger would ask him to extend his stay at KMF for additional research.

"No, I have plans," Bob told his friend. "In fact, I'm meeting Jack in Las Vegas this afternoon."

Kilmore nodded. "Had to ask, you know."

"Of course."

"Your flashback episodes are obviously much more than unusually vivid, strong memories. You've described them as full sensory, true-life experiences, as though you are physically present in the historical moment. It reminds me of science fiction time-travel stories I read when I was young. And of course, the heightened insight capability that follows is very intriguing. We have to consider this new phenomenon to be potentially related to your 'younging' condition and want to gather as much data as possible. Especially if you continue to experience episodes in the future."

Dr. Barlow took over. "We need your help in compiling additional information on your activities, your thoughts, and your state of mind going forward. To create a chronicle of your life, which can be correlated to the strange behaviors you are experiencing and any variations that occur.

"We have two requests, completely optional, but we hope you'll consider them carefully. We would like for you to keep a daily journal and document your thoughts, feelings, distractions, musings, doodles, anything you wish to record. If you have any sort of unusual experience, we'd like you to capture your impressions, emotions, anything and everything as soon as possible. The act of writing stimulates specific areas of your brain and your journals will provide us with timely psycho-emotional data, valuable to our research." Dr. Barlow handed Bob a bundle of small notebooks in various colors.

Doc sure likes to use lots of words, Bob thought.

"We are also providing a high-tech resource as an alternative or companion to the written journal. Our team has developed an application for your smart phone that will automatically record your location at all times, with your consent of course. You can disable it any time you wish. It has a recording feature to use if you have additional flashbacks or any new experiences or behaviors. You activate the app, describe the event, your thoughts, activities before and after, impressions, sensations, even smells. As much information as possible, even if it doesn't seem relevant. We realize this will not always be practical, but if you record your input as soon as possible after an event occurs, the app will automatically transmit the data to KMF as soon as you end the recording."

Bob took a few seconds before responding to give the impression he was thoughtfully considering their request. *Sounds like a ton of work. If my life turns out to be fantastically long, I want to spend my time living, not documenting.*

"I completely understand your request and the potential value of the information. Obviously I'm also interested in understanding what the hell is going on with me. I agree in principle, but I won't disrupt my life to comply. I'll make an effort but can't promise how much or how often you'll get anything. The app sounds like a good idea, and I'll consider journaling as well." Bob handed his phone to Dr. Barlow, who stepped out of the room briefly before returning.

Dr. Kilmore had one more proposal. "Things can change

quickly, and we'd like to initiate weekly bio-chemistry sampling in Springburg after you return home."

They discussed the details until Tony knocked and entered. He handed the phone to Bob and showed him the new app on the home screen. The app was named DELOREAN, and the icon was a stainless silver car with open gull-wing doors. *Someone's got a sense of humor.* If Bob had another flashback, he would activate the app after he came "back to the future." Tony shook Bob's hand and wished him well before leaving.

The voice of his driver brought Bob back to the present.

"Mr. Dodd? Would you mind if we stopped for a minute? I'm sorry, but I'm not feeling well and think I should get to a restroom." Nick's face in the rear-view mirror was pale.

"Of course, Nick. Absolutely. Anything serious?"

"No, I don't think so. Something I ate last night. I'm sorry, I won't be long."

"Sure, whatever you need."

They took the next exit and found a convenience store. Nick bolted for the men's room and Bob decided to stretch his legs and buy a snack for the flight to Las Vegas. He walked past a lanky, thin man with a thick mustache wearing a wide-brimmed hat and sitting on the hood of an old beater. He was smoking a cigarette, one boot on the fender and the other on the pavement. He looked like one of those sheet-metal leaning-cowboy silhouettes sold at art festivals. Bob nodded to the man and noticed a young boy in the front seat playing with a handheld video game. It was hot; the car's windows were down and the man was sweating as he smoked.

Bob went inside and purchased a couple of granola bars. On his way back to the car the thin man spoke as Bob approached.

"Excuse me, sir?"

"Yes?" Bob said, glancing at the boy in the front seat.

The man stood and ground the cigarette butt under his boot. "I was wondering if you could maybe spare a few dollars so I can buy some gas? I just got custody of my son yesterday and we're heading home to Bakersfield. I'm low on cash and nearly out of gas, too. Maybe just a few bucks to get us down the road a bit? Please?"

Everything turned gray, then brightened —

— and the man in the Dodgers cap extended his hand. "I think this is yours?"

A wave of relief washed over Bob. He hadn't realized he'd dropped his wallet. "Oh, wow. Thank you!" Bob said, shaking the man's hand. A small boy, maybe five or six years old, stood behind his father, peeking around.

"I'd like to repay you for your kindness," Bob said, pulling a twenty-dollar bill from the wallet. They were standing in the shade of the ticket booth outside the entrance to the IMAX movie theater in Los Angeles. Linda had gone ahead to get in line at the concession stand while Bob purchased tickets to the show.

The man shook his head, he didn't want the money.

"Please, I want you to have this. I really appreciate what you did for me," Bob said. "If you hadn't found it and chased me down, I'd have a huge problem. Thank you very much. Please, take this." He held out the twenty.

The man shook his head again. "No, it's fine, glad to help. I didn't really do anything. It was my son who found it and picked it up. He asked me what we should do. I saw you walking away from the spot and guessed it might be yours. Glad it worked out."

"Well, I'd like to thank your son. May I?"

The man nodded and nudged his son forward. Bob took a knee and gave the kid a friendly smile. "Thank you for finding my wallet..." Bob glanced up at the father, eyebrows raised.

"Richie," the man said.

"Richie, you did a very nice thing. Thank you."

The boy said nothing and shied away, trying to get back behind his father. Bob waved the twenty at the father, who gave in and nodded.

"Richie, I'd like to give you this. Maybe you can get something fun. Okay?"

The boy looked up to his father. "It's fine, Richie. Go ahead." Richie took the money and pushed it into his pocket.

"What do you say, Richie?" the father said.

"Thank you," the boy said, barely audible.

"My pleasure," Bob said. He stood and reached to shake the man's hand again —

— the boy in the car had stopped playing his game and stared through the windshield, waiting for Bob to answer the man's question. The transition from past to present was abrupt but not as disorienting as his previous episodes. *Maybe I'm getting the hang of this time-shifting business.* The thin man was waiting, clearly hoping for a positive response.

Bob anticipated what would happen next and raised a hand to the man: wait. Time-flow became mushy and thick, and Bob fought the urge to step back to create space for the data bridge between the man and himself. A gust of emotional wind touched his mind, signaling the arrival of a torrent of information.

The boy in the car was the man's son. The boy's mother was unstable, dangerous. Something happened, deep and nasty, putting the child in danger. The father drove many miles to rescue his son. He was grateful to the judge, and fully accepted his responsibilities. He hated begging from strangers, but he had no choice, he had to get his son home, to start a new life for the boy…

Time normalized and Bob's response was crystal clear. He opened his wallet, pulled out all the cash and folded it over neatly. He offered it to the man as Nick stepped outside from the store.

"Hey!" Nick yelled and rushed forward until Bob held up his hand.

"It's okay, Nick, hang on a minute."

The man looked from Nick to Bob, unsure what to do. Bob continued to hold out the money.

"It's all right, take it. My pleasure."

The man unfolded the cash and sifted through it, breaking into a big smile. He raised his head, eyes moist. "Sir, this is so nice. Really great. This will definitely get us home, with lunch and dinner too! Thank you."

Bob shook the man's hand. "You two have a safe trip."

"Yes, sir. Thanks again."

Bob and Nick returned to the town car and watched as the man moved his car across the parking lot to the gas pumps.

"Feeling better, Nick?"

"Much better, thanks." They sped up the ramp to get back on the highway. "That was a nice thing you did back there, Mr. Dodd."

"Nah, just paying it backward." Bob said. He'd need to find an ATM later at the airport, but he remembered what he was supposed to do now. He pulled his phone from his pocket and thumbed DELOREAN. The app opened and a blinking red light indicated the app was recording. *Might as well have a little fun.*

"The air was hot, dry and dusty as Missouri Bob and Albuquerque Nick parked their horseless carriage next to the general store. It was the kind of heat that made a man thirsty enough to drink an entire river..."

Chapter 43

Monday afternoon

Bob didn't really mind the forty-minute wait in baggage claim. There were dozens of interesting people to watch and he was still preoccupied with the flashback from a couple of hours earlier.

Using the DELOREAN app he reported the episode in great detail for KMF, including the PFI that validated the man's story of gaining custody of his son and needing help to get home. Bob's phone rang seconds after he closed the app, Roger Kilmore with an immediate follow-up. Kilmore and Barlow were both probably throwing fits that his flashback occurred within an hour after he left KMF. Bob let the call roll to voice mail. He had complied with their request and needed time to process it for himself.

Bob hadn't thought about losing his wallet at the IMAX theater since shortly after it happened, many years ago. The time-shifting replay seemed perfect, every detail as real and vivid as it actually happened long ago. The lack of transition match points was something new. All the previous episodes, even the quick mini-flash when Tony removed the headgear, included physical and visual similarities between the current and historical situations.

This time the relevant "match" seemed to be money: the man asks Bob for cash. *Flash back.* A stranger and son return his lost wallet. Bob convinces them to accept twenty dollars in appreciation. *Flash forward.* Wait for his trusty mental 8-ball to verify the man's story. *All signs point to YES!*

Were his flashbacks now going to be triggered by relevant intellectual content instead of visual images? He only had one data point, but if so it might be a good thing. *Maybe my insight "power" is evolving, growing stronger. Do I need to start shopping for a cape?*

Bob's large bag finally tumbled from the chute and he searched for the exit to catch a taxi. It was his first trip to Las Vegas since he drove through sixty-something years earlier, and he was looking forward to seeing the sights.

A huge number of travelers were queued up for taxi service. Bob patiently snaked through the rope lines behind a bachelorette party, already in progress. The bride-to-be was wearing a sparkly tiara identifying her as The One, to be constantly feted in royal style at all times. The bride and her entourage all carried yard-long cocktails in neon-colored plastic tubes conveniently sold in the concourse near the arrival gates. With their free hands the girls attempted to navigate rolling stacks of luggage over rough pavement while wearing high heels and tight dresses. Bob joined the party after neatly catching a toppling vanity case. He was rewarded with a sloppy kiss on the cheek and named an honorary attendant by the bride. Eventually they reached the taxi stand and the airport valet skillfully split the bachelorette party and their luggage into three taxis. Bob declined an invitation to share a ride and wished the bride good luck.

He held up one finger to the valet who directed him to number twenty-nine. Bob looked down at the number painted on the curb where he stood: six. He turned left and walked, weaving through people loading luggage and entering cabs. There was a lot of confusion. Instead of parking directly next to the numbers on the curb, the taxis parked several feet ahead. People did not know which cab went with their assigned number, the one parked ahead or the one behind? Bob watched a bewildered elderly couple pile into taxi eighteen, apparently thinking it was seventeen. The trio assigned to eighteen were a few steps behind and became frustrated when they found their taxi occupied. They turned back to taxi seventeen but it had already been commandeered by another speedy couple, already settled inside and ready to depart. It was a total cluster. The angry trio pushed their way back toward the valet to get another assignment.

Forewarned, Bob scanned ahead for number twenty-nine while keeping several steps behind a young couple heading for twenty-eight. Sure enough, they walked right past twenty-eight and piled into twenty-nine. Bob had timed his pace perfectly and smoothly stopped at taxi twenty-eight. That's how he met Ruthie.

The trunk popped opened and the driver stepped around to the back of the car. She looked like she was Bob's bio-age, short and stooped but still spry. Despite the desert heat she wore a deep purple stocking cap topped with a bright pink pom-pom, a rainbow-colored sweatshirt, gray capri pants and red sandals. Bob had never seen that many wrinkles on a single person. Even her ankles looked dry and shriveled. She reached for Bob's luggage.

"Thanks, I'll get it," Bob said. The driver shrugged and got back in the car. Bob loaded his bags in the trunk and slid into the backseat. It was frosty inside, the air conditioning fan set on "blizzard." Bob adjusted the vents away from his face. Before he could fasten his seat belt the driver floored it and squealed into traffic, cutting off the cab Bob was supposed to be in. He heard driver twenty-nine yell through an open window in a language he didn't recognize. *Assholian?* Bob's driver casually flipped a bony middle finger and they were on their way.

A Las Vegas city taxi permit was taped to the back of the front seat. A picture of his driver, Ruthie Begosian, glared at him. She hadn't asked where to go, so Bob spoke up.

"Ruthie, I'm going to Bellagio." When she didn't respond Bob said it again.

"Heard you the first time!" she snapped. Her raspy smoker's voice conveyed frailty and domination simultaneously.

Bob looked out the window. The pyramid of Luxor first caught his eye, then the castle parapets and flying pennants of Excelsior further down. When the cab stopped at a traffic light some kind of switch got flipped and Ruthie blossomed socially.

"How long you staying?" Ruthie's eyes were sharp and cold in the rear-view mirror.

"Until Friday."

"Been here before?"

"Not recently. Drove through a long time ago, never stayed."

"Are you by yourself?"

"Meeting a friend. He's already at the hotel."

"You boys going to the titty bars?"

"What?"

"Titty bars. Strip joints. You going to get your pickle wet?" There was a gleam in her eyes now.

"Uh, why do you ask?"

"Most guys go. I pick 'em up at the airport and sometimes pick up the same guys later at a strip club, two or three in the morning, all drunk and stupid. Sometimes they have a girl or two with them, stripper chicks. They fool around, you know, sucking and fucking right where you're sitting." She stared at him from the mirror. Bob refused to give her a reaction and changed the subject.

"Ruthie, how long have you been in Vegas?" He studied the placard and memorized the permit number.

"Came to Vegas when I was seventeen, ran away from home in Iowa. I was a stripper for a while, used the name Trixxie, you know, with two X's, 'cause I was X-rated. Let guys screw me for cash. Lots of money back then from horny high rollers. Made enough to live for a while on the top floor of a fancy hotel, you know? Had a good body and knew how to use it. Sometimes guys got kind of rough, but most of 'em were okay. I gave them what they wanted, they paid me. Good times."

Ruthie drove in silence until they stopped at the next light.

"Course, my body eventually crapped out, so I learned how to do other things. Some of them were legit, too. Then I got tired, and old. Been driving cab now for close to fifteen years."

She glanced at Bob in the mirror. "So, handsome, you came to Vegas to get laid, right?"

"Nope," Bob said firmly. "Just see the sights, maybe go to a show, eat some good food. Probably won't even gamble."

"Right, right." They started moving again and Bob watched a roller coaster zoom into a tunnel on the roof of New York-New York casino.

The last time he and Linda made love was a few weeks before she got sick, and since then Bob had no interest in sex. Even after the Reversal he had no desire to pursue any kind of romantic relationship. Over the last few years he occasionally caught himself admiring Betty, feeling both guilty and slightly relieved that he still appreciated an attractive woman. Still, he considered himself to be sexually retired.

Maybe not. Last two weeks say different. How about Betty in the kitchen? He thought he handled the situation pretty well but had to admit she got him riled up.

HR Betty in the lab? Wired for monitoring, people watching, cameras recording. *We have liftoff!* The experiment proved his ancient rocket wasn't completely inert.

Gena Lindon? Okay, not real time, but why that particular flashback? Triggered from Betty's flirting? Or was his ever-younging brain trying to tell him something? Once again, he wished for the power of flashback selection. If these "back in time" trips were to continue, why not let him relive a sexy romp with Linda, the love of his life?

Ruthie was staring at him. He couldn't see her mouth in the mirror but serious scrunching of her crow's feet meant she was grinning.

"Got you thinking, huh? If I was in better shape, I'd show you a good time, maybe teach you a thing or two could come in handy later."

"Thanks, that's, uh, very nice of you." *What a stupid thing to say!* Ruthie had him rattled. He'd have to give the subject some deep consideration in the future. There were a number of possibilities and scenarios to evaluate, and potentially serious implications to—

Ah hell, Bob, just admit it! At some point you'll need to get laid. Maybe not like the geriatric ex-stripper taxi driver has in mind, you'll probably try a more conventional approach when you finally decide to dip your "pickle."

"Almost to Bellagio, then you boys can start your party."

Bob watched the famous Strip pass by and tried to decide how much to tip Ruthie for the interesting ride.

187

Chapter 44

Monday afternoon

Bob dropped his bags and stepped to the window to check out his view from the twenty-fourth floor. The Eiffel Tower in Paris stood tall across the Strip, a dazzling inverted image reflected in Bellagio's fountain lake below. A giant Ferris wheel to the back and left of Paris gleamed in the late afternoon sun, a huge gleaming coin standing on edge, perfectly balanced.

Jack had sent a text a few minutes earlier, he would meet Bob in the casino bar near the poker section in an hour after "finishing up something" first. Bob unpacked, then took the elevator down to the casino. It wasn't crowded, a number of dealers in green-vest uniforms stood patiently behind empty tables. Many of the games had unfamiliar names and Bob realized he was completely out of touch with the gambling scene. He walked a loop around the casino until he came to the poker section and took a seat at the bar. He ordered a fifteen-year-old whisky and twisted around to check out the games. Serious players, most wearing dark glasses, stared in silence at their cards and each other as dealers narrated the game and prompted when bets were due.

On the far side of the poker tables, columns of brightly lit numbers towered above the roulette stations. The image of the little ball circling in the opposite direction of the spinning wheel reminded him of the Costanza strategy.

He finished his drink and charged it to his room. He pulled all of the airport ATM cash from his wallet and walked toward the nearest empty roulette wheel where he was greeted pleasantly by the croupier.

"Good afternoon, Simone," Bob said, reading her badge. "I'd like to place a bet. Is cash okay?"

"Yes, sir, I can make the exchange for you."

She handed him a stack of chips and he looked at the board. His first instinct was to choose black, he put the entire stack of chips on red.

"Let her rip."

She spun the wheel and flicked the ball in the opposite direction. The combination of the super smooth rotation and the soft clicking sound appealed to Bob's engineering nature, the device was well-designed. The wheel eventually slowed and the ball dropped, bouncing a couple of times before landing on number fourteen.

"Fourteen Red. Congratulations, sir."

Bob smiled to himself, enjoying the moment as Simone matched his stack of chips with another.

"Would you like to play again?"

It was exactly what he wanted to do, so Bob shook his head. He thanked Simone, pushed a couple of chips to her and scooped up the rest. At the cashier's window he cashed out and tipped the attendant five dollars. He pushed his wallet into his front pocket, returned to his seat at the poker bar and ordered a thirty-five-year-old whisky. Jack arrived twenty minutes later.

"Good to see you man!" Jack said, shaking hands. "Really glad you decided to come, it's going to be fun." He ordered a beer and told the bartender to put it on Bob's tab.

"What were you 'finishing up'? I've been here an hour and a half."

"I was deeply immersed in the study of advanced Greco-Roman grappling techniques in gelatinous media."

Bob tilted his head. "Really? Strippers wrestling in jello?"

Jack nodded. "Place called Jiggly's, not far from the Strip. I love jello, cherry's the best."

"Is that your favorite flavor or the name of the winner?"

"Both. Hey, here's some good news. Guess who's staying here at the hotel?"

"I give up, who?"

"The Norwegian Bikini Team!"

"No shit?"

Jack nodded. "Yep. They're here for their forty-year reunion, but still…could be fun, right?"

Bob gave Jack one thumb, not quite pointing up. "How did it go at your uncle's B&B?"

"Mostly great, except a couple of rambunctious newlyweds kicked over a candle and the drapes caught fire. Had to evacuate a few guests and air out the smoke for a while. Could have used some help from your sexy fire-fighting neighbor." Jack tipped back his beer. "How about KMF? They get your head screwed on right? Didn't cross-thread it like last time?"

"It went fine," Bob said. "After a week of examinations and dozens of tests, their only recommendation was to significantly reduce the time I spend with one-eyed ass clowns." He grinned at Jack and they clinked glasses. "It's been an interesting couple of weeks for sure."

Bob told Jack about his altercation with DJ and the third flashback, and the creative efforts of Dr. Barlow and staff to induce flashbacks in the laboratory. Jack seemed especially interested in the experiment with HR Betty.

"Poor Bob, I'm soooo sorry you didn't get to enjoy that next-door neighbor fantasy again. I feel bad for you, man." Jack shook his head sadly.

"Yeah, it didn't work, but there's more." Bob described the mini-flash with Tony and the episode at the convenience store.

Jack was impressed. "Man, you're going through a lot. How are you handling it?"

Bob shrugged and sipped his drink. "Okay, I think. Obviously, something strange is happening and it's got me a little preoccupied. All I can do is roll with it." He signaled to the bartender for the check. "Let's find some place to have dinner. I have one more thing to discuss with you."

Chapter 45

Monday evening

"You wanted to talk about something?" Jack asked. The fajitas had mostly disappeared, and a third round of margaritas had just been delivered.

"Right," Bob said. "You already know the big stuff that happened over the last couple of weeks. As I was working through it, I stumbled on an idea. Sort of a new-old philosophy I'm test driving. It's one reason why I decided to join you on this trip."

"Glad you did. What is it?"

"*Seinfeld.*"

Jack's eyebrow went up. "Yes, and?"

"There's an episode in season five where George is talking to Jerry and Elaine at the diner and feeling sorry for himself."

"Pretty sure that happens in every episode."

"You sound like Marley. Anyway, George says—I'm paraphrasing here—every life decision he's made has been wrong. Jerry says if that's true, then he should make opposite decisions, which would have to be right."

Jack nodded. "I think I remember this. Doesn't George meet a good-looking woman?"

"Yes. He introduces himself by telling her he is unemployed and lives with his parents, and somehow she is still intrigued. I was watching the episode the day after the fight with DJ and it got me thinking. I don't feel like everything I've done lately has been wrong, but over the last seventeen years I've just been drifting along."

"What do you mean?"

"I think I was just overwhelmed. Since I thought I was dying I didn't really need a plan going forward. Then the remission, and later the Reversal, and I received way more attention than I ever wanted after it all went public. When things finally settled, I rolled back into neutral geezer mode and just floated. I was getting younger and healthier every day, but instead of seeking opportunities I was waiting for whatever happened next."

Jack drained his margarita. "Think I know where this is heading. Go on."

"Something changed when I flipped on the sprinklers and soaked the kid's truck. Not that it was some great act of courage, just a baby step. Then I got into that fight with DJ and—"

"You went all George on his ass!"

"—and I was in way over my head but somehow it worked out okay."

Jack leaned forward. "Bring it home, buddy. I gotta take a leak."

"Okay, here it is. I'm implementing the Costanza Strategy. I'm going to do the opposite of what I'd normally do. Maybe not all the time, but as much as I can get away with."

Jack grinned. "I love it! When do we start?"

"I already have." Bob pulled a fistful of hundred-dollar bills from his wallet and dropped them on the table.

Jack's eye opened wide. "You mugged a high roller? Holy crap!"

"No, you ass! While I was waiting for you, I put five hundred dollars on red at the roulette table. One spin, doubled my money."

"Only one? You didn't go again?"

Bob shook his head. "No, because that was my instinct, to go again. I did the opposite and walked away."

Jack thought for a second, then his eyebrow crinkled.

"But your decision to walk away, wouldn't the opposite of *that* be to stay and play again?"

Bob nodded. "I thought you might say that. Ever heard of a DO LOOP?"

"No, what is it?"

"It's a coding thing, software programming. I learned about it in Fortran class in college. You set up a series of instructions that include IF-THEN statements. IF this condition occurs THEN do that, IF another condition occurs THEN do something else. One of the potential response actions is GO BACK to a previous step and repeat. Sloppy coding can lead to a bad DO LOOP, where the instruction just loops back on itself and repeats, stuck in an infinite number of cycles. Eventually bad things happen, or if you're lucky the program will time out and terminate."

Jack got excited. "I know! Like the directions on the shampoo bottle: LATHER, RINSE, REPEAT. Somewhere there's an idiot who's been stuck in his shower for years." They both cracked up.

"Great example," Bob said. "To avoid getting caught in an opposite version of an infinite DO LOOP, it's best to adopt a rule of only applying it once in a given situation."

"Okay," Jack said. "Lemme see how this works. I think I want another drink. But I also think I should slow down, as the night is young and we need to pace ourselves. What should I do? Order another round? Or go against that instinct and tab out? What is the opposite when you have too many choices?"

"Well, I'm pretty sure your immediate instinct now is to head for the men's room before the opposite of what you want happens. Let's ease into this idea, maybe start Opposite Day tomorrow, after breakfast."

Jack nodded and stood up. "All right. It *sounds* like a great plan, but it might be the opposite. Tomorrow, then." As he turned, two women dressed to thrill approached their table.

"Hi guys, would you like some company this evening?"

Jack whistled and turned to Bob.

"Can we start Opposite Day tonight? Pretty please?"

Bob stood and pointed toward the restrooms. "No, Jack. Go." He turned to the women. "Thank you, ladies, maybe some other time."

Chapter 46

Monday evening

After a quick bio-break, Bob found Jack admiring the view at Bellagio's indoor garden. "Man, the eye candy here is non-stop."

Bob laughed. "Yeah, and it takes you twice as long to see it all."

"Hey, be nice."

They joined the flow of people walking toward the casino until Jack peeled off to check out a window display of wrist watches. He pointed at a high-tech model with a royal blue face and a rich leather band. "I always wanted a decent watch."

Bob leaned in to look. "Three grand? Don't you think you'd be happy with, oh I don't know, a nine-hundred-dollar watch instead?"

Jack shrugged. "You're right. You're the one with money. Maybe you can buy me one for Christmas."

They walked on until they came to a bar strategically located where three walkways converged. It was a perfect spot to enjoy a cocktail and people watch.

After ordering drinks, Jack nudged Bob and tilted his head toward the opposite end of the bar. A pretty woman with auburn hair and wearing a tight red dress had just sat down. A middle-aged man, wearing black eyeglasses and going bald, sat two seats away intently working his phone. The man glanced at the woman when she ordered her drink, then went back to work. The woman lit a cigarette and gave Bob and Jack a nod and a quick smile across the bar. Bob frowned.

"What?" Jack asked.

"Smoker."

"Smoking hot, you mean."

"Well, yeah, but I hate cigarette smoke."

"Then we really came to the wrong place to relax. It's a casino. In Vegas. It's almost mandatory to smoke in here."

"Then I guess I'll have to take mine second-hand."

Bob and Jack talked and watched people strolling past the bar, occasionally glancing at the woman in red. She seemed to be putting on a show, slowly blowing smoke from ruby red lips and posing glamorously with the cigarette between puffs. The bald guy seemed oblivious and continued typing on his phone. The woman finished her cigarette and immediately lit another.

"What do you think her name is?" Jack asked.

"Who, Red?"

"Yeah, who does she look like?"

Bob gazed over his scotch glass. "Yvonne?"

"Wow, where did that come from?"

"Don't know, just popped into my head."

Jack shook his head. "Naw, too exotic. I mean, she is dressed to kill, obviously, but if you put some regular clothes on her I think she'd have a girl-next-door look. All nice and sweet but would still make a man think of interesting things."

Bob looked at his friend. "You seem to have given this a fair amount of thought."

"Just dreaming. We are in Vegas." Jack continued to stare, then said, "Sandy. Her name is Sandy."

"Perfect!" Bob agreed. "Makes you think of the beach, and waves, and bikinis, and—"

"Okay, listen," Jack interrupted. "Sandy is the middle of three kids, from a small town in…Kansas. She was in a bad relationship and took a lot of grief for it from her family and friends. She finally had enough, broke it off and decided to blow town. She packed a large suitcase, took all her money out of her bank account and drove west in, let's see, a 2001 Toyota Corolla."

Bob picked up the thread. "Sandy stops in Denver but the city feels too big. She doesn't know anyone and keeps driving. She sees a highway sign, 'LAS VEGAS 723 MILES' and thinks 'why not'?"

Jack's turn. "She arrives in Vegas and knows she can't afford to stay on the Strip or anywhere nice. She finds a small motel downtown, puts on her best pair of jeans and takes a taxi to New York-New York."

Bob grinned. "You're on a roll, keep going."

"Sandy wanders through New York, but it feels strange and crowded, you know, like a big city back east. She walks outside, sees the big castle across the street and heads on over. She walks into Excalibur and instantly gets a different vibe. It's an old casino, everything is a little worn and crusty, including the people. She sees girls dancing on elevated stages scattered behind the blackjack tables. She takes a seat at a bar to watch and orders a gin and tonic. She's never had a drink before and it was the only one she could think of. Sandy is watching the stage and one of the dancers catches her looking and gives her a big wink." Jack stopped and waved his empty glass at the bartender. "Your turn."

Bob accepted the challenge and rubbed his hands together. "On her next break the dancer comes over and sits next to Sandy. 'What's your name, honey? New in town?' Sandy is surprised. 'How can you tell?' The dancer says she had the same look when she arrived in Vegas four years earlier. Tells Sandy to call her Roxy, but it's not her real name."

Jack brought it home. "The girls get acquainted, and Roxy offers to show Sandy around town after her shift. Over the next hour Sandy discovers she really likes gin. Then Roxy shows up, takes her by the hand and one thing leads to another. A year later two old farts from Missouri are gawking as Sandy and her dress slowly seduce a balding used-car salesman at a bar in Bellagio." Jack nodded across the bar.

Bob turned and said, "Holy cow."

Sandy had moved over next to Baldy, who had stopped fiddling with his phone to give all his attention to his new friend. Sandy's right arm was below the bar and it was easy to imagine her hand on the guy's leg. *Or something,* Bob thought. Sandy smiled continuously as they talked and let the guy light her next cigarette. Bob felt an elbow in his ribs.

"She's got him," Jack said.

"What do you mean?"

"I'll bet you twenty dollars they leave together."

"Really? She looks, I don't know, too nice. Too normal."

"Trust me," Jack said. "She came to the bar by herself. She didn't take the empty seat next to you, she could tell we were together. She takes a seat at the other end, close to the guy who is obviously alone. They don't speak, don't even greet each other, she orders a drink and sits with a cigarette. Five minutes later they're side by side and she's helpfully scratching that pesky itch on his thigh."

Bob was impressed. "You seem to know what you are talking about. Personal experience?"

Jack nodded. "I was in the navy, remember? Played Spot the Hooker years ago, with my buddies." Jack pointed with his chin. "Check it out."

Sandy and the bald man stood up. The man left cash on the bar, then Sandy took his hand and led him away, in the direction of the hotel elevators. Bob passed a twenty-dollar bill to Jack.

"Well played, sir. Use that to buy us another round."

* * *

They were on their fifth round of drinks and Bob was feeling it. He was about to suggest they call it an evening when he spotted a trio of stunning young women coming their way. He nudged Jack to look and was embarrassed when the blonde in the middle saw him do it. The girl said something, and her two companions stopped as the blonde approached. Both men stood up.

"Good evening, gentlemen." She stood unnervingly close, and Bob fought the urge to step back. She appeared confident, and Bob guessed she was in her early thirties. "Having a good time tonight?" Both men, nodded. Bob was unsure what to say. *Where's my damn insight when I need it?*

The woman took a half-step closer to Jack. "Wow, I really love your eye! I mean, your...you know. It's quite striking. Makes you look sexy-dangerous." Her expression said *just like me*.

Jack recovered and jumped into the game. "Hey lady, stop staring at my eye. My dick's down here." All three cracked up.

"You guys in the mood to party? There's plenty to go around," the girl said, waving a hand toward her two friends.

Bob and Jack glanced at each other.

"What do you say, Costanza?" Jack asked. "Ready to implement your plan?"

"No, Jack. We've already settled this. Not going to happen."

The blonde looked confused.

"Thank you for the invitation," Bob said. "You ladies have a nice evening."

The girl nodded and opened her small carry purse. She pressed a business card into Bob's hand. "If you change your mind, please give me a call," she said and turned to rejoin her friends.

Jack put his hand on Bob's shoulder and peeked at the card. "Quite the professional. I see a trend developing. We're a couple of bona fide chick magnets, you know?"

"You're full of it, Jack. You said it yourself: we're in a Vegas casino, and we're not gambling. By definition we are prime targets for a particular class of entrepreneurs in the adult services industry."

Jack stared at Bob. "Him talk funny, use big words. Come on, I'll buy one more round, a nightcap."

"Okay, last one. I need an eight-hour nap."

As they turned around to their seats both men stopped and stared. Sandy had returned, perched on the same seat at the opposite end of the bar. She had a cigarette in her hand and acknowledged the men with a small, knowing smile.

"Wow," Jack said. "She's quick."

"More likely he was," Bob said.

The bartender delivered their drinks, and Bob and Jack openly admired Sandy from across the bar. She didn't seem to mind. When her phone buzzed she read the message, then paid her tab. She waved to them and headed once again to the hotel elevators.

"Jack, you're the champ. I'll never doubt your Spot the Hooker skills again."

Chapter 47

Tuesday morning

As the winner of last night's contest, Jack was given the honor of setting the time to meet for breakfast and he optimistically chose nine am. Bob was ten minutes late but still beat his friend by a good thirty minutes. He was on his third cup of coffee when Jack slid into the booth. He looked like he had been awake for several seconds.

"Morning, beautiful!" Bob said, more cheerfully than he felt.

"So, this is death. Not as bad as I thought," Jack mumbled, rubbing the grit out of his eye with the heel of his hand. He squinted at Bob. "Must be in Hell if you're here too." He grimaced from the effort of engaging in pre-caffeine hangover humor.

"Nice try, buddy."

They both ordered hearty breakfasts to soak up the residual alcohol. They ate in silence for several minutes until Jack's brain rebooted.

"What was the thing, the plan we had for today?"

"You mean the Costanza Strategy? Opposite day?"

Jack nodded as he was taking a bite and his nose knocked

scrambled eggs off his fork and into his lap. "Shit! Right. I mean wrong. The opposite of right."

"Hey, that's going to get old fast if you keep it up. Let's make it simple," Bob said. "This is our first time in Vegas together. How would you expect a couple of boring geezers like us to spend a normal Tuesday in Sin City?"

Jack took his time before answering. "We'd probably start with lots of coffee. And breakfast."

"Too late to counter-program that action. What else?"

"Well, after breakfast we'd probably walk the Strip and get a little exercise, scope out the sights, take some pictures and make fun of people. Maybe check out some art galleries and walk through the shops at Caesar's. Maybe play some slots. Do you gamble?"

Bob shook his head. "Not really. The roulette thing yesterday was an anomaly, opposite of my usual self."

"Okay, today you gamble. And we do the opposite of all the stuff I just said."

Bob nodded. "What about you? What's a normal Jack day in Vegas?"

Jack took a slug of coffee and gave it some thought. "A normal day for me would be to avoid pretty women as much as possible, probably just stay in my hotel room and read classic literature. I wouldn't drink or play any blackjack and I definitely wouldn't want to be titillated in any way."

Bob laughed. His friend was perking up. Since he was late, Jack charged their breakfast to his room. On the elevator up to their floor Bob proposed meeting in the lobby in fifteen minutes.

"I vote for the opposite, a nap," Jack said. "Or at least a shower. Meet you in an hour. Oh, one more thing. In this Costanza plan you are obviously George, therefore, I'm, Jerry. Right? The funny, clever guy."

"Sure, you bet," Bob said. *Sorry, Jack, you're obviously Kramer in today's episode.*

* * *

"Costanza" and "Kramer" had a terrific afternoon, challenging each other with new experiences they would normally not consider. After enjoying the roller coaster on top of New York-New York more than they expected, they decided to raise the stakes and check out the fantastic rides at the top of the Stratosphere hotel. There were three stomach-churning wet-yourself thrillers, each involving spinning or dangling more than 800 feet above the Strip without a net. Despite their best "opposite" intentions all three rides proved too intimidating for the not-so-dynamic duo. They settled instead for a ride on the giant Ferris wheel behind Paris, followed by thirty money-wasting minutes in an oxygen bar promising "youthful rejuvenation" from breathing specially enriched air. Bob wondered if it would have the reverse effect on him but felt no different after the session.

Accepting a double-dog dare from Jack, Bob donned an X-rated "I'm the Bride" tiara he found on the floor of a tram and wore it through two beers at an outdoor bar near Treasure Island. A man wearing a penis-crown sitting with a one-eyed companion was an irresistible image and they affably posed for photos with giggling tourists.

Late in the afternoon they decided to spend a couple of hours resting in their rooms before dinner. On the tram ride back, Bob decided to pay it forward and left the tiara as he found it, on the floor beneath an empty seat.

Chapter 48

Tuesday evening

Bob stepped into the empty elevator, punched for the lobby and checked his watch. Jack was probably two drinks ahead of him in their spot at the casino bar.

The car stopped on the twentieth floor. Bob stepped to his left as a pretty woman stepped inside, giving him the tiniest of smiles as she moved into her half of the space. She was dressed in the standard "Vegas Girl" uniform: a tight black dress, high heels, perfect hair and make-up. Bob guessed she was still on the fun side of forty.

The elevator descended for about three seconds, shuddered, and stopped. The lights went out, then blinked back on, half as bright. The woman grabbed the brass railing and glanced at Bob with big eyes. He gave her what he hoped was a reassuring look and took another step left, away from her, trying to convey that he was not a threat. He tried the emergency call button on the control panel, nothing happened. He pulled his phone out of his pocket: NO SERVICE.

"Do you have a signal?" he asked.

She pried a phone out of her tiny carry purse. "No."

Bob looked at the woman as she fiddled with her phone, apparently trying to send a text in case it might go through. She seemed nervous and uncomfortable as would be expected, but something in her expression and posture suggested she had been unsure of herself even before stepping into the elevator.

Bob studied the floor, thinking. Bellagio was a high-end establishment; no doubt hotel security and maintenance crews were aware of the malfunction and were scrambling to respond. But since the emergency button didn't seem to work and no one had spoken to them through the speaker on the control panel, it could be more complicated than the usual failure. They might be stuck for a while.

His instinct was to stand still on his side of the elevator with his hands in his pockets to make sure the woman would feel as safe as possible. Eventually he would come up with something to say, something innocuous and light, and probably stupid. She kept fooling with her phone, maybe trying to look busy, probably thinking through the situation too.

What would George do? Bob decided to break the ice. "Well, here we are in a classic fantasy situation." The woman immediately lifted her head.

"I mean, what are the odds?" he continued. "Stuck in an elevator with a gorgeous, sexy...man." He gave her a grin and asked, "How's it feel?"

She smiled slightly at his joke but still looked unsettled. Bob kept going.

"Let's break it down further. You're dressed to kill, obviously about to embark on a fantastic night on the famous Las Vegas Strip. I'm guessing you're on your way to meet friends in the lobby, right?"

She nodded. "Yes."

"As for me, I've been riding this elevator up and down all thirty-six floors nonstop for three days now, primed and waiting for the inevitable power loss that would leave me isolated in here with an attractive young woman.

"And you? You find yourself intrigued by this strange yet somehow awkward man with the round face, thin gray hair with a touch of pepper, and sexy paunch. Never-the-nonetheless, the man sets you at ease with his wit and engaging personality."

She was catching on and started to relax. "Please, go on," she said.

He backed up to lean against the wall and folded his arms. "She couldn't believe her luck. For more than a month she had dreamed of being stuck in an elevator between the seventeenth and eighteenth floors with a studly stud, a virile, passionate Latin lover sporting two and a half days of stubble. And now, thank the gods, here she is, trapped in a box in the sky with a retired engineer from the Midwest, her dream come true." He paused to take a breath and work out something to say next.

"Running short on his narrative, the old man in the corner didn't know how much longer he could continue, and he hoped the nice woman would do her part and help keep the story going." *Okay lady, your turn.*

The woman took a moment and brushed her hair back. "The nice man had done his best to put her at ease, and it mostly worked. Apparently, he was harmless with a great sense of humor. She asked him his name, and he said...?"

"Radicchio. Radicchio Macaroni, at your service," Bob said, bowing.

She laughed. "'Radicchio', it took her breath away."

Bob's turn. "And you are...?"

She barely hesitated. "Brandeee. With three E's."

Bob laughed. "Nicely done!"

"Radicchio, may I ask you a favor? These heels are awful, I'm not used to them and we may be here a while. Will you please help me sit down? This dress is so tight I might pull a muscle."

"Of course." He pulled a clean handkerchief from his back pocket and spread it out on the floor of the elevator. Then he pulled a second handkerchief from another pocket and spread it next to the first. She raised her eyebrows.

Bob shrugged. "Always best to be prepared."

She looked impressed and held his hands as Bob lowered her gently to the floor, silently enjoying the view of her legs. He sat down in the opposite corner as she slipped off her shoes.

"What happens now?" she asked.

"Exhausted from the strenuous act of assisting Brandeee, the old man craved a nap but knew that would be very bad form." He was rewarded with a smile, and Bob hoped it was from his attempts to keep things light and easy. *Or maybe she's just humoring an annoying old man.* He asked her to talk a little about herself and her trip to Las Vegas.

She dropped the act. "I'm from Chicago, this is my first time in Vegas." She worked in marketing for a retail clothing company, was thirty-six years old, divorced several years earlier after a classic married-too-young scenario. Single and uncomfortable with the idea of dating again, she threw herself completely into her job. Feeling burned out the last few months, she needed a vacation. After several weeks of badgering, her best friend convinced her to have a girl's weekend in Vegas.

"Four of us flew in this afternoon and everyone took a nap, planning for a late night out. I was told to dress up and meet everyone in the lobby at seven, and now I'm here with you." She seemed at ease now.

Bob started to reply when the elevator car shuddered for a few seconds, then stopped. They heard voices talking somewhere above.

"I'm sure they know we're stuck and trying to get it moving again," Bob said. He checked the control panel again, still dead. He looked at the ceiling. Nothing to see, but he gazed up anyway.

"What are you looking for?"

He decided to be honest. "Nothing, really. You're very attractive, and I'm trying to be a gentleman and not stare at your legs." He held his eyes on hers and she blushed.

"Uh, I understand. I'll take that as a compliment. I thought this dress was too short." She shifted, trying to get comfortable. "Let's change the subject. What's your story?"

Bob was about to say he was here with a friend for the weekend, then remembered the Costanza Strategy. Against his instinct, he decided to open up completely.

"Do you remember many years ago hearing about the guy in the news who was getting younger each day?"

Her eyes opened wide. "That's you?" She stared at him. "Now I see it, I remember! Only you look—"

"About ten years younger. Yeah, it's me. I'm getting my hair back now, at least some of it."

"Wow! I can't believe it! Your real name is Robert? Richard? Something like that?"

"Robert Dodd. Please call me Bob, Brandeee."

"It's Christine, actually. Oh my God! They called you the most unique person in the world, right? Oh, I'm sorry, I mean, it's nice to meet you, Bob. Holy shit, I'm stuck in an elevator with... oh my God, I'm so sorry."

He laughed. "It's okay Christine, nice to meet you too."

She realized she was staring at him and looked away, then right back again.

"If you don't mind me asking, how old are you? I mean, how many—"

"I turned ninety-one a couple of weeks ago. And, I figure I'm close to fifty-seven years young too."

A voice called out from above. "Hello in the elevator! Can you hear me?"

"We hear you!" Bob answered.

"We apologize for the malfunction, but we have a handle on the problem and should have things working again in about a half hour. Hang in there, and we'll check on you every few minutes."

Christine leaned forward. "Bob, since we are here for a while, I'd love to learn more about you, if you feel like sharing. Your story must be fascinating! But I understand completely if you'd rather not, you must run into a lot of crazy people who won't leave you alone when they find out who you were, I mean, who you are." She had flipped the script and was now trying to reassure Bob he was not trapped in the elevator with a crazy person.

"It's okay, I brought it up. I haven't talked about it in a long time, as a matter of fact."

He told Christine about the cancer, and how, two days after his seventy-fourth birthday, he was ready to die. He talked about hoping he would be with Linda again, and feeling surprised and strangely disappointed when he woke up, somehow still alive. How his recovery astonished his doctor, who told him it was a "significant spontaneous remission" and he should enjoy life while he could as the cancer would surely return soon and finish him off.

Bob described how he discovered he was getting younger and the efforts of Dr. Kilmore and his medical team to confirm and understand how and why it was happening. He described the chaos and anxiety of the public announcement of the Reversal, and how Frank Weaker and a group of courageous CHUMPS had saved him from being abducted by fanatical church leaders.

Bob was surprised how comfortable he was telling all to Christine. Other than Jack, who knew most of it, he had never told anyone the story from start to finish like this. Christine seemed captivated, hanging on every word.

He skipped some details knowing time was short, but it seemed important to get through all the main points before the elevator started moving again. Sharing his abbreviated life story with a complete stranger was a perfect application of the Costanza Strategy, and it felt great.

"I decided to meet Jack in Vegas and here I am, with you."

Christine eyes were soft, her voice quiet and calm. "Thank you for sharing, I don't know what to say. It's an incredible story, hard to imagine going through all of that. The way you describe it, you don't view your, uh, *situation* as negative, but you don't seem to think it's wonderful, either."

He thought for a moment before responding. "Christine, I have cycled through every emotion you can think of over the last several years. At one low point I considered whether suicide made any sense, and ultimately decided it didn't. While I don't understand why this happened—perhaps I'll never know—there must be some purpose for it all. After years of just sitting around, I finally decided to steer into the skid, get back on track, and let it play out."

Christine nodded. *She's so easy to talk to.* "Would you like to know my current plans?" Bob asked. "I mean, how I'm going to handle this going-forward-in-reverse thing?" He knew it was a loaded question.

"Absolutely!"

"Okay. After a bunch of hours in therapy with the psych team at the Kilmore Foundation, a huge number of scotch-and-sofa sessions of deep introspection, and some recent encounters with fidiots—sorry, *idiots*—who behaved badly, I realized that before the Reversal, I was a decent guy but kind of passive. Overall, things went pretty well. But now, with another," Bob paused to dramatically look at his watch, "five and a half decades to go, it feels like it's time to make some adjustments.

"I have ninety-plus years of life experience. That's a metric butt-load of accumulated knowledge, wisdom, foolishness, history, trivia, facts, and a fair amount of pure crap stored in my brain. All of it is mixed into my personality, my outlook, and my philosophy. I'm trying to keep in mind I always have this terrific resource, this massive archive I can draw on anytime I need to react to a situation or make a decision. Hopefully, it will result in better outcomes most of the time, and maybe even help others, too. The Reversal has set me up to live for a long time. Be a shame not to make the best of it, right?"

"Well, you sure helped me tonight," Christine said. "It's like some kind of comic-book superpower, magic knowledge whenever you need it."

Bob nodded. "I'm going to try some new strategies, be the opposite of who I used to be in some ways. Take more risks, try new stuff, have more fun. At the same time, I believe I have learned which principles and values are important and good, and I don't want to give those up."

He paused. "You're the first person I've talked to about all this.

Jack knows some of it, but you got the whole story. You're a great listener, Christine. Thank you."

Her face lit up, her eyes misty.

Uh oh. Time to lighten things up.

"I'm not sure I get to say 'life is short' anymore, but I guess my point is this: when you find yourself stuck in an elevator with a friendly, attractive woman, make sure you see the bright side." He flashed her a grin. "Your turn. What are your life plans?"

Before she answered the voice from above called down.

"Hey folks? Have you moving again in two minutes. The hotel manager will meet you in the lobby. Sorry again for the delay."

Christine laughed. "You'll have to hear Brandeee's life plan some other time, Bob. But you've sure given me a lot to think about. Help me up, please?" She held out her hands as Bob got to his feet.

He pulled her up and she held his arm as she slipped into her shoes. Before letting go she gave him a quick hug. "Thank you for turning an hour stuck in an elevator into such a pleasure."

He nodded, his brain automatically searching the archives for Things a Gentleman Says.

"The pleasure was all mine, Christine."

Chapter 49

Tuesday evening

Denton Rafter made his way through Hell to the bar. He ordered a beer and scanned the room but didn't see Betty. He checked his phone, thankfully there were no more updates from Casstown. Things were stable for the moment.

He was tired of dealing with the lesser brains in the lowest ranks of his organization. Every time he considered hiring someone to manage the staff, he talked himself out of it to avoid cutting into the profits. Overall, he thought he was managing things pretty well and hoped to rise to a higher position in the Company soon. The disaster of the last few days probably meant waiting for a while longer. One more fuck up and he might even have to find other opportunities, maybe in a hurry. That's why he had insurance. A big-ass, Plan B safety net.

Unless DJ had screwed it all up.

A hand touched his shoulder and Betty sat down next to him. She was as pretty as he remembered, wearing tight jeans and a clingy green sweater. She smiled a lot last time, not so much tonight.

"I'm really glad to see you," Denton said. "Thanks for coming."

Betty turned to the approaching bartender and ordered a glass of chardonnay. "I almost stayed home. Thought you might stand me up again." She focused on her phone instead of him, and Denton smiled inwardly. He figured that's how she'd play it; he knew exactly what she wanted. He'd give it to her, but not quite yet. *I know how to play too.*

"Be right back," he said, and left for the men's room. He took twice as long as he needed, reading the advertisements posted above the urinals and checking his phone again. When he returned to the bar Betty was sipping her wine and watching ESPN on the television. He put his hand on her back and she turned to face him with a blank expression.

"I'm sorry about last week," he said. "I had to leave town suddenly for a business situation. I should have called but in all the chaos I forgot. I apologize. You can forgive me and we can have a nice evening. If not, I'm out of here. Either way is fine with me, your call." Denton set his jaw and waited for her decision. If he guessed right, she'd get over it and they would continue the dance. If he was wrong, he'd leave and hit the strip club a few blocks away.

He watched her work things out. It only took two seconds.

"Buy me another drink, please?" Betty raised her glass and tipped her head back to finish off the wine, nicely stretching her sweater in the process. Denton appreciated the view but somehow managed to turn to the bartender and swirl a finger for another round.

For the next half-hour they chatted about nothing, Betty occasionally making a point to touch his arm and Denton acting like he didn't notice. Betty made a trip to the ladies' room. When she returned, she looked pale and worried.

"Hey, you okay?"

"No, not really," Betty said, holding her stomach. "I feel sick, maybe from something I ate. I don't know…" She swayed and Denton caught her arm.

"Let's get you home," he said, signaling to close out their tab. In the parking lot he steered her towards his truck until she stopped.

"Thanks, I'm okay. I can drive myself."

Denton shook his head. "Friends don't let friends throw up in their own cars." He grinned at his own wit.

"No, I'm not leaving my car here."

"Well, at least let me follow you, to make sure you get home safe."

"That's sweet. Thank you." She took his hand and they walked to her car.

Denton followed her through town and surprised himself by not being disappointed that nothing physical was going to happen. Earlier in the day he had fantasized that Betty would finally tell him what she needed him to do to her, and exactly how to do it. But his lust changed immediately to genuine concern when she told him she was ill. He still wanted it to happen, of course, no doubt about it. But it wasn't going to be tonight, and it was fine. He'd be a perfect gentleman and keep dancing. They'd get serious the next time they got together. Probably. If she wanted to.

He followed her into a residential neighborhood, vaguely familiar, and parked at the curb in front of her house. Betty pulled her car into the garage and met him in the driveway.

"What's with all the cars?" Denton waved at the street.

"The kids across the street are always having a party."

Denton nodded, and looked at the house being repaired next door. "What's the story with that? Storm damage?"

"No, it was a fire," Betty said. "About two weeks ago. I saw it first and woke up Bob, we were trying to put it out when the fire department showed up. It was pretty scary." She grasped Denton's arm and leaned against him.

"Wow! This Bob guy is lucky to have you living next door."

"Actually, I'm the lucky one. Bob's great, a perfect...gentleman." She let go of his arm and stepped away with a serious expression. "He treats me really well. You might have heard of him, Robert Dodd? The guy in the news a long time ago, the man who stopped growing old and is getting younger?"

"Yeah, I remember. I knew he lived in town but didn't know where. How 'bout that? Right next door." He noticed the bricks piled around the broken mailbox, and the house across the street looked familiar. Neurons nudged each other inside his brain.

DJ gave the flashlight to some guy after knocking down his mailbox. In the neighborhood where Denton had picked him up once...

My fucking flashlight is there, in that house!

Denton turned to Betty. "I'd like to meet Bob. Do you feel well enough to introduce me tonight?"

Betty shook her head. "He's out of town, his nephew is house-sitting during the repairs. Some other time." She gasped and wobbled, clutching her stomach.

"Okay, let's get you inside and call it a night." He held her arm as they walked toward the garage, his eyes locked on the house owned by the famous Robert Dodd.

Chapter 50

Tuesday evening

This is pointless.

Bob sat up in bed less than a minute after lying down, his thoughts churning on the mind-blowing head trip a couple of hours earlier. He walked to the window and opened the drapes. The Bellagio fountains below swirled in the lights, enjoyed by hundreds of people gathered on the sidewalk despite the late hour. If anyone happened to look up, they'd probably see him outlined in the window wearing only his briefs, but he didn't care. *Enjoy the show, folks, I've got bigger things to worry about.*

Bob took a slow, deep breath, focused on the dancing waters below, and replayed the entire crazy scene in his head, one more time.

* * *

During dinner Bob suggested, in the spirit of Opposite Day, that he and Jack get tickets for the Cirque du Soleil show, *Bodies in Flow*. As expected, Jack threw a fit, vehemently rejecting the idea and accusing Bob of taking the "opposite thing" way too far. Bob was ready with another option to which Jack quickly agreed. A short time later they were standing in line to buy tickets for the Blue Man Group, the show Bob had wanted to see all along.

They took their seats as the pre-show entertainment began. A monstrous inflatable creature, vaguely fish-like in bright neon colors, floated over the crowd, remotely controlled from offstage. Occasionally it hovered in place and gazed eerily down at a delighted fan in the audience before moving on in silence.

The stage curtain parted and a second, smaller inflatable was released, a giant, unblinking eyeball outlined by pulsating rings of color. It made a circuit around the theater and paused, hovering directly overhead. Bob looked up at the crazy balloon and chuckled at the weird symmetry: Jack with one eye staring up at the bizarre floating eye staring back.

The pulsating rings changed from soft colors to a dazzling bright white, and a jolting sensation of intense pain spiked in Bob's head. He ducked his head and shut his eyes, but the burning residual image of blinding white circles persisted in his vision for several seconds.

He clenched his eyes closed as tight as possible. Seemingly in response, the image of the rings dissolved into separate swirling particles before coalescing into a solid wall of flashing gray and white color. Instantly Bob recalled the black and white console television in the living room when he was a boy. Any time a thunderstorm knocked out the antenna connection, the screen only displayed flashing snowy pixels.

The particles swirled in ghostly, shapeless forms before morphing into a series of distinct visual images. Each lasted only a few microseconds, but Bob recognized them as snapshot memories pulled from the personal photo album stored deep within his mind:

The first page of an English homework assignment with HOPE+ stamped in green at the top—the Star Child from 2001: A Space Odyssey floating toward him with a familiar face he could not identify—an aerial view of a huge spider-like insect, etched across the Nazca desert in Peru—a cartoon image of Ringo Starr picking up a black spot from the floor, stuffing it into his pants and declaring "I've got a hole in me pocket"—a black sky shattered by a lightning bolt, identical in shape to the crack in a monkey skull displayed in a glass museum case—his son and daughter playing in the sandbox while he tended burgers on the charcoal grill—Linda weakly smiling in her hospital bed—

The random sequence of thousands of images flashed through his inner vision, a confused collage compiled from a lifetime of memories. The pain in his head increased as the transition speed between images became irrationally fast and Bob could no longer process them individually. His mind was forced to relax and flopped open to accept the massive flow of input and associated pain.

It stopped. Relief was instantaneous. His closed-eyes vision was dark and normal. He had a sense of completeness, as though the reservoir of memory-images was now depleted. He remained still for several seconds before opening his eyes. Beside him, Jack was still watching the great eye floating overhead, the surrounding neon rings flashing in their original soft colors, now almost soothing. The mother-ship fish-thing hovered nearby, delighting a group of laughing teenagers. Apparently, no time had elapsed during whatever-the-fuck. Bob had no vocabulary to describe what he just experienced.

He mumbled to Jack he'd be back and carefully stepped past the people sitting in their row. He exited the theater and spotted the sign for the rest rooms on the far side of the lobby. As he entered the men's room he was struck with another memory, this one retrieved on his own and not nearly as disturbing.

In countless movies and television shows, after surviving an intense, harrowing experience the hero or victim would inevitably be shown leaning over a sink, splashing water on their face before anxiously looking into the mirror and trying to process what had just happened.

"What the hell," Bob muttered and moved to the nearest sink. He splashed water on his face three times and reached for the paper towels. Drying his face, he lifted his head.

He didn't recognize the man staring back in the mirror. He was decades too young, in his mid-fifties. His face was too smooth, the eyes wild and intense. The guy in the mirror wasn't him, it was someone else.

Someone's here. Bob turned around slowly, scanning the room. He bent to look under the stall doors: no one there. He tossed the paper towels and splashed water on his face again. Shaking his head and flinging water like a cartoon dog, he tried to clear the persistent sensation that someone else was inside his mind.

For the second time he raised his head to the mirror and stared. He looked tired, exasperated. There was a subtle mind-shift and the presence grew less obtrusive, an imaginary guest quietly settling into new accommodations.

He toweled off again and cautiously probed the I-am-not-alone sensation. Something was there and not-there. No movement, no sound, no bizarre thoughts or images, but a definite nagging sense that a tiny amount of previously empty brain-space was now occupied. A new idea popped: *the lights from the floating fish-eye triggered a bad headache.*

"It's just a migraine, that's all," he said to the guy in the mirror, who mouthed back the same words. Bob had suffered from migraines when he was young, nasty headaches lasting several hours with unusual neuropathic and visual side effects. His last one was decades ago, but the migraines back then were nowhere near as disturbing as this.

After a few moments he was better, still a bit light-headed and thirsty but otherwise okay. He purchased two bottles of water at the concession stand, returned to his seat and handed one to Jack.

"Thanks," Jack said. "You okay? Your shirt's all wet and you look like you scared yourself in the mirror."

"I'm fine," Bob said. "Just had to see a man—"

"About a horse?"

"Something like that."

The lights came down and ultra-loud music fired up. Three blue men in dark gray clothing walked cautiously onto the stage. They didn't say a word but stared in apprehension at the audience.

I know exactly how they feel.

* * *

Bob drew the curtains closed and sat on the edge of the bed. He wanted to sleep but had a nagging idea he should be working to understand what happened to him. As if growing younger for seventeen years and dealing with uncontrollable flashbacks wasn't enough, life had apparently tossed him an uninvited guest to host. Like the feel of a chipped tooth on his tongue, Bob was constantly aware of the tiny presence in his mind, dark and dormant. The sensation was odd and spooky, and for some reason brought to mind the old joke about the large man standing alone in a crowded elevator.

A Fortune of Reversal

It has to be a side effect of the migraine, some kind of residual trauma. He went over the initial memory-images he recalled from the psychedelic parade before the rush became incomprehensibly fast. The twelfth-grade English assignment was some of his best work, Mrs. Hope only marked HOPE+ on papers she considered best in class. It was the only time Bob had received the honor.

He first saw the floating embryo in *2001: A Space Odyssey* with his dad, a rare father and son Saturday afternoon at the movies. He didn't understand the significance of the weird star baby until he read the novel years later.

Ringo Starr picking up a black spot from the Sea of Holes. It was the only scene he remembered from *Yellow Submarine*, and it still struck him as hilarious.

Something had entered his brain and accessed his mind, his memories, his life. *This can't be real! Am I finally going nuts?*

Dementia was certainly possible, especially at his bio-age of ninety-one. While there was no way of knowing if he was actually crazy—like the fish who doesn't realize it's wet—the ideas circulating in his head were crazy for sure, dredged up from movies, television, and sci-fi novels. *An alien life force has taken over my mind; right now E.T. is pedaling across my cranium on a kid's bicycle. Are my brain cells mutating from too much alcohol lately? Or damaged from riding the New York roller coaster? Maybe Ruthie is really an ex-stripper voodoo shaman who put some sort of bizarre curse on me?*

Was his mind cloning itself, reprocessing all of the data stored in his memory banks for transfer to Bob 2.0? That might explain the flashbacks and the streaming memories tonight. Perhaps he now shared mind-space with a developing alternate version of himself. That's why he hadn't been surprised or frightened when he realized he had company in the men's room. You can't tickle yourself, and you can't scare yourself either. Bob had been alone, and in the next instant he was not alone.

Crazy idea number seventy-two: right now, an alternate-universe version of Bob could be doing the same thing, trying to figure out who the other guy in the mirror was. Bob knew this was all nonsense, but he also remembered his engineering training: during a brainstorming exercise all ideas, realistic or not, should initially be considered plausible.

Eventually the mysterious thing in his head resolved itself into an imaginary lumpy, almost massless object. Bob was exhausted and lay down on the bed. He forced himself to apply William of Occam's famous principle.

It was just a bad migraine.

Chapter 51

Wednesday morning

Despite a restless night, Betty felt marginally better, enough to try some toast and tea. As she pulled the mug of nearly boiling water from the microwave it slipped out of her hand. She jerked back to avoid the splashing hot water and smacked her elbow against the refrigerator. The mug shattered on the floor. Betty leaned against the refrigerator and cried.

When she'd received Denton's text asking her to meet him in Hell's bar, she tried not to care but couldn't help the shiver inside from the familiar thrill. Another man wanted her. Of course she would meet him. She'd crafted her response carefully to keep him guessing, but there had been no doubt: Betty was going to Hell.

But when she arrived Denton acted like he barely cared. No kiss hello, not even on the cheek, then running off to the bathroom and leaving her alone at the bar for a really long time. And his apology for standing her up didn't seem sincere at all. Plus, he only touched her after she started feeling woozy and sick. Still, he followed her home, which was actually kind of sweet. Then it seemed like he was more interested in Bob Dodd living next door than her.

She got up from the floor, stepped carefully around the glass and collapsed in a chair at the kitchen table. *My life is shit.* She pulled the psychological insecurity blanket tightly around herself. No one wanted to be with her. Ray was gone all the time because he couldn't stand to be in the same house with her. The neighbor guys all enjoyed the view when she paraded around the yard, but they were all married cowards who never came close. And Bob, that was the most humiliating. She couldn't get a ninety-one-year-old widower interested, even after unbuttoning her top just two hours after literally saving his life. She held her face with both hands and sobbed until she heard a ding from her phone.

HOW ARE YOU FEELING? BETTER I HOPE. I'M DRIVING TO CASSTOWN AGAIN TODAY BUT WOULD LIKE TO SEE YOU THIS WEEKEND. MAYBE WE CAN GET AWAY FOR A COUPLE OF DAYS?

Betty wiped her eyes with a tissue, her desperation suddenly replaced with hope. Maybe Denny's finally waking up. Go away for the weekend? Surely he'll make his move then, tell her how much he needs her, and exactly what she should do to him.

And I'll give him whatever he wants.

* * *

Denton dropped his phone in the cup holder and started the engine. *If this doesn't work, I'm done.*

He thought he played it exactly right last night, showing concern and making sure Betty got home okay. Hell, he didn't even kiss her, just a quick hug at the door. And even though the world just took another massive dump on his head, he still remembered to send her a how-you-doing text this morning.

Boyfriend of the Fucking Year!

One of the new backup delivery guys Denton hired last week got himself killed in a rollover crash overnight. The good news was the kid riding shotgun wasn't hurt too bad and had the good sense to call Brutus right away. They were able to secure the packages before the cops arrived and made the deliveries only a couple of hours late. Now, he had to go to Casstown one more fucking time and put out yet another fire.

He laughed and shook his head at the same time. At least one of his problems was solved: he knew where the flashlight was. He didn't need to find DJ anymore. He'd get the flashlight himself as soon as he got back into town.

The phone buzzed, his boss in Edgar. Denton let it roll to voice mail, he needed a couple of minutes to figure out what to say and update the plan: go to Casstown and hire another goon. Drive home A-S-A possible and get the flashlight back from whoever was at Dodd's house. Celebrate over the weekend with Hot Betty at the cabin.

Maybe a romantic walk through the woods or around the lake will get the juices flowing, and Betty will finally wake up, take control, and demand that Denton worship her body.

And I'll give her whatever she wants.

Chapter 52

Wednesday morning

Bob said goodbye and ended the telephone call with doctors Barlow and Kilmore. He dialed a number and Jack picked up on the seventh ring.

"Shine and rise, bright eye! It's after eleven. You ready for some food? It's lunchtime but you can call it breakfast if you want."

Bob heard Jack rubbing the sand out of his eye over the phone. "Can't. Body not working," Jack mumbled. "Need more sleep."

Bob laughed, as loud and annoying as possible. "Okay, buddy. I'm going to that In-N-Out Burger we passed the other day. See you later."

"Wait!" Jack said, apparently drawing energy from an internal auxiliary power source. "It's too hot to walk that far, you'll get fried. Use my rental car, the valet ticket number is... just a sec...twenty-four seventy-three. Wait, twenty-four seventy-eight. Maybe. Everything's kinda blurry."

"Thanks, Jack. I'll see you this afternoon, or maybe tomorrow? Do the world and me a favor and get as much beauty sleep as possible."

* * *

It took over an hour for Bob to reach the end of the drive-through line and pickup his order at the window. He spent the time going over the crazy psych-trip again and his conversation that morning with Kilmore and Barlow. *Sounds like a comedy duo hosting a TV variety show. "Please give a warm welcome to Bob Dodd and his singing brain-worm!"*

Bob took inventory immediately after he woke. He was both relieved and disturbed that his new companion was still resting quietly in place. He held nothing back from his doctors and described everything as accurately and truthful as possible. They were fascinated by the extra-mental presence but neither doctor could suggest a quick working theory.

Schizophrenia was discussed and quickly discarded. Both physicians also rejected Bob's idea of a bizarre side effect from a migraine. They insisted Bob return to KMF immediately for additional research and testing and were clearly frustrated when he refused. Bob was surprised to realize he didn't really care.

He was determined not to allow whatever-it-was to control all of his life. For too many years he'd floated along without a plan or purpose, and tasting life again during the last two weeks left him craving more. He still wanted to know what was happening to him, and why, and he'd make the necessary adjustments to his new Life Plan, currently under construction. In the meantime, he would continue to experiment with the alternative motivational strategy of that crazy New Yorker, George Costanza.

Exiting the restaurant, Bob turned right, salivating from the tantalizing smells of a double-double cheeseburger and fries.

Instead of returning to Bellagio he would find a place in the shade to enjoy his lunch. He wound his way through a large residential neighborhood and came to the entrance of a medium-sized cemetery. Large trees were scattered around the grounds, so he drove through the gates and found a quiet, shady spot. No one was in sight; he had the place to himself.

Not exactly a cheeseburger in paradise, but it'll do.

He rolled down all the windows and turned off the engine. It was hot but not unbearable, and he liked the atmosphere of quiet serenity. The cheeseburger was awesome, and he remembered helping his father with Saturday night barbecues when he was a boy.

Bob probed his consciousness. His new companion had been in his head for several hours now and almost felt normal. In his imagination he visualized it as a lumpy, gauzy cocoon, custom spun to conform to the twisted brain furrow-space it inhabited. The logical part of his mind wanted to reject this clear invasion from another life-entity. *Occupation complete, Captain. Commencing assimilation program.*

But emotionally there was an odd sense of familiarity. The shadow-presence gave him a strange feeling of comfort. Bob's lump—*Blump?*—seemed like an extension of his self, the psychological equivalent of discovering you had sprouted an extra finger or toe.

Bob finished his lunch and got out to stretch his legs. Emotions and memories surged, as expected. The last time he had been in a cemetery was Linda's funeral. He felt tremendous gratitude for the time they had together, then a deep sadness and sense of longing washed over him. *I miss you terribly. I wish I could see you again.*

He stared at the nearby gravestones and markers, a variety of sizes and styles carefully aligned in perfect rows. He turned the idea over in his mind, letting it play out. Part of him was intrigued, and part of him thought it was nonsense. Blump didn't offer an opinion at all. Bob knew what George Costanza would do.

What the hell, nothing to lose. He shut the car door, walked across the road and into the graves.

Chapter 53

Wednesday afternoon

Bob walked past the ornate wrought-iron sign indicating he was entering an area called ROSEBUD. The only roses in sight were a half-dozen made of plastic, gently scattered across a grave by the wind. He gathered and replaced them in the metal vase affixed to the marker before continuing his careful walk among those he hoped were resting peacefully.

He found what he was searching for on a stone marker in the fourth row. LINDA KAY BORNADELLO 1947 - 1992. Bob didn't remember where he first heard the expression but it popped in his mind instantly: *your entire life is right there, in the tiny little dash between the dates.* There were no other Bornadellos buried nearby, Linda was alone. Bob wondered what kind of person she was, and why she passed so young. *She died at forty-five, and I get to enjoy life at ninety-one in a fifty-seven-year-old body? That's not right.*

He scanned the cemetery and saw no one. Taking a deep, slow breath, he focused on the name LINDA, etched forever in stone, and tried to decide which happy memory he would try to resurrect.

The summer trip to Canada, hiking the Rockies. Walking around Lake Louise to the ice-blue glacier sprawled at the far end.

Bob stared at LINDA, his heart pounding.

I'm ready, take me back. Now!

His vision would fade, then brighten, and he and Linda will be strolling by the lake, holding hands...

The memory-image of Linda and the lake vanished, replaced in an instant with her face, drawn and thin, eyes open and sightless. Her lips were parted, her head back after arching for her last breath—

Bob gasped and stumbled before collapsing on the ground. He fought to breathe and clear his mind of the horrible image, the awful, final moment of Linda's life.

His attempt to initiate a happy flashback not only failed, it seemed as though his mind actually *punished* him for trying.

He got to his feet and walked. The rows of markers and headstones, peaceful just moments ago now were ominous and unsettling. The desert air smelled hot and beads of sweat ran down his neck. The blue-gray sky was too big, Bob dropped his head and scanned the ground for insects, counted small rocks, and focused on individual blades of grass. He needed to see, to absorb, to fill his mind with anything and everything to displace the terrible memory he had inadvertently summoned.

* * *

Still shaken but feeling slightly more normal, Bob put the car in gear and left ROSEBUD behind, promising himself never to return. Driving slowly along the narrow cemetery road he remembered Blump and probed. It—*he?*—was still there, hiding inertly in a lost corner of his mind.

What the hell's the point? I feel you taking up space, but otherwise you're pretty fucking worthless. Blump had no response.

The car crested a small rise and Bob spotted an olive-green awning erected over a pedestal. Two men in dark overalls were setting up rows of chairs. Grateful for the distraction he parked a discrete distance away to watch the funeral preparations.

Minutes later a hearse arrived and two men wearing suits stepped out. They extracted the casket from the back and wheeled it under the awning. All four men placed it carefully on the pedestal. The driver went back to the hearse and returned with a large flower blanket. Bob watched as the man placed the flowers on one end of the casket before sliding it toward the center.

A ring of darkness closed, cutting off Bob's vision, then just as quickly dilated—

—and Bobby watched as the funeral director placed the flowers on top of Grandma's coffin and stepped back, buttoning his suit coat. Bobby stared at the casket, tired and mostly quiet after crying hard for several minutes. He shifted closer under his father's arm. Mom sat on Dad's other side, holding his hand tightly. Dad kept hugging Bobby and his mother, asking if they were okay. Bobby didn't understand why his father was so calm with his mother lying dead in that box, just a few feet away.

Organ music played and the service began. Ministers preached and led prayers, and a woman sang a slow song that took forever before it was over. The church was full, Bobby didn't know this many people had liked Grandma. He heard his mom crying as she leaned against his dad, who sat very straight and still.

The service ended and curtains closed around the family. Bobby heard people talking and shuffling as they left the church through the main entrance. The funeral director removed the flowers from the coffin, handed them to an assistant, and opened the lid. Bobby stared at his grandmother lying frozen in her dark blue dress. The director stepped away and motioned with his arm, inviting the family to approach.

Dad took a slow, deep breath and stood up. Mom moved around to take Bobby's hand and they followed his father to the casket.

Grandma looked like she was sleeping. Why did she have her glasses on? They stepped closer and Bobby saw a tear fall from his father's eye. It made Bobby start to cry again. For some reason his Mom wasn't crying now, but she had a serious expression on her face. Dad leaned over the casket and put his hand on Grandma's shoulder. Bobby gasped. You weren't supposed to touch a dead person!

His father stepped off to the side but still close, making room for Bobby. Bobby looked up at his dad, who nodded. "It's okay, son. If you want to."

Trembling, Bobby forced himself to step closer. Grandma's face was strange and white, her lips bright red from lipstick. It made Bobby think of the clown who came to his sixth birthday party. He slowly reached out his hand, the tears made it hard to see. He patted Grandma's shoulder twice, just like Dad, then jerked his arm back and moved next to his father.

It was Mom's turn but she didn't touch Grandma, just looked for a moment before turning away. The family followed the funeral director through the chapel's side door into the bright sunshine outside.

His mom got in the big black car first and scooted across to the other side. Bobby climbed in beside her, his stomach hurting. He was mixed up inside. He was sad Grandma died, and it was scary seeing his father cry. But he was proud and excited too. Even though he'd been really scared he had touched a dead body!

His father slid in next to him and the director gave the door a push—

—the car door slammed shut and Bob watched a gray-haired man offer his arm to an elderly woman, the first mourners to arrive.

Bob's vision blurred again. He leaned forward and rested his head on the steering wheel, his body convulsing. It was the first time he cried in over twenty years.

Chapter 54

Wednesday afternoon

"By Friday, Larry! I'm not spending another weekend in this shithole. Make sure you get it done or I'll cut off your nuts and send one to your wife and the other to your girlfriend."

Megan ended the call and handed the phone back to the guard. Randall pushed the phone into his pocket and clumsily unfastened his pants, holding a nightstick in one hand while he freed his own. A big toothy grin spread across his face.

"About time," he grumbled. "All right, let's get this party started."

Megan glared at him and shifted her stance, one foot slightly in front of the other. Randall looked like he was a couple of months on either side of enrolling in Medicare. "You bring an oil can, Randy? Your equipment looks kinda rusty."

The teeth disappeared as Randall stepped forward and shoved Megan in the chest as she expected. She stood her ground, her body wavering only a couple of inches.

"Hey, Grandpa, I hope you can push it better than that or we'll be here all night," Megan said. Randall was the fourth guard she had entertained this week but the first one who agreed to let her make a call first. When Larry finally answered she could smell his fear through the phone. No doubt the slime-bag attorney was now frantically scrambling for the cash to post her bail.

Might as well get this over with. Megan moved to the bed and lay back. "Hurry up, you don't want to miss dinner tonight at the nursing home, I hear they're having pudding cups for dessert."

"Shut the fuck up!" Randall growled. He kept the nightstick in one hand and shoved his pants down to his ankles with the other.

Megan closed her eyes and went to her unhappy place.

Chapter 55

Wednesday afternoon

Bob gripped the steering wheel, eyes locked on the visor mirror. He didn't see his puffy, red eyes, he gazed *through* them, his mind focused beyond on a fantastic mix of swirling colors, not-quite-there shapes, and roiling ribbons of emotions. One panicked thought burst through.

I've lost my marbles! Wait, maybe...

He was seeing—no, *feeling*—his mind, his...soul? Whatever, it was *himself*, stripped of inconsequential flesh, bones, fluids and organs. The intimate essence of his own existence, rendered in his imagination as a superbly-cut emotional gemstone with innumerable facets. A few were mentally visible, a great many more were hidden, only vaguely sensed. After flashing back to his grandmother's funeral, he was now receiving another powerful surge of insight, *from his own mind.*

The shapes and sensations shifted, flying apart before coalescing into strange but familiar forms. There, *floating*—not accurate, he had no language for this—was the non-corporeal entity known terrestrially as Robert Dodd, a human life-form

239

battling pain, confusion and uncertainty from complex mysteries thrust unwanted into his time-line, all enclosed within an external shield. A calm, accepting demeanor concealed the turmoil inside.

An amorphous shape appeared, bright but without color. He recognized it instantly as an abstract thing: an idea, a concept, an option. A path of reversal, his undoing. The shape changed, its brightness contracting to a misshapen circular form, telescoping around a small, dense space of shifting darkness: a tunnel at the end of the light. Beyond, a great mass of life: his.

A buzzing sensation increased in intensity until Bob shifted his focus to the source. It appeared instantly, a far-off turbulent cloud of minuscule objects. He knew every particle, each one important: Linda, Jonathan, Jack. Trevor, and Lindsay, his son and daughter, long lost but somehow still present. Grandma, Marley, DJ, Ray, and Betty. His parents and many others, individual life energies overlapping his own in various degrees.

The particle cloud diminished, and a new emotion-shape bloomed, obscuring all else. Glowing purples and blues swirled to contain a compressed sphere of heat and lust, straining to expand. The intent was crystal clear: it would not stay bound much longer. And underlying the entire experience was the familiar sensation of a soft cluster of warmth, tucked out of the way in an unused corner of his mind. Intimidating, yet somehow comforting.

His mind cleared with disturbing suddenness, and his external vision returned. A weepy-eyed doofus stared back from the mirror; a troubled man obviously leaning way too far over his skis. Bob took a deep, slow breath and was astonished to feel sad but mostly normal. And a bit sleepy.

I just relived a close encounter with Grandma's corpse and took a carnival freak-show ride through my own mind, accompanied by an alien presence isolated backstage in a sound-proof cocoon. And all I need is a nap?

After resting a couple of minutes, Bob started the car, then remembered his promise. He picked up his phone. *This is going to blow Roger's mind. Again.*

He paused, his thumb hovering over the DeLorean icon. He looked to his right at the funeral service. About twenty people stood respectfully as the minister spoke. Bob wondered what comfort and wisdom was being offered. In the end, does any of it really matter? Life was generally pretty short for most people, but for him it was the opposite. *Why me?*

He looked down at his phone and gave the DeLorean icon a long press. An option window popped open and he pressed DELETE APP. Another window opened.

DELETING APP WILL ERASE ALL DATA PERMANENTLY. ARE YOU SURE?

He pressed YES. The DeLorean disappeared and the remaining icons shifted automatically to fill the empty space. Bob decided to watch the end of the funeral and turned off the car engine.

He had plenty of time.

Chapter 56

Wednesday evening

The early evening air was hot but dry, and the famous Las Vegas Strip was choked with the usual crowds, dominated in numbers by young drinking-age adults surging along the sidewalks to the next party spot. Except for their relatively senior appearance and being dressed for weekend yard sales, Bob and Jack fit right in. They had an early dinner at a Mexican restaurant in Luxor and were walking back to Bellagio.

Once again, Bob was trying to act normal just a few hours after experiencing another traumatic paranormal event. This one had left a psychological mark, something inside himself had changed, something he did not yet comprehend. Bob said nothing to Jack about going to the cemetery.

As they walked, they conformed to the flow of people and frequently passed through a gauntlet of men and women noisily slapping decks of cards in their hands and extending one to every person who came near. Printed on the cards were raunchy advertisements for escorts and assorted other adult services. Thousands of cards littered the sidewalk, sometimes piling up in spots and occasionally causing girls to slip in their high-heeled shoes. Bob declined to accept even a single card, but Jack looked forward to each new handout, sorting and arranging them like a poker hand.

"Hey! If I get one more of these Tranny Sally cards, I'll have a full house!"

"Don't touch me, Jack. You don't know where those cards have been."

Without realizing he was doing it, Bob's brain engaged in a cost/benefit analysis of the X-rated advertising campaign. Groups of six or eight card slappers were staged about a hundred feet apart along the sidewalk on both sides of the Strip. They each had several packets of cards stuffed in their pockets and backpacks and were obviously well-trained to annoyingly draw attention by slapping the cards against their palm before optimistically offering them to as many pedestrians as possible.

Most people ignored them and kept moving. The few who accepted a card looked at the picture, showed it to their companions, then dropped it to the pavement. Was there any way this could possibly be a money-making venture? How many "escorts" had to be hired each night to offset the costs of printing and paying hundreds of slappers for distribution?

As they navigated the last street intersection before reaching the fountain lake in front of Bellagio, Bob fell a few steps behind as he weaved through the counterflow of people. Up ahead Jack turned left toward the sidewalk up to the hotel entrance. Bob was still pondering payouts and profit ratios when a short, beefy man with a bored expression stepped in his way, slapped a card against his palm and held it out chest high. Bob shook his head, implying a silent thank you, and started to move to his right to go around the man. He got bumped from behind mid-stride, lost his balance and fell forward into the card slapper. They both toppled over and down in a confetti cloud of pornographic cards. Bob heard a whoosh of air as he landed on the man, knocking the wind out of him.

The card-slapper violently push-punched him and Bob rolled off to the side, feeling a sharp pain in his ribs. Both men lay on the sidewalk trying to recover as people stepped over and around the two gasping idiots.

Slappy got up first, then reached down for Bob's hand and pulled him to his feet. Bob started to apologize when Slappy shot out a fist and caught Bob just below his right eye. Bob staggered back but stayed on his feet.

I'm in another fight! Other than his battle with DJ, of which he remembered almost nothing, Bob had not been in an actual fist fight since he met Lewis Kertz behind the school back in seventh grade. That epic battle quickly morphed into a harmless wresting match by unspoken mutual agreement. The spectators had not been impressed.

Bob's limited knowledge of physical combat was acquired from watching fight scenes in movies, and in ninety-one years he had seen hundreds. He adopted a defensive stance like Clint Eastwood in the monkey movie *Every Which Way But Loose*, his fists up, protecting his face.

I hope I'm doing Clint and not the orangutan, he thought. What the hell, he was in it now. Slappy grinned and raised his fists, apparently no longer bored. People yelled and shifted around, forming a small, tight fight circle. Bob stood his ground and waited for his opponent to throw his next punch.

Instead, Slappy let out a yell and charged. Bob backtracked, lost his footing and went down on his back, his hands flat on the pavement at his sides. Slappy couldn't stop, it was his turn to fall onto Bob. Switching his internal database from movies to television, Bob channeled Chuck Norris as *Walker, Texas Ranger* and instinctively lifted his legs in time to get his feet under Slappy's stomach. He rolled back and kicked up.

People scrambled out of the way as Slappy somersaulted over Bob, gaining just enough altitude to bounce on top of the ornamental concrete fence surrounding the Bellagio fountain lake. Slappy's momentum carried him over and he splashed into the shallow water below.

The crowd clapped and cheered their approval. Bob lay flat on his back, breathing hard and wincing from the pain in his ribs. His face hurt from the sucker punch to his eye. *I'm getting too young for this shit.* He looked up at the Eiffel Tower until Jack's head eclipsed the view, staring down at Bob with concern.

"Are you crazy? That sidewalk is filthy!" Jack said.

Bob took a deep breath before answering his friend.

"Help me up, Obi-One Kenob-Eye. You're my only hope."

Jack grinned and extended his hand. "How long have you had that one chambered?" he asked, pulling Bob to his feet.

Bob hitched up his pants. "I thought of it the day we met in Mooncups, two years ago. Come on, I need a drink or three."

Chapter 57

Wednesday evening

"What was that all about?" Jack asked.

"Oh, just a quick conference with a marketing specialist from the adult entertainment industry. You know, opposite day." Bob was holding his side with one hand and the escalator rail with the other. They were standing on the moving sidewalk approaching the lobby entrance of Bellagio.

"Sorry I wasn't any help. I thought you were right behind me when I made the turn."

"It's okay," Bob said. "If you took a punch in the eye you'd be totally blind." It was weak cheese and he knew it. "Never mind. Scotch, now. And lots of ice on the side."

"Maybe another round of Spot-the-Hooker?"

"Sure," Bob said.

They made their way back to the same bar where they had spent most of Monday evening. "Let's take our drinks over there," Jack said, pointing to a large area with several couches arranged around a big-screen television. An NFL pre-season game was on.

As they approached the bar Bob nudged Jack and pointed with his chin. On the other side of the bar Sandy and a tall, rangy man were just leaving, her arm entwined with his. They were heading in the direction of the hotel elevators.

"He kind of looks like Kramer from *Seinfeld*," Jack said. "Well, you won the first round, I'll buy the drinks."

They dropped onto the couch and Bob poured ice from a glass into his handkerchief and pressed it to his eye.

"Would you ever hire a hooker?" Jack asked. "Or have you already?"

Bob shook his head, hand and ice pack moving in concert. "No. Not even on Opposite Day, not my thing. I doubt I could even pick up a woman the old-fashioned way, with charm and wit. What about you? Ever pay to...dip your pickle?" Bob grinned, remembering Ruthie.

Jack kept his eye on the game as he answered. "I officially admit to nothing, but I did attend a couple of rowdy stag parties back when I was young and dumb and—"

"Did you say 'stag'?" Bob interrupted. "I thought I was old."

"Anyway," Jack said, "I get all puckered up now just thinking about it. Way too stupid and risky, you know? Not that I'm opposed to having fun, it's just been a while. I'd like to get back in the game sometime soon. I mean in a conventional way, organic. Not a business transaction. Know what I mean?"

Bob didn't answer as he spotted Christine in a group of women coming their way. They were having a great time, laughing and dancing along in stocking feet, holding their high-heeled shoes with one hand and yard-long plastic margarita tubes with the other.

As they made the nearby turn Christine stopped and the group held up for her. She handed her drink and shoes to a friend and made her way directly toward Bob and Jack.

"Uh-oh," Jack said. "Danger! Danger, Will Robinson!" Bob laughed. The *Lost in Space* reference had to be ten or fifteen years older than the woman who approached.

"Hi guys!" Christine stopped directly in front of them with a big smile, one hand planted suggestively on her hip. Both men said hello, gazing up from the low couch.

"Oh, my!" Christine said. "What happened to your eye?" She seemed genuinely concerned.

"Well it's kind of an interesting story," Jack said. "A long time ago—"

"Not you." Christine took a step closer and put a hand on Bob's shoulder. "*You*."

"Punched myself shaving," Bob said, shrugging. "It happens. I'm okay."

"You poor thing!" Christine leaned over, giving both men a terrific view. Jack's eye opened wide.

Christine took Bob's face gently in both hands. "Maybe this will help," she said. She kissed him on the mouth, long and slow. For the second time that day, Bob's mind was blown from a complete sensory overload. He wanted to stop time and take it all in: the intoxicating scent of perfume, her warm breath sweetly flavored with lime and tequila, the softness of her lips.

Christine ended the kiss, then leaned in to whisper in Bob's ear, loud enough for Jack to hear. "Thank you, Bob. I had a fantastic time last night." Her lips brushed his ear and she stood up with a satisfied smile, clearly enjoying herself and the effect she was having on both men.

Bob somehow managed to recover. "I had a great time too, Brandeee. Thank *you*."

Christine winked and said, "Give me a call if you want to take another ride sometime. See you around." She walked back to her friends who giggled and hugged her before moving on.

Jack was staring at Bob.

"Close your mouth, buddy," Bob said. "Something's gonna fly in there."

"What the hell was that? I thought you said you weren't that kind of guy?"

"No worries, Jack." Bob grinned and raised the ice pack to his eye. "It was totally organic. Buy me another whisky and I'll tell you about it."

Chapter 58

Thursday evening

The Sports Book area of Bellagio seemed overly crowded for a Thursday night in August. Jack and Bob took the only empty table near the back of the viewing area. The opposite wall was filled with large and small video screens live-streaming a variety of sports, from horse racing in California to jai alai in Florida. But they were here to watch two of their favorite teams simultaneously. The St. Louis Cardinals were taking on the Chicago Cubs at Wrigley field, and the Kansas City Chiefs were hosting the Los Angeles Chargers in a preseason football game. To make things interesting, Bob bet a hundred dollars on the Cards and Jack bet the same on the football game, taking the over on total points.

After several days and nights of drinking and staying up late, Bob was worn out. There was a lingering sense of being unbalanced, an emotional hangover from his visit to the cemetery the day before. He was more than happy to spend their last night in Vegas watching sports over a couple of beers.

Late in the third quarter of the Chiefs game, three guys at the next table left and two women immediately sat down. The older of the pair was pretty and looked close to Bob's neo-age. She wore dark pants and a lemon-yellow blouse which contrasted perfectly with her auburn hair and striking green eyes. Her younger companion was a stunning brunette, dressed in a purple sweater dress, mesh stockings and red heels. The ladies ordered drinks and chatted, occasionally laughing. Jack looked at Bob with his eyebrow arched and Bob nodded in agreement. Their seats had just been upgraded for no additional charge.

The Chargers scored on a nifty catch in the corner of the end zone and the brunette stood up and cheered. Jack booed and the woman playfully stuck out her tongue, then froze when she saw his face. She rushed to their table and leaned down close to Jack, her eyes alive and bright.

"Oh my gosh, I love your face! That is so fricking cool!" She held out her hand. "Hi! I'm Amy, and that's Tracy."

Jack fumbled through the introductions, flustered by Amy's attention and proximity. Bob glanced at Tracy, who seemed to be enjoying the show too.

"So, Amy, you're a Chargers fan?" Bob asked.

Amy continued admiring Jack's face as she answered. "No," she said, dropping a hand to Jack's shoulder and giving it a squeeze. "I just don't like the Chiefs."

"Aw, come on!" Jack said. "You can't be serious!"

Amy laughed. "I'm kidding. I like football, I like touchdowns, and I love to have fun. What about you, Jack? Do you like to have fun?"

Jack mumbled something and picked up his beer, clearly flummoxed. Bob had never seen his friend tongue-tied before.

"Ladies, why don't you join us?" Bob asked. "I'll get the next round."

Steve Moore

Amy immediately sat next to Jack and Tracy brought over their drinks and took the seat to Bob's right.

"Thank you," Tracy said.

"Tell me," Bob said. "How many E's are in 'Tracy'?"

"What do you mean?" She looked confused.

"Sorry, inside joke." Bob explained he had recently met a young woman with a surplus of vowels in her name.

Bob and Tracy got acquainted, keeping an eye on their friends. A few minutes later Amy stroked Jack's face with the back of her hand and told him he had the sexiest eye she had ever seen. Bob exchanged a glance with Tracy, closing one eye and rolling the other. Tracy burst out laughing and Jack flushed a deep crimson. Amy moved closer to Jack, holding on to his arm with a smug expression. She was young and sexy and knew it. Tracy was more mature, with a soft face and laugh lines around her eyes that enhanced her smile.

The games ended and both men lost their bets. Amy asked Jack to teach her how to play blackjack and they left, hand in hand.

"You know, it's possible those two might be hitting it off," Bob said.

"I think you're right," Tracy replied. "Do you like jazz? There's a combo playing in the lounge on the other side of the casino."

Bob hesitated for only a second. He was still unsettled from the crazy mind trip the day before. Maybe music and a change of scenery would be good, especially in the company of an attractive lady.

"Sounds great," Bob said and motioned to their server for the check.

Chapter 59

Thursday evening

The lounge was packed, but as they stepped through the entrance Bob spotted a couple rising from a love seat along the wall. Bob and Tracy settled onto the overstuffed soft leather couch, their bodies naturally leaning in against each other. Bob's pulse quickened as they touched, but Tracy seemed at ease and he soon relaxed. The funky, smooth jazz was a touch too loud for conversation. They listened to the band and enjoyed the music.

It was a perfectly nice moment, so Bob was surprised and irritated at a growing sense of uncertainty, a nagging shift in perception causing his mind to psychologically squirm. Something was not quite right, off center. He was trying to work it out when Tracy nudged him and nodded toward the casino. Amy and Jack walked past in the direction of the room elevators, her hand tightly gripping his arm. Jack looked bewildered, an old dog that finally caught the car he'd been chasing and now had no idea what to do with it. Bob grinned. *Good for you, buddy. Have a great time.*

Bob refocused on the music, tapping his foot to the beat and letting his thoughts float free. The band finished the song and he mentally snapped his fingers. *Got it!* The closing drum flourish had opened the box in his mind and revealed the answer.

The lead guitar player announced they were taking a short break and the audience began talking and milling about. Bob shifted around to look Tracy in the eye.

"What?" she asked, her lips tight.

She's uncomfortable. She knows I know something.

"I think it's time you told me what's going on," Bob said.

"What are you—"

"No," Bob shook his head. "Just tell me. Say it. Come clean. Spill the beans from your guts. Let the cats out of the barn, and the cow out of the bag."

Her smile returned, barely. Tracy turned away, confirming his suspicions. "Okay," she said. "It's not what you're thinking." She turned back and met his gaze. "Uh, what *are* you thinking, Bob?"

Bob said nothing.

"All right," she said. "I was working up to it, but you jumped way ahead of me." Tracy sat up straight, back in control. "I'll explain everything but not here. Can we talk somewhere private? Maybe…go up to your room? I promise to behave, and I believe you'll find my…*proposal* interesting. It's nothing bad. I'll even order champagne from room service and charge it to my account." She put her hand on his arm. "Please?"

Bob studied her lovely, green eyes. Whatever it was, it didn't feel dangerous, just mysterious. A pretty woman he met two hours earlier just invited herself to his hotel room with the promise of an intriguing proposal. What was the Costanza protocol for this situation?

Don't overthink it. He stood and held out his hand to help her up. "Sure, why not?"

Chapter 60

Thursday evening

Tracy signed the room service ticket and thanked the porter. She expertly opened the champagne, capturing the cork in her hand, and poured two glasses.

"To your health, Bob."

"To yours as well. And to a complete, no-bullshit explanation."

They clinked glasses and drank. Tracy perched on the foot of the bed, holding the flute with both hands in her lap. Bob sat in a chair by the table near the window. The curtains were open and the bright neon lights from the Strip cast crazy patterns on the glass.

"I'll explain everything, Bob, that's actually the reason I'm here in Las Vegas. First, will you please tell me what tipped you off? How did you know something was amiss?"

Bob gave her a half-smile. "I have a third sense about these things."

"Don't you mean—oh. You're joking." It wasn't a question, but Tracy didn't seem sure of herself.

Why is she worried? That she failed?

255

"Kind of, yeah," Bob said. "Okay, here it is. I didn't feel quite right all evening, but I thought it was from something that happened yesterday. I finally put it together when the band took their break. First, those three guys at the table next to us in Sports Book. I didn't notice it at the time but realized later one of them never turned to check out the sports, even when the crowd cheered a touchdown. He just drank his beer facing our way the entire time. Then they got up and left and you and Amy were right there to snag the table. Nothing unusual about that, except it happened again when you and I stepped into the lounge. The place is packed, I'm scanning for a place to sit and a couple stands up from the couch at the exact moment I turned my head in their direction. That was twice but still could have been a coincidence.

"Then I thought about Amy going nuts over one-eyed Jack, stroking his face and all that over-the-top flirting. I know we're in Vegas and pretty much anything is possible—and I've been led to believe when something does happen it stays right here in the city—but it seemed like too much.

"The kicker was you, Tracy. You're pretty much the opposite of Amy. Mature, laid back, sweet and pleasant. Attractive, great smile. Frankly, you're my kind of woman. It all fits a little too nicely together, and with a bit of hindsight I realized you and Amy were playing roles." As he said this, Bob knew it was more than deductive reasoning or a clever hunch. It was some version of higher-level insight, minus the usual preceding flashback.

Is that you, Blump? Hiding somewhere in my brain, screwing with me?

"Bob? Are you all right?" Tracy looked concerned.

She's genuinely worried. About me.

"I'm fine." Bob took a big drink of champagne. "This is great stuff. Thank you."

"My pleasure," Tracy said. "Please, go on."

"I still wasn't a hundred percent sure but lately I've been trying new things and I decided to call you out. When I asked you what was going on you didn't seem surprised, so I knew I was right. But I still don't know what it is I'm right about. Why don't you tell me?"

Tracy blew out a long breath and visibly relaxed. "I'm glad you and I have reached this point. Our analytics team advised there was a probability of seventy-six percent you would discover our deception earlier than we planned to reveal it, but it was always our intention to eventually inform you who we are, who we represent, and why we wanted to make contact with you."

"Analytics team? What—"

"I'll explain everything," Tracy said, then chuckled. "And Amy? She really is interested in Jack. His ultra-smooth skin graft is really eye-catching, pun intended. She was really looking forward to getting to know him."

"What do you mean 'looking forward'? You were planning to meet us?"

Tracy slowly sipped her champagne before answering. Bob's insight failed him now. Was she being dramatic, or just thirsty?

"Bob, I'm sorry to be the one to tell you this. We've had you under surveillance since shortly after the announcement of your Reversal, nearly ten years ago."

Chapter 61

Thursday evening

Huh. That's something I don't hear every day.

Marley got up from her desk and walked across the studio into the climate-controlled utility closet that housed a rack of servers. She pulled out a keyboard, typed a command and studied the output on the small service monitor.

The notification alarm she heard a few seconds earlier was ancient, the "Robotz asterisk" WAV file from a Microsoft Windows 98 sound scheme. Marley had selected it for its relative obscurity to serve as an ear-catching alert for a specific, rare event: when a third party *stopped* trying to hack into one of her systems. Since this was the opposite of a security threat, she had designed a passive notification protocol, a simple audible sound every two minutes. If the alert was not canceled after ten minutes Marley would receive a text message on all of her devices.

She scrolled through the log file, located the event that triggered the warning, and disabled the alert. A few more keystrokes and she had the details. The hack attack had ended, and—

Oh. Interesting...

When Bob hired Marley to be his personal IT department, she set up a firewall and an industrial-strength security system to protect the devices and data of her famous client. Digital attacks started immediately, but Marley knew what she was doing and there had not been one successful breach in four years.

But the danger was real and attempts to invade Bob's system were ongoing. One entity in particular was unrelenting and apparently fond of autobot hacking strategies, persistently trying to gain entry past Bob's firewall an infinite number of times with minor tweaks to previous attempts. Marley's security system easily handled the attacks but they continued to occur daily for several years.

Until they stopped, two hours ago. Someone had called off the digital dogs.

Chapter 62

Thursday evening

"You've been spying on me?"

Bob surged from the chair to his feet. Tracy stood almost as quickly and started for the door, stopping when Bob stepped away and faced the window. He focused on the rotating neon lights of the giant Ferris wheel, arms at his side, his hands clenched in fists. He struggled to slow his breathing and regain his calm while frenetically processing three thoughts simultaneously. The first two were emotionally jarring but unrelated. The third was an analytical attempt to synthesize the first two and arrive at a new level of understanding.

Spying on me for ten years! Son of a bitch, how in the—Oh, I scared Tracy. She thought I was coming after her, I have to apologize. I would never—How about that? After a decade of surveillance they don't know me at all. I would never attack someone, especially a woman…

Bob slowly let out a deep breath and unclenched his hands. From the reflection in the window, he knew Tracy was watching him carefully. He turned slowly, hoping the expression on his face was non-threatening.

"I'm sorry I scared you, Tracy, if that's your real name. All better now." He wouldn't take a step until she indicated she felt safe. "I was just surprised. And pissed. Please, relax. You're free to leave if you like, or prop open the door if it will help. I'd like to hear more about who has been watching me from the shadows, and why."

Tracy nodded but otherwise didn't move. "I represent an organization called Alaxis, and I'm here to offer you a proposal."

"You mentioned that earlier. Let's hear it."

"First," Tracy said, "I need to tell you a story."

* * *

Tremonian Alaxis was the only child of brilliant Austrian parents. His father taught mathematics and economics at the university. His mother held doctorate degrees in psychology and psychiatry and ran a thriving private practice. Young Trey satisfied his voracious appetite for knowledge with constant support from his parents and virtually unlimited access to university resources through his father's tenure.

After a normal childhood—as normal as an extraordinarily gifted child could have—Trey entered the university to begin his studies. He quickly rejected the convention of completing highly structured course work and passing examinations to earn a degree in a particular field of study. He wanted to learn about *everything* as quickly as possible. He dove into a variety of subjects in an energetic self-study program, quietly approved by the university administration after his parents made a substantial financial contribution far exceeding the cost of tuition. When Trey achieved what he considered a satisfactory level of pragmatic knowledge of a subject (what his professors would have described as "total mastery") he immediately moved on to the next area of study as zestfully as the last.

This rapid accumulation of knowledge created intriguing educational threads. Studies of philosophy and religion led to investigations of history and archeology. Trey's long fascination with near-earth space exploration and the moon landings in the 1970s (and the frustration of seeing the programs reduced or eliminated by funding limitations) sparked deep excursions into astronomy, physics, and quantum mechanics. The challenges of humans living and working in space captured Trey's imagination and he turned next to aeronautical engineering, human physiology, and biochemistry.

After seven years spent mastering more than a dozen subjects, Trey arrived at two cornerstone beliefs which would define his remaining life's work. First, humanity was not destined to be confined to a single planet. Humans would ultimately expand within and beyond the solar system through deep-space exploration.

Second, the true limitations of long-term, long-distance space travel were not technological but *biological.* Besides coping with the environmental and physical challenges of living in and traveling through space, human bodies and minds must also survive for incredibly long periods of time, far beyond the normal life span of seven to nine decades. Tremonian scoffed at multi-generational schemes for traveling to distant star systems, considering them nothing more than science fiction fantasies.

He believed humans were originally "designed" to rejuvenate, to replenish and replace worn-out cells, tissues and organs through natural biologic processes. Assuming the avoidance of accidental or malicious death, a human body theoretically should live forever. But something disrupted the genetic program thousands of years ago, a monster defect which caused physical aging, mental deterioration, and death from "natural causes." Tremonian dedicated the rest of his life to finding a cure for this defect, to initiate an evolutionary upgrade of his favorite species. He dreamed humanity would achieve the Star Trek mantras to "boldly go" and "live long and prosper" by expanding their presence throughout the solar system and beyond.

With the help of his parents and wealthy, like-minded individuals, Tremonian founded Alaxis, dedicated to the advancement of human genetics, biology, and longevity with a companion mission to promote human deep-space exploration. The company remained private to operate without restraint as much as possible. Alaxis expanded rapidly over the next few years and established discrete operations in dozens of countries, all managed from the corporate headquarters in Frankfurt, Germany.

Tremonian hired the finest minds in biomechanics, space technology, and medical science. They did the heavy lifting while he pursued his own activities and passions, including the extension of his own life. Obsessed with his own mortality, Tremonian feared he would not live long enough to see Alaxis succeed in its many endeavors. Despite adopting a fanatical personal health regimen which kept him alive and vibrant many years beyond the norm, Tremonian Alaxis died alone in his home at the age of 109.

Chapter 63

Thursday evening

Tracy finished her champagne. She had moved to the table across from Bob, the champagne ice bucket between them. Bob refilled her glass.

"That's impressive. One hundred nine is a great run."

"Definitely," Tracy said. "But Tremonian did not die of natural, old age causes. In a horrible, ironic twist the healthiest man in the world for his age died at home from a fall in the shower. He bled to death from a head injury. No one knows why he fell but everyone who hears the story immediately imagines he slipped on the proverbial bar of soap. I suppose it confirms the influence of all those cartoons we watched as children."

"All right, from your story so far I can guess at least part of the deal," Bob said. "Alaxis is interested in me for my 'not getting any older' thing."

"Absolutely. The announcement of your Reversal was exciting news for everyone at Alaxis."

"Why have I not heard from them until now, ten years later? And why all the skulduggery?"

"The simple answer is we wanted to verify the validity of the announcement, to confirm your reverse-aging condition was real. As for our discrete methods, are you familiar with the Hawthorne Effect?"

It seemed familiar, maybe from one of Bob's college classes. "Something about people participating in an experiment change their behavior when they know they are being observed?"

"That's right. After significant discussion, our leadership team concluded direct, early contact with you might skew the information we needed, especially if your claim was fraudulent. By setting up passive surveillance, we could establish baseline data and verify you were growing younger by obtaining various data over time. And by passive, I don't mean spies lurking around corners, but high-tech resources such as security cameras at various locations in Springburg. We obtained access—"

"You hacked into security systems? Is that legal?"

Tracy shifted in her chair. "Yes. Also no. Some of it is a gray area. Our digital teams are very good, the small chance of detection was considered an acceptable risk."

"Did you hack into my home? My computer, my email?"

Tracy shook her head. "No, but I admit we tried. Your assistant, Miss Carducci, has exceptional skills, we were unable to penetrate the firewalls and other security measures she has in place to protect your digital life. We're very impressed and have discussed the possibility of recruiting her to join Alaxis after we made contact with you. She is an outstanding talent."

"I agree," Bob said. He made a mental note to take advantage of his own world-class hacker and have Marley check out Alaxis. *Turnabout, fair play, yada yada.*

"By the way," Tracy said, "as of earlier this evening we have terminated all surveillance programs, including the attempts to hack your digital information."

"Why talk to me now?"

"We are aware you have had some new experiences recently. It is impossible to know for certain, but we believe you are the only human on Earth currently experiencing a Reversal of aging. You truly are the most intriguing man on the planet."

"You said 'currently'?"

"There is a significant amount of evidence suggesting a small number of others may also have experienced a reversal. Some during ancient times, others more recently."

"You've got to be shitting me," Bob stared at her. "Name twenty."

Tracy laughed. "Sorry, not that many. The most famous is the Egyptian pharaoh Tutankhamun, who supposedly died at age nineteen. Our reinterpretation of historical records indicates he was almost certainly well over one hundred when he died, but reversed aging caused him to look like a teenager. There is some interesting evidence that his father Akhenaten may also have been extremely long-lived, but unlike Tut he did not benefit from the 'younging' condition."

Bob's mind instantly pulled Steve Martin from the archives, doing the flat-palm Egyptian dance in costume and singing praises to the great boy king.

"More recently there's William Henry Harrison, the ninth president of the United States who died in office at age sixty-eight, only a month after his inauguration in 1841. Our investigation revealed a successful election campaign conspiracy that concealed the fact that his actual age was over ninety. We speculate he refused treatment for his pneumonia to avoid discovery of his true biological age. If true, it was a fatal decision."

"That's...incredible." Bob tried to wrap his mind around the idea he might not be all that unique after all.

"There are just a handful of others," Tracy said, "including a possible set of triplet brothers who lived in rural Idaho in the mid-nineteenth century. The evidence is sketchy, mostly local lore."

"Isn't 'rural Idaho in the nineteenth century' redundant?" Bob asked, attempting to sidestep his swirling emotions.

Tracy ignored the joke. "Bob, I apologize for the surveillance, and for the deception tonight. From this point forward we will be completely honest and not hold anything back. While we were not able to penetrate your digital security, we know from other sources you have recently experienced some unusual psychological episodes and side effects."

Bob made the connection instantly. "Tony."

"Yes, he works for Alaxis. By the way, the code name we used for you at KMF was 'Ponce', short for Ponce De Leon. It was Tony's idea."

"Clever guy," Bob said. Ponce De Leon was a Spanish explorer known for his search for the mythical Fountain of Youth.

"Tony reported you probably suspected something after the final flashback experiment in the lab. We were already aware of your adventure in Costco—well done, by the way, a very happy ending for that little girl—the fire at your house, and the altercation with the teenager on your front lawn. We suspect you may have had another incident last Monday, in the parking lot of a convenience store near the airport in Albuquerque. The nearest security camera was offline, we only have distant video from another camera down the street."

Holy crap, they're everywhere!

"And of course, later we obtained a copy of your entertaining report from the DELOREAN app."

"Got it," Bob said. "Very impressive. No use fighting the

almighty Oz, the force is strong in Alaxis. So why are we here, Tracy?"

Tracy rose and stepped to the window. Bob stood and joined her. The fountains were just starting another performance, the brilliant underwater spotlights creating dancing water patterns slightly distorted by the window glass. The Eiffel Tower of Paris provided a striking backdrop. A crescent moon was high in the sky, but the lights of the city obscured all stars but one. Bob guessed it was a planet, maybe Venus or Jupiter.

Tracy broke the silence. "As Tremonian chased his curiosities down various intellectual rabbit holes, he studied the mythologies of primitive peoples and early civilizations that included tales of strange visitors from the skies or heavens above. The evidence of their beliefs was derived from archaeological investigations, written texts and illustrations, and oral traditions passed down through multiple generations. Tremonian became enamored with these stories and fielded a team of specialists to conduct his own studies."

Tracy turned and faced Bob. "Are you familiar with the theory of ancient alien astronauts?"

Chapter 64

Thursday evening

Bob's head flooded with memories and images. Not a flashback, but a normal mind-collage of references to ancient astronauts extracted from his archives:

Sprawled on the living room carpet as a boy and listening to his father argue with Pastor Wilkins over the interpretation of a biblical passage from Ezekiel, something about wheels within wheels...late-night television documentaries presenting hard-to-believe origin stories for the colossal statues on Easter Island...reading a paperback copy of *Chariots of the Gods,* then seeing the movie at the theater with his dad, amazed by the aerial photographs of strange geoglyphs carved into the plains of Peru—

The Nazca lines! They were in that crazy fever dream, at the Blue Man show...

"Bob?" Tracy stared at him. "Are you all right?"

He shook his no, but said, "I'm fine."

"Where did you go? It must have been interesting, you looked...far away."

"Never mind. Made me think of something. Yeah, I remember the ancient spacemen theory. Strange creatures arrive from the sky in flaming chariots and start messing with the locals. Drinking Tang and smoking weed with tribal chiefs. Hosting wine and cave-painting parties. ET entertaining the kids with Velcro strips and peanut butter candy. Eventually they leave, but—"

"—promise to return," finished Tracy, laughing. "Very funny. Tremonian was obsessed with the theory and often met with Von Daniken and other proponents. They put together several talented research teams, some of the finest minds in the world of whom you've never heard. They financed dozens of expeditions and acquired thousands of artifacts. Alaxis teams have completed a great deal of impressive, far-reaching work completely unknown outside of our organization.

"Remember, Tremonian was also obsessed with space exploration. He believed humans had significantly underachieved after reaching the moon and failed to exploit the opportunities of additional lunar exploration. He hoped to use the scientific and research programs of Alaxis to support humanity's ultimate quest: deep space exploration and eventual intergalactic expansion. Besides the obvious technical challenges, Tremonian knew fantastic advances in genetic and biological engineering were required to control—or, ideally, *eliminate*—the aging process so humans would have the longevity to travel beyond the known planets."

Tracy paused, apparently for dramatic effect. Bob suppressed a chuckle but a tiny, disconcerting thought started growing in his mind.

"Back to ancient history. Tremonian was absolutely convinced extraterrestrial life not only visited Earth eons ago, but also seeded the planet with the biological materials and genetic instruction codes which guided human development over the centuries to our current physiological form. Tremonian believed the fantastic structure and persistent mysteries of human DNA proved his theory of intelligent design. The people of Earth did not evolve naturally but by deliberate manipulative processes initiated by the intergalactic 'gods' who arrived from the sky in those flaming chariots."

Tracy once again faced Bob, her eyes bright.

Finally! Bring it home, Tracy, I'm not getting any older.

"Under the leadership of first Tremonian and now Elizabeth, his wife, Alaxis is on a path to produce—in just a few years—incredible advancements in technology and human capabilities essential for deep space exploration. Humans are finally on the verge of expanding beyond our solar system, as originally intended by ancient extraterrestrial visitors to our planet."

Bob ran a hand through his hair, his thoughts racing ahead. *Is it possible? Is this why—*

"I'm sure you are unhappy with our methods, but you can understand how exciting it was to learn of your enhanced powers of insight associated with the unusual flashback experiences."

Tracy took both of Bob's hands in hers. "The science teams and leadership of Alaxis believe the Reversal, along with your recent memory-insight experience, is literally living proof: you are the first modern human to reach a new, predetermined level of evolution. Another 'giant leap for mankind' as Armstrong said so well."

Bob immediately recalled the thrill and emotion of watching the black-and-white television images of the Apollo 11 moon landing and hearing those famous words for the first time, nearly a half-century ago.

Tracy's next words brought him back to *now* and blew his mind.

"We also believe your Reversal is the result of a genetic trigger designed by extraterrestrial beings who engaged with hominids on Earth two million years ago."

Chapter 65

Thursday evening

If someone had told Bob he would end his last day in Las Vegas in a Bellagio hotel room with an attractive woman and an expensive bottle of champagne, he would have imagined a scenario vastly different from the hour he just spent, sitting at a small table patiently listening to a long, detailed briefing on the intergalactic travel plans of a dead Austrian polymath.

At least there wasn't a timeshare pitch. So far.

It took Bob eighty-seven seconds to process everything Tracy had said, including her final statement. He replayed the origin tale of Alaxis in his mind, then considered the final two-point summary:

Bob was the first human to experience a new—and presumably higher—state of evolutionary development. And two: Space Invaders made it all happen a long time ago, in a galaxy not far away at all.

He realized Tracy gave him the extensive background to make the final revelation sound at least a tiny bit plausible. "Gee, Tracy, you kind of buried the lead, don't you think? Some big-footed alien trips over an extension cord and two million years later my hair starts growing back?"

"I'm sorry I dragged it out so long," she said. "I wanted to give you enough of the backstory to make the conclusion sound more or less plausible. What? Why are you smiling?"

"Nothing," Bob said. *Wow, this enhanced insight thing is pretty cool. I kind of miss the flashbacks though.* "I'm not sure you totally succeeded, but I understand."

"Good."

"So, the Ancient Ones prophesied Alaxis would one day offer me some kind of proposal?"

"Ha. Not exactly," she said. "I'll keep this short and straight. We'd like to invite you, Dr. Kilmore, and the entire KMF staff to join forces with Alaxis. And Miss Carducci, too. Together we will continue to investigate your amazing transformation and recent psychic experiences, and eventually apply what we learn to enhance and accelerate Alaxis projects in human longevity and space exploration."

"I can understand how all that makes perfect sense to Alaxis," Bob said. "But I'm going to need some time to think about it. There's a couple of sticky points too, such as the double-secret spy-on-Bob program. You said Tremonian's wife Elizabeth is now running Alaxis?"

"Yes. Elizabeth was nearly forty years younger than Tremonian when they married, she's somewhere around eighty now, no one knows her exact age. She shared many of her husband's interests and passions, including a fanatical devotion to maintaining youthful and healthy minds and bodies. Unlike Tremonian, Elizabeth took full advantage of the medical resources at Alaxis and had a number of successful cosmetic and structural surgeries. She looks and acts decades younger than her actual age, and has proved to be a worthy successor to Tremonian as our leader."

"I'd like to visit with her before making any decisions on your proposal," Bob said.

"Great! She's here in Vegas, and hoping you will join her for breakfast tomorrow morning before you leave."

Bob's spidey sense tingled. "Wait, let me guess. *You* are Elizabeth Alaxis?"

Tracy laughed and shook her head. "No, my name really is Tracy."

Damn, swing and a miss. Insight not so hot after all.

"Tremonian was my grandfather. My mother was Trey's daughter from his second marriage. Mom passed away a long time ago."

"I'm sorry, I thought—"

"It's okay, really." Tracy said, a twinkle in her eye. "Elizabeth *Amelia* Alaxis is here, in Bellagio. She goes by Amy and she's just down the hall, getting rowdy with your buddy Jack."

Chapter 66

Friday afternoon

"There's one." Bob pointed out the window at a motel up ahead. "Take this exit."

"Right." Jack eased the rental car over to the off ramp. It had been a fun week topped off by interesting—and radically different—adventures for both men on their last night in Vegas. After eight hours of driving they reached Albuquerque and were ready to find a room for the night and enjoy a steak dinner.

Early that morning Bob met Amy and Tracy for breakfast in the casino restaurant. Amy immediately apologized for being deceptive the night before, for years of secret surveillance, and for wearing Jack out so completely she thought it best he skip breakfast and get some extra sleep. Bob told Amy that was a good call, all was mostly good between them, and they would be discussing the surveillance issue again in the near future.

Amy reiterated their intentions and, in a show of good faith, offered Bob and Marley complete, unrestricted digital access to the entire Alaxis organization. She invited them to visit Alaxis headquarters in Frankfurt and urged Bob to be sure to bring Jack.

Bob promised to consider it. When the meeting ended, Tracy gave him a goodbye hug and whispered in his ear.

"I hope I can share another bottle of champagne with you soon under friendlier circumstances." He needed no special insight to understand her message. Tracy kissed him on the cheek and hurried to catch up with Amy.

Bob rousted Jack from bed and called the valet for their rental car. Bob offered to drive the first shift while Jack recovered with coffee and bright sunshine. After a half hour Jack broke the silence.

"Why haven't you asked me how it went with Amy last night?"

Bob stared straight ahead and tried not to smile. Jack didn't know anything about Alaxis, the breakfast meeting, or who he had spent the night with. Amy just kissed him goodbye and left him in bed.

"None of my business," Bob said. "Besides, I think by law that stuff has to stay inside Vegas city limits, right?"

"Bob, old boy, it was amazing! I've never...maybe came close once, but I was just a kid, didn't know what I was doing. Amy, she *knows* stuff, you know?" Jack's fingers gently massaged his face where his eye used to be. "She taught me some tricks too. I'm telling you, Bob, if you ever get a chance to have wild animal sex with a girl almost half your age, I strongly recommend it. You'll still feel like a tired old man, only much less crabby."

Bob decided not to tell Jack his Night of a Thousand Pleasures was with an eighty-something-year-old CEO of a mysterious international conglomerate working to achieve the galactic ambitions of ancient spacefaring geneticists. He'd learn all about it soon enough.

Jack asked Bob how his evening with Tracy went.

"We listened to some jazz and got acquainted."

"You don't want to tell me what happened," Jack said.

"Nope."

"Bummer." Jack shook his head sadly. "I was pulling for you."

Bob spent the rest of the trip thinking through what he had learned about Alaxis and considering their proposal and his options. The idea that he was living through some kind of epic transformation on behalf of humanity with extraterrestrial origins was far-fetched and overwhelming. As he tried to process it all, his mind kept returning to the recent mind-trips in the theater and the cemetery. He realized it was too much to handle at the moment and decided to table it until they got back to Springburg.

A few miles out from Albuquerque Bob proposed they continue the Costanza Strategy and stop at the first dive motel they came to, just for the hell of it. Jack parked the car outside the office and they got out to stretch. Bob glanced up at the big neon sign he had spotted from the highway. The letter 'A' wasn't working; they were about to check in at the RO DRUNNER INN.

A bald man with massive sideburns wearing a ripped Metallica T-shirt was sitting behind the counter, reading a newspaper. Bob asked if they had rooms available.

"Only one. You boys want to share?"

"Didn't see many cars in the parking lot," Bob said. "You only have one room vacant?"

"Didn't say that. Only one is clean. You want it or not?"

Bob looked at his watch, it was nearly six o'clock. "What do you say, Jack? Shall we do *Planes, Trains and Automobiles* and take the room?"

Jack nodded. "I think we have to 'cause it's the exact opposite of what I want to do. Just keep your hands away from my pillows."

Sideburns chuckled. "I've seen that movie. No worries, there's two beds in the room."

They parked the car in front of room 113 and unloaded their bags. Bob started to slide the key with the green plastic tag into the lock when he noticed the door was already cracked open. He remembered a joke someone told him when he was a little kid.

"Hey Jack, when is a door not a door?"

"Huh? What the hell are you talking about?"

"When it's ajar." Bob grinned and pushed the door open. He fumbled for the light switch then froze. Two cowboy boots were sticking out from under the nearest bed, toes up.

Jack bumped into him. "What's wrong?"

Bob held up his hand. He stepped slowly to the bed and bent down to look, then grabbed one of the boots and tugged. Empty. He pulled on the other, let out a yip and dropped it. Part of a leg extended from the boot. It was a prosthetic, sawed off at mid-shin with a sharp ragged edge. Jack burst out laughing.

"We're not in Kansas anymore, Bob-O!"

"No, we are not," Bob said. "If these boots could talk. Probably an interesting story."

"This is the *clean* room?"

Bob dropped the boots outside the door next to the noisy air conditioning unit in case the owner hopped back for them. "I hope this guy isn't signed up for tonight's ass-kicking contest down at the fairgrounds."

Jack came out of the bathroom. "All clear in there except for some cockroaches holding a square-dancing class. What do we do next?"

Bob set the timer on his phone for forty-five minutes. "I'm going to take a nap. Then we dine."

Chapter 67

Friday evening

They really wanted steak but neither of them wanted to get back in the car. They walked across the street to the Waffle Box and had breakfast for dinner.

"Look, I made a happy plate," Jack said, pushing it to the edge of the table. "All gone."

"What are you, four?" Bob asked.

"We still doing Opposites?"

Bob nodded. "Yep. Trip's not over yet."

"Good. You and I normally wouldn't go to a bar and talk to ladies who wouldn't have anything to do with us, right?"

"Sounds good."

They paid their bill and the cashier suggested Nicky's, a short walk up the street. It had an old-time western saloon feel with smoke in the air and sawdust on the floor.

"Keep your eye out for a barefoot one-legged cowboy," Bob said.

"A man with one eye looking for a man with one leg," Jack replied. "Sounds like a twisted nursery rhyme written by Stephen

King."

They ordered the requisite long-neck beers, clinked bottles and turned to watch the crowd. Dozens of guys patiently stood around the perimeter watching a girls-only line dance. All of the women wore cutoff shorts, boots and tied-off shirts, and each one knew the moves and lyrics of the song. Bob and Jack were ignored even though they were completely out of place by not wearing hats or boots. The next song started and all the guys stepped in between the girls, holding their beer bottles in one hand and lassoing the air with the other in perfectly synchronized movements. Everyone was clearly having a great time.

Bob nudged Jack and pointed to a sign on the far wall: KOWBOY KARAOKE. A feathered arrow pointed the way to the next room. Jack nodded and they made their way through the crowd.

It was an entirely different vibe. A middle-age couple stood on stage belting out the words to a slow country song at high volume. Dozens of people were seated at tables eating and drinking, mostly ignoring the singers.

They found an empty table and Jack sat down. Bob walked to the karaoke station, mustering his courage as he went, and added the name Ralph McGillicutty to the list. He selected an old Buck Owens song he recognized.

After a half-dozen songs the deejay announced it was Ralph's turn to sing. With the complete opposite of confidence, Bob climbed onstage and picked up the microphone. He studied the crowd during the lead-in music. Everyone seemed perfectly oblivious, which suited him fine. When the cue for the vocals appeared, he ignored the prompter and sang his own made-up lyrics.

"Oh-oh, well my dog died this mornin', and my wife this afternoon.

It might as well keep rainin', right on into June."

Momentarily distracted when he spotted Jack laughing, Bob missed the next verse but covered it by slapping his thighs, hambone style.

"Got a blister on my foot, and two flat tires on my truck. They shut off my 'lectricity, but I don't give a fuck."

He had the crowd now, many were clapping along. The DJ flashed him a thumbs up. It was time to bring it home.

"Life's been kickin' my ass, but I don't give two hoots. I know that I'll be good and fine, long as I got my boots!"

Jack stood up, hooting and clapping. Bob cracked up and called it good. He waved and stepped off the stage to a nice round of applause and cheers.

"How's that for Opposite Day?" Bob asked.

"Outstanding!" Jack said, giving him a fist bump. "That line about the boots was hi-larious!" As they sat down Jack shifted his gaze toward something behind Bob.

"What?" Bob started to turn but Jack stopped him.

"There's a woman standing by herself against the wall over there. She keeps looking at you."

"How do you know she's not looking at you?"

"Because she stared at you the whole time you were on stage. Why don't you go introduce yourself?"

"Is it safe for me to turn around and see?"

"No," Jack said. "Unless you want her to know you're checking her out. Trust me, she's a babe, and older than most of the kids here. She's only about half your real age, you old coot."

"It's still Opposite Day," Bob said. "Here's the deal. You walk over and talk to her, find out what you can. Act like you're interested."

"I *am* interested, it's just that she's obviously interested in you."

"Go on, do me a solid, opposite boy."

Jack stood up. "Okay, here goes something."

After he slipped by, Bob moved over to Jack's chair to watch. Jack was right, she was attractive. He matched eyes with her for a quick second and she smiled, then Jack stepped forward and blocked his view.

Chapter 68

Friday evening

Jack sauntered toward Bob's mystery fan, still feeling a residual amount of euphoria from his spectacular night with Amy. If he had to guess from the way Bob acted today, he and Tracy hadn't romped at all. He was happy to serve as Bob's wing man tonight.

"Hi there, I'm Jack, and I've had my eye on you for quite a while," Jack said, flashing his friendliest smile.

The woman chuckled. "That's not a bad line. Does it work?"

"You tell me."

"Nice to meet you, Jack. I'm Julie."

"I noticed you watching my buddy sing?"

"Yes, he reminds me of someone."

"Your great, great grandfather?"

Julie laughed. "No, he just seems familiar."

"Well, he's a nice enough guy but as you saw on stage, he's kind of shy and boring. I'd be happy to introduce you if you'd care to join us?"

Hesitating only a second, Julie accepted and followed him back to the table. Jack made the introductions.

"I thought the DJ introduced you as Ralph?" Julie asked.

"That's just my stage name," Bob said.

"It was a great performance, looked like you were having fun up there. I recognized the song but not the lyrics."

"Thanks. I'm a poet but don't realize it," Bob said.

Come on, Bob! Jack thought. He leaned back in his chair and crossed his arms. *That was lame, you can do better than that.*

"Are you here by yourself?" Bob asked.

Nope, maybe not. Jack started preparing an intervention. This was too painful to watch.

"I was here with a friend, but she wasn't feeling well and left. I was about to finish my beer and leave when you started singing. What's your story? I'm guessing you two are just passing through as we don't see too many men without hats here at Nicky's."

"Probably don't see folks doing 'The Safety Dance' standing in parallel lines, either." Bob grimaced, apparently realizing how stupid this must have sounded.

Julie stared at Bob like worms were crawling out of his ears. Bob shifted awkwardly as though he was suffering from a bad case of earworms. Jack was embarrassed for his friend. *What the hell's the matter with you? Come on, buddy, you're losing her.* He went for the save.

"Bob, Julie said you remind her of one of America's founding fathers." He turned to Julie. "It was randy old Ben Franklin, right?"

Julie laughed. "No, I was thinking of an uncle." She looked at Bob. "My favorite uncle, actually."

Bingo!

"Tell me about those song lyrics. Were they inspired by true events?" Julie asked.

"Not really," Bob said. "I used to hear that Buck Owens song when I lived in Bakersfield once upon a time ago. I just made up the words to spoof C&W music."

"Well the crowd loved it. Are you singing again tonight?" Julie briefly touched Bob's arm with her hand before picking up her beer.

Okay buddy, she's waving you around the bases. I might need to find another place to sleep tonight. Jack excused himself and headed to the men's room. He'd take his time and hoped Bob didn't blow it by himself.

Chapter 69

Friday evening

"No, I'm done singing tonight," Bob said, still unsure of himself. *"Safety Dance"? What the hell is wrong with me? Pull it together, you fidiot.* "And I won't be coming out of retirement to go on tour."

"Retirement? You don't look old enough to be retired!" Julie's eyes were bright and inviting.

What have I got myself into? Bob shifted in his chair. This was his third encounter this week with an attractive woman and for some reason it was the most difficult. Julie was terrific. She was open, relaxed, easy to be with. She had touched his arm, lingering for a moment before picking up her beer. Bob knew Jack stepped away to give them some time alone, but for what? He felt stupid, frozen with doubt. *It's been a while, but you can do this. Just visit with her, get acquainted. Get her to talk about herself.*

He glanced at Julie and started to ask a question, then realized what was happening and tipped back his bottle of beer instead.

Julie's funny and nice and cute, and I like her.

It had been a really long time but the sensations were still familiar. He didn't feel like this with Christine in the elevator or sitting cozy with Tracy on the love seat in the jazz lounge. Betty had certainly tried to spark a physical reaction that morning in his kitchen and might have succeeded if not for his solid moral firewall.

Bob might be wrong—*where's my Blumping insight when I really need it?*—but he was fairly sure Julie was sending him signals. Bob took a second drink and finished off his beer, stalling for a few more seconds of analysis. When was the last time he felt this way? Not counting his favorite flashback with Gena Lindon, but in real time? With Linda, of course, many years back. So long ago novelists would describe it as "another lifetime."

Linda would want you to enjoy yourself. She would hate that you lived all these years without a companion. Maybe it's time to jump back in the pool and hope it's the deep end. And that it's filled with water, too.

"Actually, Julie, I am that old and retired, for the moment. Let me ask you something. Do you remember a story in the news several years ago, about a guy who stopped getting old and started growing younger every day?"

Her eyes opened wide. "Oh my gosh it's you! The Reversal guy! That's why you look familiar!" She recovered and blushed. "Oh wow, Bob, I'm so sorry. I didn't mean...I don't know what to say."

Bob laughed, hoping to put her at ease. "Nice to meet you too. No worries, it's fine. I just wanted you to know."

Julie had tons of questions and Bob started to relax as he told his story. As with Christine a few days earlier, he was surprised how good it was to talk about his experiences with someone other than Jack or the doctors at KMF. It was almost therapeutic. Verbally reliving the Reversal and the associated attention and drama seemed to relieve inner tensions Bob didn't realize he had.

After several minutes there was a natural break in the conversation and Julie took Bob's hand and stood.

"Come on, I love this song. Let's dance."

"Sorry, I don't know how to do that line-skedaddling thing."

"Skedaddling? Wow, you really are old. Get up, I'll teach you. It'll be fun, I promise." She pulled him up and as they walked to the dance area Bob spotted Jack leaning against the wall where Julie stood earlier. Jack pointed a gun-finger at him and pulled the trigger, then turned it into a thumbs-up sign.

George would be proud. The Costanza Strategy was working.

Chapter 70

Friday evening

Bob, Julie, and Jack danced and talked for more than an hour. Bob never got the hang of line dancing, but he gave it his best Opposite Day effort. His reward was watching Julie, she had all the moves down. Bob couldn't take his eyes off of her.

Jack suggested dessert at the Waffle Box and the trio left Nicky's and walked to the restaurant.

"Where are you guys staying tonight?" Julie asked.

"We have a suite at the Rodrunner," Bob said. "Do drop in, take off your boots and stay a while." Jack cracked up and they explained the joke to Julie.

"Oh, you worked that bit into your karaoke song. Nicely done!" Julie said.

When they reached the restaurant, Jack announced he had a headache, said goodbye to Julie and crossed the street to the motel. Bob appreciated the obvious gesture by his friend, and Julie seemed fine that it was now just the two of them. They settled into a booth and ordered iced teas and a giant cinnamon roll to share. It was Julie's turn to tell her story. She was an assistant principle at a junior high school in Albuquerque after teaching science classes for twenty-two years. Never married and coming close only once, she spent her summers traveling around the southwest visiting friends and attending festivals.

"I heard Jack say something earlier about opposite day. What's that about?" Julie asked.

"You're probably too young to remember the show *Seinfeld* on TV?" Bob joked.

"Aw shucks, Mr. Dodd, you're such a gentleman," she said in a silly, naive television voice. "Why, I'm old enough to know *lots* of things, and even though you're super old I bet I could show you some things you've never seen before." She blinked her eyes at him several times, obviously trying not to laugh.

Bob knew he was turning red and laughed a little too hard, hoping Julie wouldn't notice. For the second or third time that night he worried he was in way over his head. *She's so sexy! Great sense of humor too. I wish I remembered how to flirt. Wait—did I ever know?*

Julie cut him a minor amount of slack. "Yes Bob, I am aware of *Seinfeld*. I learned all about it on a junior high field trip to an ancient history museum."

Bob explained the Costanza strategy and how he was inspired by the episode where George meets Victoria by doing the opposite of his natural instincts.

Julie sat up straight, imitating Victoria. "You just ordered the exact same cinnamon roll as me," she said.

Bob recognized his cue. "My name is Bob, I'm ninety-one years old. I'm unemployed and I live with my parents."

She almost broke character but recovered. "I'm Julie. Hi!"

They both laughed until their server arrived with the pastry and drinks.

They talked about their favorite episodes and other television shows until it was obvious that awkward, special time of the evening had arrived. Bob paid the tab and they stepped outside. Glancing up at the sky, Bob recognized the familiar moon and planet grouping. This time last night he was trying to get his mind wrapped around an unbelievable theory explaining his bizarre life. Now he was wrestling with an equally unbelievable situation, with a pounding heart and a knot tightening in his gut. He had a general idea what he wanted to do but no idea how to make it happen. *I have the complete opposite of insight.*

Fortunately, Julie made it easy and switched back to Victoria. "Would you like to come to my place for some coffee?" she asked. "It's not far."

Ah, right. Okay, I got this. Unlike George, Bob had no intention of doing the opposite and declining her invitation. He raised his right hand as though taking an oath and stared off into the distance.

"I, Bob, do solemnly declare Opposite Day is officially, unequivocally over," he said in a serious tone. He turned to Julie. "That sounds perfect, I'd like that very much."

"Good." Julie took his hand in hers. "Let's walk back to Nicky's, we can take my car."

Chapter 71

Friday evening

Jonathan turned the corner and was not surprised to see cars parked in the street in front of his uncle's house—the kids across the street had a never ending stream of visitors—but he was surprised to see a pickup truck parked in the driveway. A man he did not know was sitting on the open tailgate, smoking a cigarette.

It was a tight fit but Jonathan parked next to the truck and managed to squeeze out the door.

"Hello. Are you waiting for me?" Jonathan asked.

The man looked serious and slightly ominous. "You must be Dodd's nephew," he said, standing and flicking his cigarette into the street.

"How do you know that?"

"Next-door Betty told me. We're friends."

"Oh. What can I do for you?"

"My son gave your uncle a flashlight. It belongs to me, and I need it back."

"Right, your boy was here last weekend asking for it. Bob took it with him on his trip. Didn't he tell you?"

"No, he didn't say nothin' about that." The man looked at Betty's house for a few seconds, then seemed to make up his mind. "What's your name again?"

"Jonathan. What's yours?"

"Jonathan, I want you to give your uncle a message for me. Why don't you run inside and get paper and a pencil so you can get it exactly right?" It was clear he wasn't asking.

"Sure, I can do that. Or, if you want, you can use my phone and just call him."

The man blinked, staring at Jonathan, then seemed to relax a tiny bit. "That's a pretty good idea. Dial his number, then go stand over there until I'm done."

Jonathan made the call, handed the man his phone and walked to the far side of the yard. The man frowned and waited several seconds before speaking, too low for Jonathan to hear. *Probably rolled to voice mail.*

The man finished the call, turned and heaved the phone in Jonathan's direction across the yard. Jonathan fumbled the catch and dropped the phone in the grass. He picked it up and inspected the screen, then watched as the man got in his truck, backed into the street and drove away.

Jonathan dialed his uncle again as he walked to the front door of the house.

Chapter 72

Friday evening

Julie unlocked the car with her remote key, but before Bob could open the driver's door for her she grabbed his arm, spun him around and surprised him with a soft kiss lasting several seconds. She pulled away with a sweet smile, leaving Bob light-headed. He was surprised a second time by the familiar movement in his pants.

"I'm sorry, let me shut this damn thing off," he said, pulling his phone from his front pocket: JONATHAN. He sent the call to voice mail and got in the car. Julie turned left out of the parking lot and a minute later Bob's phone lit up again: JONATHAN.

"Guess I better take this," Bob said. "Jonathan? Is everything okay?"

"I'm not sure, Uncle Bob. Sorry to call so late. I just got home from a movie and there was a man waiting for me at the house. He didn't tell me his name but said he was the father of the kid who was here last week asking about the flashlight. He wanted the flashlight too, I told him you had it. I let him use my phone to call you, but it looked like he left you a voice message."

"Yeah, I'm a little busy at the moment." Bob glanced at Julie, who grinned but kept her eyes on the road.

"Is something wrong? Something I should know?"

"Everything's fine, Jonathan. Thanks for taking care of my house. We should be home late tomorrow," Bob grinned as Julie shook her head vigorously, "or maybe Sunday. I'll let you know." Bob ended the call, started the voice message, and held the phone close hoping Julie wouldn't hear.

"Hello, Mr. Dodd. You have something of mine, and I want it back. I have something too. Betty, your hot, friendly neighbor. Man, she's a fine-looking woman but she's got some issues, you know? I bet you do. She's told me a lot about you, Dodd. What a great guy you are, how you're such a gentleman. Don't know how you do it, man, if I lived next door I'd be hitting that every chance I got. She needs it bad, you know? Her husband's a dipshit to leave her alone all the time.

"But hey, I'm a businessman, let's get down to it. You have the flashlight, I have Betty, a perfect setup for a trade. I know you're on a trip so I'll give you the weekend to get back here. Give me a chance to have a little fun with bouncing Betty. I'm dying to find out if she's as kinky as I think she is. If not, maybe I can teach her, right?

"You're probably already thinking about calling the cops. Go ahead, if you want, and I'll be sure to leave Betty's beautiful body where it will be easy for someone to find. If you want a happy ending instead, bring the flashlight to the old appliance warehouse at Sixth and Broadview, north of downtown. Monday night, eleven sharp. Come alone and park in the back. If I see cops or anyone else around, the deal's off. I'll be pretty disappointed not to get my property back, but you'll have to explain to Betty's old man why you've got a flashlight and he's got a dead wife."

The message clicked off.

Bob stared through the windshield. They were driving through a residential neighborhood, the houses mostly dark except for decorative landscape lights. Families safe at home and asleep. A wave of crushing guilt rolled over him.

Ray asks me for one favor, to keep an eye on Betty. I've got nothing going on but instead of keeping my promise I fly halfway across the country for a freaking vacation and Betty gets nabbed by a small-time drug-running asshole. I'm such a fucking idiot!

"Julie, I'm sorry, there's an emergency back home. Please take me back to the motel." Bob dialed Betty's cell phone number and was not surprised when it rang four times and rolled to voice mail.

* * *

Bob watched the taillights of Julie's car fade as she drove away. He fought with two swirling storms of emotions. He was furious at himself, embarrassed by his colossal mistake of leaving town after telling Ray he would keep watch over Betty. Logically, he was aware of the true nature of Ray's request (general, not literal: *hey, keep an eye out for her, okay?*) and the appropriate level of commitment required (*no need to cancel your KMF trip, just check on her once in a while*). Based on results, it was obvious Ray and Bob both had completely underestimated the potential for trouble.

At the same time, he was massively disappointed to bail on what surely would have been a special time with Julie. He was surprised how fast his attraction to her developed over the last few hours. Again, logically he was aware of the potential for lust and even love to occur from a first encounter. But it was a new experience for him and he really enjoyed the feeling.

To the mound of guilt over Betty he piled on more for disappointing Julie. There was no question he had to call it off, he and Jack needed to get back home as soon as possible. Julie was great and said all the right things. She took Bob's phone and dialed her number so he'd have it, then kissed him long and soft, leaving him dazed and conflicted and vowing to return soon.

"Let's stay connected, I want to see you again," she whispered as she hugged him goodbye. Then she got in her car and drove away.

Bob forced himself to focus and stepped inside the motel room. Jack had left the bathroom door cracked with the light on but Bob flicked on the ceiling light.

Jack rolled over in bed, squinting. "Bob? Figured I might not see you again for a few days. Geez, you're speedy. Didn't figure you as a love 'em and leave 'em type."

"Get up and get dressed. We have to leave, right now."

Jack sat up. "What's going on? Julie got a jealous husband?"

"Jonathan called, problem back home. I'll fill you in later but for now get moving."

"Right," Jack said and pulled on his pants.

Bob dumped the contents of his bag on the bed. He picked up the flashlight and flicked it on. The light was weak.

"DJ Rafter gave me this flashlight after our fight, some kind of weird payback for setting my house on fire. I usually travel with a light so I tossed it in my bag. His father just called and wants it back, really bad."

Jack watched as Bob twisted off the top, looked inside the barrel, then shook out the contents. A roll of cash wrapped tight with a rubber band, a small plastic bag half-filled with white powder, and a single-D-cell battery. Bob examined the light; it had been modified to work with a single battery instead of three, leaving extra space for storage.

"Cocaine?" Jack said, picking up the baggie and holding it up to the light.

"Beats me." Bob slipped off the rubber band and thumbed through the money roll. All fifties and twenties, a few thousand dollars at most. One of the bills in the middle had two small, yellow notes stuck to it. On each a series of mixed-case letters, numbers and symbols was neatly hand-written.

"These might be passcodes," Bob said. "I'm guessing they're way more important than the cash or that party-in-a-bag you're holding."

Bob took a picture of the two notes with his phone, then rolled up the money as before and put everything back in the flashlight.

"We need to leave as soon as we can. I'll fill you in on the road. You drive the first shift so I can call Jonathan and Marley."

Chapter 73

Saturday afternoon

Bob and Jack left the motel in Albuquerque a few minutes after one am Saturday morning. Bob called Marley to brief her on the situation and asked her to meet them at Bob's house mid-afternoon. Other than stopping for gas and bio-breaks they drove thirteen hours straight, alternating turns driving and trying to sleep. They argued back and forth over whether to call the police—Detective Bent was already familiar with the Rafters—but Bob decided against it for now. Denton's ties to drug operations and cartels strongly suggested the potential for violent behavior, and he had been clear in his threat to harm Betty if Bob notified the cops.

Going over the chain of events that led to the current debacle, Bob realized it all traced back to his decision to soak DJ's truck in a stupid act of minor revenge. He was responsible for putting Betty in serious danger, which meant he was also responsible for resolving the situation and getting her back safely.

He knew the desire to handle it himself was more than a guilt-driven gut instinct. He felt a strange, intense certainty. He would succeed in rescuing Betty—with the help of his friends, of course. Bob speculated his pumped-up confidence was somehow related to the mysterious entity silently camping inside his brain. He took mental inventory and it was still there, still inert. *As useless as a Blump on a Bob.*

He suddenly realized that during his time with Julie last night he hadn't thought of Blump at all. In fact, if you didn't count the sawed-off prosthetic leg, singing a made-up Karaoke song, line dancing, playacting *Seinfeld* episodes with an attractive new lady-friend, and an irresistible invitation only a serious personal emergency would prevent him from accepting, it had been a perfectly normal day. No flashbacks, fisticuffs, or fantastic insights.

* * *

Bob and Jack had been home less than an hour and were sitting at the dining room table, drinking coffee with Jonathan. Marley let herself in the front door and pulled a laptop computer and a mini-projector from her backpack. She rigged the gear to display the monitor image on the wall. Jonathan set a mug of coffee on the table for Marley, careful not to spill it on the equipment.

"Thanks," Marley said. She got right to the point. "After Bob called last night, I pulled together additional info on the Rafters." A picture of a run-down house with an overgrown front yard appeared on the wall. "No one's home, but I—"

"Wait." Bob saw grass moving from a breeze. He pointed at the wall. "Is this a live feed of Rafter's house?"

"Yes. I went over there this morning to scope it out. I stuck a battery-powered mini-cam on a piece-of-crap Caddy sitting on cinder blocks one house over and across the street."

If the men had been characters in a classic Saturday morning cartoon, the sound of three lower jaws striking the table-top would have clanged and echoed around the room.

"You went to Rafter's house this morning?" Bob asked.

"Yes. The house looked empty, and no one has come or gone since I was there. I'm recording video and..." Marley stopped. All three men were staring at her. "What?"

"That's crazy!" Jack said.

"What if Rafter caught you snooping around?" Bob said.

"It was still early. I was careful."

The men continued to stare. Marley blew out a slow breath.

"Look, I've worked for...I mean, I've got some experience I can't really talk about. Let's focus on the problem, okay? If Denton or DJ returns home I'll see it on the cam with my phone. We can tell who it is by these." She showed the next image, side-by-side rear-view pictures of two dark pickup trucks. Bob recognized one of the pics, he had taken it with his phone from his front yard. "The Rafter pickup trucks look similar except for the nuts hanging from DJ's."

"Do we have any idea where DJ is?" Bob asked.

"Not currently, he's been mostly off the grid since Sunday night. As for Denton, I don't believe he'll go home because I think he's holed up with Betty, here." The display changed to a satellite image of a lake shore bounded by woods to the south. To the east were a pair of buildings and a large boat dock.

"This is Krager's Landing on Lake Thompson. And this," Marley tapped for the next aerial picture, "is a double-wide trailer on the south side of the woods, about a half-mile from the lake shore and the boat dock. Care to guess who owns this rustic hideaway?"

"Warren Buffet?" Jack said.

"Denton Rafter. According to the county tax records he's owned it for sixteen years."

"How did you get the satellite picture?" Bob said.

Marley ignored him. "I think Denton is at the trailer. At the time this picture was taken two days ago there were no vehicles parked anywhere close. I can't get a new satellite image for two more days, so we'll need eyes on site to confirm someone's there. We have two options..."

Bob and Jack exchanged glances. Marley clearly had her shit together.

"This is a dirt or gravel road from the trailer back to the main highway," she said, using a red laser pointer. "The trailer isn't visible from the highway. To see if a vehicle is parked there you have to drive part way down Rafter's private road, which means anyone in the trailer can hear and see you coming. The other option is to stage from Krager's Landing, trek through the woods a half-mile and observe the cabin from the trees. More effort and time but much lower risk of being seen."

"What about a drone? Scope it out from above?" Jonathan asked.

Marley frowned. "That would be perfect. Unfortunately, I let a friend borrow my drone last week for...something. He wasn't careful and someone shot it all to hell. He's going to replace it soon but I don't have it yet." She looked at Bob. "And if I understand the schedule, we don't have enough time to find another one."

Bob nodded and said to Jack, "You're the only one of us that hasn't been seen by Denton or DJ. Maybe you could take a wrong turn down his road, see if anyone is home, then back right out?"

"Sure," Jack said. "But what schedule? What are you thinking?"

"Tell you later. Marley, any info on DJ?"

"No recent debit card purchases, no ATM withdrawals, no phone calls. There were a few pings from his cell phone during the last week, a couple in town, and one from here." Marley switched back to the satellite image and pointed to Krager's Landing. "DJ may be at the cabin too."

The men nodded, no longer surprised by Marley's ability to obtain information. "We need to give Marley a new nickname," Jack said. "Like Trinity, or Blue Angel, something like that."

"Marley's just fine, thank you," she said.

"Aren't we forgetting something?" Jonathan said. "Betty is in trouble. Shouldn't we be talking to the police right now instead of making jokes?"

"No, we haven't forgotten," Bob said. "I appreciate your concern, though. We're all tired and stressed, and trying to respond to a situation none of us, except maybe Marley, has been through before. A little humor to release some tension isn't going to derail our focus for more than a few seconds. But you're not wrong, we need to move things along a bit quicker. As for calling the police, Denton promised to hurt Betty if we did, and I'd like to consider our options before making that decision. Understood?"

Everyone nodded.

Bob continued. "I have an idea, and I'll explain in a minute. First I'd like to hear Marley's interpretation of the two sticky-note codes that were rolled up inside the flashlight money."

Marley displayed the picture of the notes Bob sent earlier from Albuquerque. "Each note has a sequence of twelve characters neatly printed, easy to read to avoid mistakes. Each is a mix of numbers, lower and upper-case letters, and a variety of typical keyboard symbols. I launched several search algorithms for both full and partial sequences from both notes, so far the results are null. My guess is these are passcodes, but I don't know what they might access. Could be financial or block-chain accounts, or communication passwords. They might even unlock files containing other passcodes."

"Why would Denton keep something that valuable in a flashlight?" Jack wondered.

Marley shared a glance with Bob. "We know Denton isn't really all that smart. My guess is these codes are personal, and he wanted to keep them close. They'd be more secure in a safe deposit box, but Rafter's business requires him to avoid dealing with banks. These are obviously important; a bag of party powder and a couple of thousand dollars isn't enough to risk felony kidnapping. Denton's not demanding ransom money and a getaway helicopter, he just wants the flashlight back."

"And that's our leverage," Bob said. "Rafter can have it all, the light, the cash, the cocaine, and the codes as long as we get Betty back unharmed. Marley, please show the aerial shot of the woods and the trailer again."

Bob rubbed his chin while he studied the layout. He was barely aware of his mind smoothly shifting to analytical mode, a residual skill from his engineering days half a lifetime ago. *Solve the problem.* He was only slightly surprised how quickly he came up with a plan.

"I have an idea, but we need to confirm Rafter is at the trailer. Jack, get the directions from Marley and go ahead and make your run out to Rafter's place. Take binoculars—or I guess a telescope would be best for you? If there's a black truck parked at the trailer, try to see if it's male or female. If it's DJ's truck maybe he can tell us where his father might be. If the truck is *sans* balls, we'll assume Denton has Betty at the trailer. Either way find out what you can, get out of there fast and call me from Krager's Landing."

"Roger that," Jack said and left.

"Jonathan, you must have told Denton I was out of town. That's why he said to meet him at the warehouse Monday night."

Jonathan nodded.

Bob stood, moved to the wall, and pointed at the image. "Marley, how wide would you guess this space is, between the edge of the woods and the back of the trailer?"

"Maybe seventy, eighty feet?" Marley said. "What are you thinking?"

"I think we have a good chance to surprise Denton at the trailer and get Betty back. Tonight."

"What?" Jonathan exclaimed. "Are you serious?"

"Approach the trailer from the woods across open ground?" Marley asked.

Bob nodded. "We'll need a diversion, and I'll take care of that. Now, here's what I have in mind…"

Chapter 74

Saturday afternoon

Jack jumped over the drainage ditch and made his way along the barbed wire fence back toward the turnoff to Rafter's trailer. A pair of small binoculars hung from a strap around his neck, and he held them with one hand to keep them from bouncing as he walked.

Marley's directions were perfect. Jack had turned off the highway onto Rafter's private dirt road and crept forward far enough past the trees to see the trailer. A black truck was parked beneath a carport, but he was too close to the trailer to risk being seen using binoculars to confirm which truck it was. He made a quick three-point turn as though he'd made a mistake and returned to the highway. A quarter mile from Rafter's turnoff he pulled to the side of the road and parked, his vehicle obscured from the trailer by dense woods.

He found a good spot to climb over the barbed wire fence and slowly advanced through the trees until he had a decent vantage point. He looked through the binoculars at the truck: no balls. *Dude's truck looks like a lady.* Humming a song by Aerosmith, Jack inserted ear buds and called Bob.

"Jack?"

"Bobwhite, this is Jackass, come in Bobwhite." Jack was sure he was too far from the trailer to be heard but kept his voice low for dramatic effect.

"What did you find, Jack?"

"A no-balls pickup is parked next to the trailer. Repeat: the truck has no nuts. Looks like Daddy Rafter is holed up here just like—wait. Standby, Bobwhite. Maintain radio silence."

The front screen door to the trailer opened and Betty came down the metal steps in a two-piece bathing suit carrying a towel and a floppy hat. She walked to the far end of the trailer and dragged a chaise lounge from the shade into the sunshine. As she arranged the towel on the chair a man stepped out the door carrying two bottles. He gave one to Betty, adjusted a second chair to be completely in the shade and sat down. The man lit a cigarette and blew smoke in the air as he watched Betty getting settled.

"Bob, I see Betty. She's in a chair outside with a guy, must be Rafter. She's wearing a bikini and they both have beers. This does not look like a hostage situation, more like a weekend getaway. You copy?"

The reply came after several seconds. "I copy, Jack. Maybe Betty doesn't realize Denton is using her and she's having some kind of fling. Don't let them see you but get out of there and drive to the diner at the landing. We'll meet you there in about an hour, around six o'clock."

"Negative, Bobwhite. I need to run a quick errand, won't take long and I'll meet you at the rendezvous point at oh-eighteen-hundred sharp. Jackass out."

Jack carefully backed out of the woods and returned to the car, grinning the entire time. He knew how serious the situation was but damned if he wasn't having a good time. He was just like his favorite TV spy, Maxwell Smart. Agent 86. Too bad this was a solo mission. It would have been nice to have Agent 99 along for company.

* * *

Bob parked his SUV in front of the diner and he and Jonathan got out. Marley pulled her Mini Cooper into the adjacent space. Bob shielded his eyes and looked at the sky, they still had a couple of hours of daylight left and he hoped it would all be over before dark. They stepped inside the diner and Jack waved them over to a booth with a window facing the parking lot and the woods beyond.

"What's with the camo vest, Jack?" Marley slipped off her backpack before sliding in next to him. "Isn't it too hot for that?"

"Just wanted to be prepared," Jack said, fishing a hand-sized object from a side pocket.

"Is that what I think it is?" Jonathan asked.

"I have no idea what you think it is," Jack replied.

"Some kind of electric zapping weapon? Where'd you get it?"

"It was, uh, left over from one of my previous jobs," Jack said.

"Does it work?" Bob asked.

Jack nodded. "I keep it charged at home and tested it a little while ago on my neighbor's poodle. Works fine."

Everyone stared at him.

"What? Sparky's fine. He's kind of wobbly and drooling a lot, but he's okay. I promise."

Jonathan looked at Bob, who nodded.

"Jack, after you left, the three of us agreed we would keep

things simple tonight, without weapons. Denton is a drug dealer so he's likely armed. Our plan is definitely non-violent. As Marley said, if one of us tried to use a gun or knife Rafter would probably just take it away and use it on us."

"Okay," Jack replied, "Thought it might come in handy, but I'll leave it in the car. What's the plan?"

"It's a long shot, but plan A is to use a diversion to distract Rafter out front while you and I sneak in the back door of the trailer, grab Betty and run like hell."

"I like plan B better," Jack said.

"You haven't heard it yet," said Jonathan.

"Still, it's the better plan. I can feel it."

Bob continued. "Good, because plan B is much more likely to happen. If we run into any kind of snag, I plan to confront Rafter directly and tell him we decided to move up the schedule. He agrees to let Betty go, I give him the flashlight."

"You're going to have the flashlight with you?"

"Yes and no." Bob unfolded a hard copy of Marley's satellite image. He pointed to the woods between the landing and the trailer. "Jack, Marley and I will go through the woods to the back of the trailer. Jonathan will stay here in the diner with the keys to my SUV and wait for our call. The cash, codes and cocaine from the light are in a bag in the glove box. I'll stash the empty flashlight someplace in the woods not far from the back of the trailer.

"When Denton agrees to the exchange, Jonathan will drive up and park fifty yards up the drive. Once Betty is in the car, Jonathan will leave, drive until he's out of sight from the trailer and drop the goodie bag by the side of the road. He'll take a picture of the bag on the ground and text it to my phone. While Jonathan and Betty drive back to the diner, I'll lead Denton around back to the empty flashlight. Before he freaks out, I'll use the picture to convince him his stuff is just up the road. He gets what he wants, and we have Betty and a happy ending."

Bob held up his hand before the others could protest. "I know, it seems like a big flaw in the plan, me being alone with Rafter at that point. Don't worry, I know exactly how to handle him, and when he and I are done with our business I'll call one of you to come and pick me up."

Bob tried to sound as confident as possible for his friends. The truth was he knew exactly what he was going to do with Rafter: figure it out on the fly. All day long a powerful sensation had been growing in his mind and his body. He believed—no, he *knew*—the rescue mission would end successfully. It was pointless to try to explain it to his team, he didn't really understand it himself. But this much was absolutely certain:

He and Blump were going to *solve the problem.*

Chapter 75

Saturday evening

Denton lowered his hand another fraction of an inch down Betty's arm, mentally willing her to accept the motion as natural and unforced. She shifted closer under his arm, her head below his shoulder. It was unbelievable how hard it was to fight the urge to move his hand to her chest for a squeeze.

What the hell is she waiting for? Come on, give me one tiny signal and I'll blast you to the moon!

For almost ten minutes he had micro-inched his fingers down her bare arm, hoping to stimulate a special sex nerve or trigger a suppressed nymphomania. Something, anything, to get her to yank off her top, take his hands, and make him do exactly what she wanted. How long was she going to make him wait before she finally took control? *Get with the program and start the party!*

They were on the couch watching a movie on video cassette. Denton was kind of surprised Betty picked *Gone Fishin'* from the box of tapes underneath the TV, but it was a classic. Joe Pesci was a comic genius and Rosanna Arquette was hot. Denton was just as surprised the ancient VCR still worked.

A Fortune of Reversal

It was their second day at the trailer. After apologizing several times for standing Betty up the week before, he said he wanted to make it up to her with a weekend at his place by the lake. They arrived Friday afternoon, had lunch in the diner at Krager's Landing and spent the rest of the day on the water in his boat. Betty seemed to enjoy both the scenery and all the attention he gave her, even though he was frequently preoccupied with getting his flashlight back. He'd thought it was a perfect place to hide the passcodes, but it was a huge mistake.

Denton had skimmed money from the operation from day one, tiny amounts too small for Management to notice. Eventually he accumulated enough cash that he needed to find safe storage. One of his dealers, who was a little sharper than the rest, told Denton about the new digital currency that was becoming a hot international trend. Speculators believed small investments would become millions later as the transaction technology improved over the next few years and digital money caught on with the public. Denton did a little internet research and was intrigued enough to set up an account and convert most of the cash to digital coin. Storing the passcodes was a problem. They were way too long for him to memorize, he had to avoid banks, and he didn't trust anyone. He decided to store them in the flashlight in his nightstand, hiding in plain sight. Just like in the movies.

Until DJ fucked it all up. Where are you, you son of a bitch?

When Betty fell asleep on the couch Friday night, Denton left her a note that he was making a grocery run and drove to Dodd's house. He hoped the asshole had listened to his voice message by now, surely the nephew would have told him about Denton's visit. If not, he'd have to set up the whole exchange all over again.

But if he had listened to the message, Denton knew Dodd was

313

too weak not to cooperate. He'd bring the flashlight to the warehouse Monday night, they'd make the exchange and he'd be glad to be done with Betty. She was super-high maintenance, and probably not worth the trouble in the long run. Still, he had a couple more days to get what he needed, which was for her to demand what she wanted. They were getting closer, he could feel it. It almost felt like...pain.

Time to move his hand again, just a little lower and a tiny bit closer to her—

They both jumped at the loud thumping boom of a bass drum. Betty jerked her head up into Denton's chin.

"Ow!" He pulled back his arm and rubbed his face as Betty sat up. A trumpet was playing too, and a flute or maybe a piccolo. It sounded close. Denton walked to the window and looked out, Betty right behind him.

"The fuck is that?"

Chapter 76

Saturday evening

Marley handed tiny ear buds to Bob and Jack. "We can stay in touch with these."

"Very cool," Bob said, not a bit surprised Marley was on top of mission communications. "I feel like Jack Bauer." He didn't ask where they came from, she wouldn't tell him anyway.

"Mic check, mic check," Jack said using his covert surveillance voice. "Will Mr. Michael Check please report to Lost and Found to retrieve your Lhasa Apso."

"Knock that Shih Tzu off, Jack," Bob said. "What's the range on these?"

"Two hundred yards, give or take," Marley said. "That's why I didn't give a pair to Jonathan." Jonathan was sitting in the diner nursing a soda and waiting for a phone call. If he didn't hear from the team in ninety minutes, he would call the police and lead them to Rafter's trailer. Bob figured it would all be over long before then.

They entered the woods and in twenty minutes were crouched in foliage, peering at the back of Rafter's trailer. A set of three metal steps were set below a door. Three small windows up high were evenly spaced along the back of the trailer, one on each end and one in the middle above the door. At the left end of the trailer was a large pile of firewood and Rafter's pickup truck parked a few yards beyond, underneath a carport.

"The diversion should start in about fifteen minutes. We'll cross over during the noise and hide low beneath the windows by the stairs. When Denton goes out the front door we go in the back, get Betty and hoof it back out."

"What if the door's locked? Knock and hope Betty lets us in?"

"No, she might get scared and yell, or join Denton out front. We'll just switch to plan B."

"Hope nothing goes banana-shaped," Jack muttered.

"You mean pear-shaped?" Marley asked.

"Pear, banana, whatever. Any fruit shape other than grape or orange is bad, right?"

They were far enough from the trailer that Bob let his friends yammer. If it kept stress levels low it was fine. He focused on relaxing his mind and taking several slow, deep breaths. He hoped Blump was doing whatever an imaginary psycho brain-twin did for stress management.

They all heard the trumpet and the thumping bass drum and exchanged glances. It was go time.

* * *

Denton stared out the front window at a group of five people dressed in bright colors marching toward the trailer. Betty put her hand on his back and peered over his shoulder.

A man and a woman led the group in front, the man blowing a vaguely familiar tune on a trumpet. The woman played along on a piccolo. Another couple marched behind the first, holding handmade signs on wooden poles: TOO YOUNG TOO SOON! and BE GONE WITH THEE! A large man brought up the rear, pounding on a bass drum strapped over his shoulders.

"Stay here," Denton said. Betty took his place at the window and Denton went outside, closing the door behind him.

The trumpet player waved and the gang continued to approach. Denton walked to his truck and leaned against the tailgate, arms folded. At a signal from the man with the trumpet the band stopped advancing and marched in place. Denton recognized the song now, a sorry version of "When the Saints Go Marching In."

They played through the end of the verse, the drummer marking the end with a dramatic triple-thump on the big bass.

* * *

As the band made its final approach, Denton leaned against his truck, facing away from their hiding place in the woods. "Now!" Bob whispered.

Marley stayed put as Bob and Jack sprinted across the open area between the woods and the trailer to the back doorsteps. Bob kept his ears on the song, mentally singing along. When the final verse began, he ran up the stairs and tried the doorknob. Locked. He pointed to the left end of the trailer and both men ran over and crouched behind the wood pile just as the bass drum ended the performance with a booming flourish.

* * *

"Good evening sir, my name is Frank." The man with the trumpet stepped forward, extending his hand. "And your name is…?"

Denton kept his arms folded. "What do you want?"

"We apologize for the interruption, we won't take up much of your time tonight. My friends and I belong to the Church of the Modern Peoples. We want to extend a friendly invitation to you and your family to join us next weekend at the grand opening of our new fellowship center just a few miles down the highway in Newberry."

"Church of the what?" Denton dropped his arms and stood straight.

"The Church of the Modern Peoples. Sometimes folks refer to us lovingly as CHUMPs, all in good fun. But I don't mind telling you, sometimes I wish the Founding Brothers had put just a little more thought into naming our ministry back in the day. Know what I mean?" Frank flashed Rafter a toothy smile.

"You're trespassing on private property and disturbing the fuck out of my peace. You need to leave."

"Yes sir," Frank said, taking a step back toward his group. "We'll be on our way now, but I hope you and your better half," Frank tilted his head toward Betty at the window, "will consider joining us next weekend. Let me give you one of our flyers. Curtis, may I have the flyers, please?"

Curtis shrugged the drum harness off one shoulder and opened the flap of a leather pouch hanging at his side. He pulled out a handful of pink pages and handed them to Frank.

"Thanks. Sir, here are several copies, would you mind sharing them with your friends? We'd love to have a good turnout."

Denton took the flyers. It was a hand-drawn map of main street in Newberry, with a big red star labeled CHUMP FELLOWSHIP HALL in the middle. Grand opening next weekend. It looked like someone had spent every second of two and a half minutes on the design and layout.

Denton crumpled the flyers into a ball and flung it across the yard. "You all need to leave, right the fuck now."

"Yes sir, leaving now." Frank turned and faced the group. "Okay gang, let's spread the word. CHUMPs go marching...out!" Frank raised his trumpet but Denton interrupted.

"Wait a sec, what does that mean?" Denton pointed to one of the signs. "Too young too soon?"

Frank turned back to Denton but before he could speak the woman holding the sign chimed in. "It refers to the abominable Robert Dodd, one of Satan's most fiendish minions. Surely you've heard of the infamous monster who, against all that is holy and natural, grows younger every day?"

Denton stared, his mind trying to catch up with the words he just heard. *These clowns hate Dodd? What the fuck is going on?*

"You! Get out, now!" Denton roared, pointing his finger at Frank, who looked worried and pale. Denton spun and walked back to the trailer. At the top of the steps he turned to make sure the CHUMPs were leaving, then slammed the door shut.

"What did they want?" Betty said. "I think I recognized—hey!"

Denton grabbed Betty by the arm and pulled her down the hall and into a bedroom.

"Okay! It's about time!" Betty said, beaming. Denton put his hands on her shoulders, spun her around and pushed her down to the bed. She relaxed and leaned back on her elbows, legs slightly apart, letting him look at her body.

Damn, she's hot! Denton shook his head, frowning, then turned and walked out, shutting the door behind him. He flipped the deadbolt and locked Betty inside the room that used to be DJ's. He had installed the deadbolt years ago to isolate his son when Denton needed to conduct business, party with a stripper or two, or teach the boy a lesson.

Betty started yelling and pounding on the door. "Shut up!" Denton shouted with enough volume that she actually stopped. He heard her crying as he walked back to the front room. He pulled a pistol from underneath a couch cushion and peered out the front window.

It didn't make any sense. A group of idiots who hate Bob Dodd—the guy with his fucking flashlight and passcodes—show up at his trailer one day after he leaves Dodd a message he has Betty?

Something screwy going on here...

Chapter 77

Saturday evening

The diversion by the CHUMPs worked, covering Bob and Jack's approach to the back of the trailer and their quick move to the woodpile after finding the back door locked. They heard Betty yelling and Rafter shouting before all went quiet. Bob peeked around to check the road. The CHUMPs were gone.

"Now what?" Jack asked. Before Bob answered Marley was in his ear.

"Bob, you copy?"

Bob looked back at the woods but couldn't spot where Marley was hiding. She had tucked her blue hair underneath a dark green stocking cap. Her brown T-shirt and dark pants blended into the trees and bushes perfectly.

"Yes, Marley, go ahead."

"FYI, no sign of DJ's truck at home, but a red two-door sports car just drove by Rafter's house. It stopped in the street for a few seconds like it was checking things out, then drove off. The windows were tinted too dark to see who was driving."

"Okay, thanks." Bob said.

"Yeah, thanks Wizard," Jack said.

Bob looked at his friend. "You love this shit, don't you?"

Jack grinned. "Yeah, little bit. Makes me feel alive. What's our next move?"

Bob took his time answering. When Jack reported seeing Betty casually sunbathing with Denton earlier, he assumed it meant she was here voluntarily, acting out her self-destructive impulses. But the shouting they just heard inside could mean things were no longer friendly, and Betty might be in danger.

"Jack, I assume you still have the zap gun?"

"Uh, yes. How did you know?" Jack pulled it from his vest pocket.

"Jackass, we agreed no weapons!" Marley hissed.

"I knew you couldn't resist," Bob said. "Never mind, here's what we're going to do. Rafter won't be expecting me to show up tonight to make the trade for Betty. We'll catch him by surprise. You said there are a couple of lawn chairs in the front yard, right?"

Jack nodded. "Near the opposite end of the trailer."

"Okay, you go around back and hide behind the front corner near the chairs. I'll get Rafter over there and as soon as you have a clear shot, light him up with the stunner. Marley, be ready to run in and get Betty out of the trailer while Jack and I keep Rafter down. And call Jonathan immediately if anything goes irregular-fruit-shaped."

"Roger that," Marley said.

Jack raised his index finger, pointed at his eye, then rotated it around toward Bob. With a shit-eating grin he made his way along the back of the trailer and disappeared around the far corner. "Jackass in position."

"Remember when you guys are in front of the trailer I won't

have visual, only audio." Marley said.

"Copy that, Wizard," Bob said. "Here we go."

Bob stepped around the woodpile and along the side wall to the front edge of the trailer. Peeking around the corner, he saw the lawn chairs across the yard beyond the front door. He walked toward the metal steps and wondered if it would be better to knock politely on the front door or bang on it loudly for shock effect. As he lifted his foot onto the first step the trailer door swung open and Rafter stepped out, pointing a gun at Bob's chest.

"You don't follow directions very well, do you Mr. Dodd?"

Oh. This is what shock effect feels like. Bob realized there was no point trying to hide his surprise, Rafter was way ahead of him. *He recognizes me, but does he think I'm alone?*

As if reading his mind, Rafter scanned the road and the yard, then looked back at Bob. It only took a half-second but gave Bob time to recover.

"Why wait until Monday when we can settle this tonight? I've got your flashlight nearby. You do know your boy DJ gave it to me 'cause he felt bad about trying to burn down my house?"

"The flashlight is mine, I want it back. The moron made a huge mistake stealing it, and a huger mistake giving it to you. Your house is not my problem. Betty told me she helped you put out the fire, and from what I saw the repairs are almost done."

Bob tried to stare back with the same confident expression Rafter had. "Did you just say 'huger'?"

"Where's my fucking flashlight?" Denton roared.

"Where's Betty?"

"She's fine. Let's stop dicking around. Give me the light and I'll let you take her home."

Bob shook his head. "After your friendly voice message, I

checked the flashlight. You're taking a huge risk for a little fun powder and a couple of thousand bucks. You emotionally attached to that light? Maybe used it to read comics under the covers when you were little? What's the big deal? It doesn't even work very well."

Bob waited for Rafter to work out what he just heard. There was a subtle change in Rafter's expression as he realized Bob didn't know about the codes rolled up in the cash.

Now or never, Bob thought.

"Mind if I sit down?" Without waiting for an answer Bob walked across the yard and sat in the nearest lawn chair. He pointed to the other chair and called back to Rafter, still standing on the top step at the front door. "Come on, let's talk."

Rafter scanned the road again before stepping down and crossing the yard. He kept the gun pointed at Bob as he sat on the chair, his back to the trailer. "What the hell do we have to talk about?" Rafter said. "It's gonna end up the same either way, but go ahead, I'm listening. You can have two minutes."

Over Rafter's right shoulder a forehead with a receding hairline and one eye slowly extended from the corner of the trailer, scoping out the scene. Bob leaned over and scratched his leg to avoid the temptation to shift his eyes to Jack and alert Rafter.

Come on buddy, it's up to you now.

It never occurred to Bob that One-Eyed Jack's optically-challenged condition made it difficult for him to accurately aim the weapon.

Chapter 78

Saturday evening

"What I want to know," Bob said slowly, stalling to give Jack time to creep up behind Rafter, "is why you involved Betty in our little situation?"

Rafter gave a frustrated head shake. "Man, that chick is messed up. She's hot, don't get me wrong, but your neighbor is a crazy fucking tease."

Jack used Rafter's voice as cover to get three steps closer before freezing when Rafter paused. Bob guessed Jack needed another seven or eight feet to be in optimal fry-his-ass range.

"I'm curious, how did you two meet?" Bob asked.

"Met her in Hell," Rafter answered. "She was trolling, putting out that come-talk-to-me vibe, so I obliged. She told me right off the bat her husband was out of the country and I knew what that meant. Figured we'd have some fun, but she's super high-maintenance and can't make up her fuckin' mind what she wants. Not sure it's worth the trouble." Jack was four steps closer now and holding the zapper in front of his body with both hands.

Bob concentrated on ignoring Jack in the background and

focused his eyes on Rafter's nose. Jack had stopped, waiting for more conversation. Bob gave it one more shot.

"See, that's a big difference between you and me," Bob said. "Back in my day I never sank so low I had to mess around with another man's wife. My sparkling personality attracted more girls than I could handle." Jack was clearly in range now, pointing the zap gun at Rafter's upper back. "But you, on the other hand...NOW JACK!"

Jack jumped and triggered the zapper as Rafter spun in his chair to look behind him. This reduced the target from Rafter's wide upper back to a narrow side profile, and the two barbed probes missed Rafter by several inches. One of the two probes glanced off Bob's upper left arm and landed in the grass next to the other, coiled wires trailing all the way back to the zap gun in Jack's shaking hands.

Bob uncontrollably flashed on Bill Murray in *Ghostbusters* after Egon failed to light up Slimer in the hotel ballroom. *Nice shootin' Tex!*

Rafter, still twisted, tried to rise but caught his foot on the chair leg. The chair collapsed and Rafter fell to the ground, losing his grip on the pistol. Jack sprang forward, scooped up the gun and tossed it high in the air behind him.

Bob followed the arc of the pistol as it sailed up and clattered on top of the roof of the trailer. *That's a shame, might have come in handy.* He made a mental note to ask Jack to explain his brilliant tactic later. He shouted Jack's name again and dove on top of Rafter, hoping the two of them could keep him immobilized on the ground.

Bob grabbed Rafter's arm, intending to yank it behind his back for morale-crushing leverage just like the cops on *Chicago PD*, but Rafter punched Bob in the mouth and shoved him aside. Jack wrapped his arms around Rafter's neck from behind but Rafter rose to one knee and elbowed him in the gut. Jack staggered backwards and landed on his butt, gasping for air.

Bob got to his feet and wiped his bloody mouth with the back of his hand. Rafter, apparently confident Jack was no longer a threat, straightened up on his feet and faced Bob. Rafter grinned and took a step forward.

"Hang on guys, I'm coming!" Marley said in Bob's ear.

"No! Stay where you are!" Bob yelled, forcefully enough that Rafter stopped a few feet away, looking confused.

Bob kept his eyes on Rafter as he bent over and put his hands on his knees. He sucked in lungfuls of air as Jack did the same, still on the ground behind Rafter.

"You geezers are pathetic," Rafter said.

"Yeah," Bob wheezed, "but I've still got the flashlight." Something stirred in the part of his mind where Blump hung out. Bob took one more deep breath, then stood upright. He raised his fists in what he hoped was a classic boxing pose but probably looked like an arthritic old man stretching after a nap.

Rafter laughed. "Okay, Dodd, let's dance. Come on, take your best shot." Rafter glanced back to check on Jack, then squared around and dropped his hands to his side. "First one's a freebie."

Bob cautiously took a step forward. He sensed a muted, buzzing vibration, as if Blump was anticipating the upcoming action. Rafter leaned forward and raised his chin to give Bob a clear target. Bob drew back his right arm as a bright, intense idea burst in his mind.

LEFT HAND TRUCK NUTS

The air seemed thick and distorted and Bob's sense of time went haywire. Rafter's left fist surged forward toward Bob's nose, a sluggish sucker punch. Over the next four seconds of ultra-slow time, Bob's lips formed a smile and he casually moved his head two inches to his left. He actually had to wait for Rafter's fist to drift past his right ear. Bob thought he heard air molecules being compressed, then realized it was Marley's voice in the earbud, stretched out thin, too distorted to comprehend.

Rafter's face slowly contorted in frustration as his punch failed to connect. Bob casually dropped to the ground on one knee, then the other. He pulled his right arm back and made a tight fist, taking time to make sure his forearm was parallel to the ground. He wanted this to be perfect.

The bizarre game of freeze-tag ended and time instantly became normal. Everything in sight—Rafter, Jack, the trailer, and the twilight sky beyond—zoomed back into clarity as Bob thrust his arm forward and punched Rafter in the balls with all the power he had.

Rafter let out a high-pitched little-girl scream and fell to the ground, clutching his crotch with both hands. Bob got to his feet, shaking out his throbbing hand. He'd pounded Rafter so hard he might have broken a finger or two.

Jack got up from the ground, then leaned down to pick up the zap gun. He reloaded with a cartridge from his vest pocket, aimed at point-blank range and blasted Rafter in the thigh. Rafter convulsed for a few seconds and passed out.

"Way to go!" Jack said, walking over and clapping Bob on the back. "You laid that son of a bitch out like Bruce Lee in a kung fu movie."

"Thanks," Bob said. Something shifted in his mind. "Actually, it was Johnny Cage taking out Goro in the movie *Mortal Kombat*." Something queasy rolled in his gut. *What did I just say?*

"What?" Jack was staring at him. "Say again?"

"Never mind. Let's get this asshole tied up while he's still napping."

Bob checked his mental inventory. His possibly-imaginary friend was still tucked into his regular spot, quiet and still. Bob was uncomfortable accepting Jack's praise, it was Blump who warned him of Rafter's left-handed punch and suggested the nut-busting nut punch. The fuzzy little brain-nugget had saved Bob's butt and the day. It was a lot to process, he had no freaking clue what the hell was going on in his head. Plus, he had a brand-new mystery to puzzle over. Not now, but soon.

Bob was absolutely positive he had never seen—or even heard of—the movie *Mortal Kombat*.

Chapter 79

Saturday evening

"Guys? Everyone okay? Talk to me."

"We're fine, Marley," Bob said. "Come around to the front of the trailer and bring your backpack."

In half a minute Marley came around the corner and grinned when she saw Rafter, face down in the dirt, passed out and drooling.

"Nicely done!" She shrugged off her pack and tossed a giant coil of nylon rope to Bob.

"Come on, Jack, let's hog-tie this pig."

Bob and Jack didn't want to tangle with Rafter again, so they went overboard and used almost all of a hundred feet of cord. When they finished, Rafter's hands were tied behind his back, his ankles were lashed together and dozens of loops of rope were coiled around his chest, mummy-style. Jack fashioned the remaining few feet into a hangman's noose and slipped it over Rafter's head, leaving it loosely cinched.

"Is that necessary?" Bob asked.

Jack shrugged. "For psychological effect. Keep him off

balance."

"Okay, keep your eye on him while I get Betty," Bob said. "Marley, please contact Jonathan to bring the SUV here." He stepped inside the trailer and walked through the narrow hall to the bedroom at the end.

"Betty? It's Bob. Everything's fine, I'm coming in." He flipped the deadbolt and opened the door.

"Bob!" Betty rushed forward and hugged him tight, nearly knocking him down. He put his arms around her until she stopped shaking and pulled away.

"Why are you here? Where's Denny?" she asked. "Why did he lock me up? I heard shouting outside but couldn't tell what was happening." Betty started to step around Bob into the hallway.

"Hang on a minute, let me explain first." Bob gave her a short version of how Rafter threatened to harm her if Bob didn't meet him Monday night and return the flashlight DJ gave him for setting fire to his house.

"We decided to surprise him here, tonight. Catch him off guard and get you out before anything ugly happened."

"But Denny wouldn't hurt me! He's been a perfect gentleman, and tonight we were…" Betty's voice trailed off.

Bob said nothing and waited. Betty covered her face and sobbed, her shoulders heaving. "I've been so stupid!" she wailed.

"Hey, it's—" Bob's instinct was to tell her everything would be fine but he realized that was totally wrong. Betty had fucked up big time, and he really didn't know what would happen.

"All right, let's go outside and get some air." Bob let Betty go first, and as he stepped out behind her he heard the sound of tires crunching gravel. A red sports car stopped in the driveway, throwing up a cloud of dust.

Bob stepped down the stairs and into the yard. "Marley, is that the same—"

"Yeah, looks like the car that drove by Rafter's house earlier."

The driver's door opened and Megan Jensen got out. She froze, recognizing Bob, then bent low behind the car door. When she stood she pointed a pistol at Bob.

"What are you doing here, asshole?"

"Aw shit," Bob groaned. "Not you again!"

"Hands where I can see 'em," Megan said, walking forward. She stopped and stared down at Rafter, still out cold.

"The fuck you do to my cousin?"

Chapter 80

Saturday evening

Bob, Betty, Marley and Jack sat next to each other on the ground against the trailer skirt, their hands voluntarily clasped behind their backs at the request of Megan and her pistol. Rafter was still sleeping off his electric hangover, lying a few feet away near the front doorsteps.

Megan stood over them and studied each in turn, with a double take for Jack. She poked the pistol in his chest and took a long look at his face.

"What's with the eye?" she asked, staring at the smooth patch of skin.

"All the better to see you with, my pretty."

Marley, sitting next to Jack, shook her head. "You're mixing up your references, Jackass," she said.

"Shut up!" Megan yelled. She stared at Marley, then Betty before standing directly over Bob. "I have to admit I'm surprised but really happy to see you. I've spent weeks making plans for you."

Bob could see most of Megan's teeth when she smiled. *She*

needs a good orthodontist. "The pleasure is all yours, I assure you."

Megan struck him across the face with the butt of the pistol, opening a gash in his cheek. Betty gasped as Bob fell into her, then helped him sit back up.

Megan looked satisfied for the moment and sat on one of the lawn chairs. "So, what brings you all to Denny's lakeside palace?"

"We just stopped by to invite Mr. Rafter to the grand opening of our new church over in Newberry. It's called CHUMPS and you're invited too, although you're both way overqualified. Maybe you and your cousin can do your clown act at the talent show?" Bob surprised himself with his wisecracking attitude. It seemed like the exact opposite of what he should be doing: fully cooperating with the bad woman holding the gun. He did a quick brain-check but got nothing from Blump. He looked down the line at his friends. Betty was crying, and maybe in shock. Marley was furiously staring at her feet, perhaps thinking of some high-tech escape plan. Jack returned his gaze and nodded in silent agreement with Bob's approach. It was his turn now.

"Hey, bitchmaster general! Who sprung you from the hoosegow? And are you planning to serve refreshments? I could really use a beer."

"Shut the fuck up!" Megan yelled, standing up from the chair. "I'm answering the questions here!" she snapped. "I mean, I'm asking the answers!" Flustered, she waved the gun back and forth at the group. "You know what I mean!"

"I understand now," Jack said. "I'll take 'FIDIOTS' for $200 please, Alex." Bob cracked up laughing. Betty sobbed. Marley raised her head to give Jack a look of respect. All four jumped when Megan fired her pistol in the air. Even Denton moved a little, flexing his knees in the dirt.

"Let's get to the point, shall we?" Megan said, looking down at Rafter. "I'm sure it was pretty easy to get the drop on Denny here, he's not the brightest french-fry in the toolbox." Megan turned to Betty. "I'm guessing sugar tits here was the perfect distraction, am I right?"

Betty looked up, tears streaming down her face. "Who are you?"

Megan kicked Marley's foot. "What about you, smurf queen? What are you doing with these assholes?

Marley kept her head down and said nothing. Megan paced back and forth, glaring at each of them in turn.

She has no clue, Bob thought. He tried to see it from Megan's perspective. *She gets out of jail somehow, neither Denton nor DJ is home. She decides they must be at the trailer, or maybe decides to stay there herself. She arrives and is surprised to see me and three strangers standing around her cousin, tied up on the ground.* Despite the risk of getting entangled in a Costanza do-loop cluster, Bob decided to do the opposite thing one more time and tell Megan the truth.

"Denton was keeping Betty here as leverage to get something from me. My friends and I came here tonight to get her back. Things were actually going pretty well until you showed up."

"And what exactly was he trying to get from you?" Megan asked.

"DJ gave me his father's flashlight as a gift. He sort of owed me a favor. Neither of us were aware of his father's fetish for hand-held illumination devices. Denton took Betty hostage to get his damn light back." Bob paused and rubbed his bloody cheek. "Apparently, kidnapping runs in the family."

Megan kept the gun pointed at Bob and glanced at her cousin. Rafter was moaning, starting to come around. "And where is this magic flashlight?" she asked.

As far as Bob knew the empty flashlight was still in Marley's backpack and the contents were in the glove box of his SUV. That reminded Bob that Jonathan would arrive any second, assuming Marley had made the call. "I hid the flashlight in the woods back behind the trailer," Bob said.

Megan seemed to think this over for several seconds. "Okay, nobody move a muscle." She kept the gun pointed their direction as she stepped over Rafter. A garden hose was attached to a faucet mounted on a pipe sticking up from the ground. She turned on the water and picked up the end of the hose. Megan held the stream of water over Rafter's face and he jerked awake, sputtering and shouting. Megan dropped the hose and it landed near his knees, soaking his jeans and the ground around him.

Rafter twisted and shook and finally managed to roll over and look up at Megan.

"Aw shit," Rafter said.

"Wish I'd said that," Bob muttered.

"Hi, cuz," Rafter said. "Glad you got out of jail. If you don't mind untying me—"

"Shut up, fuckhead!" Megan yelled. She kicked him in the groin and Rafter screamed.

"What the hell? Come on, Denny, I barely tapped those peanuts. Be a man for fuck's sake!"

Bob stifled a laugh. Marley and Jack were also enjoying the show, but Betty continued whimpering softly. Megan glared down at Rafter.

"Why didn't you bail me out, craphead? I know you got my message, you slime bag!" She kicked at him again but Rafter managed to roll just enough that her boot missed his crotch and got him in the ribs. He let out a whoosh of air. Megan ranted some more and kicked him again.

Might be a good time to grab her gun. Bob started to stand but

Megan spun around, took two quick steps and pushed the barrel of the pistol into his forehead, shoving him back against the trailer. Betty screamed and fell away toward Marley.

"Oh yes, please do," Megan taunted. "Come on, make your move. I owe you some big-time payback. Go for it!"

Bob didn't move, didn't say a word. He tried to look into Megan's eyes without flinching. *Shit, I screwed up. Wait…what?*

There was a growling, slobbering sound and everyone looked toward the opposite end of the trailer as a bulldog raced toward them in full gallop. Megan pulled the gun from Bob's head as she stood and turned.

The dog barked and jumped over Rafter, heading for Megan's feet. Megan yelled and managed two steps back before slipping on the grass, wet and slick from the flowing water hose. There was an ugly popping sound and Megan screamed, dropping the gun as she hit the ground hard. The bulldog locked its jaws on Megan's right boot and dug in, trying to drag her across the yard.

Bob jumped to his feet and snatched up the gun. He looked at Jack, who jerked his head up. *Good idea.* Bob tossed the gun onto the roof as DJ and Jonathan stepped around the far corner of the trailer.

"Buster! Good boy! That's a good dog!" DJ knelt and separated the dog from the half-chewed boot. Buster immediately jumped up to lick DJ's face. DJ picked up his dog and stood over Megan, who was holding her twisted knee with both hands.

"Hey, Cousin Megan. What's up?"

Chapter 81

Saturday evening

"Junior! Get over here and untie me!"

Denton Rafter, Senior had wormed his way a couple of feet from his original position trying to get free. He looked like a soggy mummy wrapped in coils of nylon rope, his expression wild and desperate.

Holding Buster in his arms, DJ walked halfway to Rafter and stopped. He looked at Bob, who shook his head. *This should be interesting.*

"Come on, Junior, cut me loose and we can get this all sorted out," Denton pleaded. "I forgive you for taking my flashlight, as long as I get it the fuck back. Now cut me loose!"

DJ bent over and released Buster. The dog immediately ran to Rafter and started licking his face, slobbering incessantly. Rafter thrashed and cursed but the dog had the better position. "Junior! Get your mutt off me!"

DJ stood over his father. "My name is DJ." He turned and walked back to the others huddled around Megan. Jack held the zap gun, just in case. Marley was holding her phone and speaking to someone through her earbud. Jonathan talked quietly to Betty, sitting on the ground against the trailer. She had stopped crying but still looked miserable.

Megan was obviously in pain but tough enough to pretend she was still in charge. She glared at Bob before trying to splatter him with a gob of spit.

"You better kill me, Dodd, otherwise I'm coming for you. You are so—." She was interrupted by a clanging sound and everyone turned toward Denton. He had managed to wrench himself over trying to dislodge Buster but had banged his head on the metal frame of the front doorsteps.

"Stupid mutt," Megan grumbled. "What the fuck did he attack me for?"

"I think he remembers you kicked him in the ear, last Thanksgiving," DJ said. "He's like an elephant, he never forgets."

"Sheriff's Department is on the way," Marley reported.

"Good," Bob said. "I assume somehow you got word to Jonathan not to drive here after all?"

"As soon as I saw that red car drive up, I sent him a text to abort. He texted back he was bringing help; I had no idea what he meant."

"We'll get it all sorted out after we turn these two over to the sheriff."

"Go to hell!" Megan yelled, trying to spit on Bob again.

"Jack? Is your zapper loaded with a fresh cartridge?"

"Yep, ready to go. Got a couple spares, too."

"Keep your eye on Megan. If she moves again, light her up."

"Roger that, Bobwhite."

Bob only took two steps before hearing a pop, crackle, and yelp. He spun back around. Megan was writhing on the ground, the twin electric barbs stuck in her ribs. Bob looked at Jack with the universal raised-eyebrow query: WTF?

Jack shrugged. "She tried to kidnap a little girl. My hand slipped."

Marley made a whooshing sound, her index finger rising in the air before arcing over and down. "Ka-boooossshhh! Game over."

Chapter 82

Sunday morning

DJ and Buster had a good time hanging out at the trailer all week, watching old movies on the VCR and hiking through the woods to the marina. He was careful to set an alarm on his phone to remind him every hour to check his father's location. When his dad seemed to be heading to the trailer Friday afternoon, DJ packed quickly and left. He and Buster spent the night in his truck parked in the lot at the diner.

Saturday, they hung around the docks, DJ using his phone to confirm his father was still at the trailer. He had just decided to drive back to town and go home when he saw Bob, Jonathan and Marley arrive and go inside the diner. Later, when Bob, Marley, and a man he didn't recognize walked into the woods in the direction of the trailer, DJ went inside to ask Jonathan why they were here.

"At that point, I thought it was okay to tell DJ what was going on," Jonathan said. "I figured whatever happened, it was all going to be over soon." The gang was debriefing in Krager's Diner, squeezed into a large corner booth with an extra chair for

DJ. It was just after five am but the place had already been open an hour serving regular early-bird customers. Everyone ordered coffee or tea except Marley, who asked for a Mountain Dew and continued typing feverishly on her laptop. Buster was sprawled across several feet below the table, snoring softly.

They had all been questioned over several hours by sheriff's deputies as well as Detective Bent, who was called to the scene as chief investigator of both Megan's kidnapping attempt and the arson fire at Bob's house. Megan Jensen and Denton Rafter were both arrested and transported in separate vehicles to keep them from trying to kill each other.

Bob glanced around the table at Jonathan and his friends, grateful for a happy outcome and proud of their efforts. Everyone looked tired but relieved except Betty, who slumped between Bob and Marley and barely spoke.

Jonathan continued. "When I got the all-clear text from Marley, I suggested DJ and Buster drive to the trailer too. But just as we were about to leave, I got the abort message. DJ said he knew a quick trail to the cabin so we hoofed it through the woods, figuring we'd check out the scene and either help or call the sheriff. When we reached the back side of the trailer Buster bolted ahead like he knew something we didn't. You know the rest."

Jack raised his cup. "To DJ and Buster, the newest members of the Dodd Squad. Thanks for bailing us out of that charlie foxtrot."

"And to One-Eyed Jack, the fastest zap gun in the tri-state area," Bob said.

"And to Bob, who puts the 'odd' in Dodd." Jack grinned. "Man, that squatting crotch death-punch you gave Rafter was sweet."

Marley spoke up. "Sounds like Johnny Cage in *Mortal Kombat*, one of my favorites. Watched it again just last week. Here," she said, typing on her keyboard before spinning it around. They all watched a video of a good-looking young actor drop to the ground and punch a giant four-armed mutant in the groin before running off.

"Is that where you got the idea, Uncle Bob?" Jonathan asked.

"No, I've never seen the movie," Bob replied. "Just a voice in my head, I guess." Jack gave him a funny look but Bob ignored it, his mind spinning. *Marley watches one of her favorite old movies, and a few days later I get a critical, just-in-time thought-weapon and use it to nail Rafter. Exactly like the movie, which I've never seen. What are you up to, Blump?*

"Well, here's something else," Jack leaned forward. "The cop I talked to didn't ask me anything about the flashlight, and I didn't bring it up. Anyone else get into it?"

"I got the flashlight and the stuff out of the SUV and gave it all to Bent," Bob said. "Told him the whole story."

Betty perked up. "When I was locked in the bedroom, I heard shouting outside but couldn't make it out. What is it again about the flashlight?"

Bob explained everything, including Denton's voice message threatening Betty to get the flashlight back. DJ nodded his head a couple of times but had yet to say anything.

"What about those sticky-notes? What are they for?" Betty asked.

"Detective Bent and his team will probably be able to figure it out," Bob said. "He has access to resources we don't—"

"I think I have it," Marley said, her fingers still flying over her keyboard.

"Have what?" Jonathan asked.

"I know what the sticky-notes are for."

They waited for Marley to speak but she continued to type,

staring at the screen.

"Marley! What is it?"

She leaned back against the booth and extended her arms in a stretch.

"Okay, get this." She took a quick drink of Mountain Dew. "I copied the codes from the two sticky notes and have been trying to figure out what they are. Each note has twelve characters, either numbers, symbols, or letters. Long strings like these are typical of high-security entry codes for secure facilities, or access codes for cripto-currency accounts. You know, digital money? Like bitcoin?

"But assuming these are passcodes, there's no way to know what they provide access to. Based on Rafter's business I assumed they were tied to financial accounts. And there are millions of ways digital currency accounts can be set up, tons and tons of options. Access procedures, security measures to avoid both detection and hacking attempts, payments, transfer protocols. It can get really complicated.

"But our boy Denny is not all that sharp, and certainly not trained in cyber-security. If I were him and wanted to set up a digital-currency system, I'd do an internet search for 'how to set up a digital currency account.' So I searched for exactly that and found this." She turned the laptop around to show a web page filled with text. At the top in large blue letters was the title: HOW TO SET UP A PRIVATE DIGITAL MONEY ACCOUNT.

"It's the first search result," Marley went on. She spun the laptop back around to herself. "If you skip down below…here it is. The article recommends using a minimum of twelve characters in a passcode, completely random. It stresses committing them to memory or storing them in a secure, safe place. Denny apparently believes the inside of his flashlight is a safe place."

"But there are two sticky-notes, not just one. Two different money accounts?" Jack asked.

"That was my first thought too. Then I saw this further down in the article." She started to turn the screen again.

"Just tell us, Marley," Bob said.

"Okay. The article recommends a separate utility be used to convert a URL to a code, and they even provide a simple macro to do this. Instead of typing a common-language web address like 'my-money-account-dot-com,' the macro converts it to a random sequence of letters, numbers and characters."

"So one of the notes is actually a URL," Jonathan said.

"I tried both codes as URLs and neither opened a site. There was nothing else in the article, and I went back to the original search results. Turns out Denny was a tiny bit more clever than I thought.

"The next link in the search results, just below the first, was another how-to article with an interesting recommendation. If passcodes are going to be physically stored, they suggest adding an additional level of security by inserting an 'underscore' between two characters somewhere in the string. Doesn't matter where, you don't mark it on the code itself, you have to memorize where you put it. For example, add an underscore between the tenth and eleventh characters and don't forget it's there.

"I wrote a simple macro and ran it, inserting underscores sequentially in both codes, between the first and second characters, between the second and third, and so on. For some reason, Denton inserted an underscore between the sixth and seventh characters, and this opened—"

"That's my dad's favorite two beers," DJ said, surprising everyone.

"Say again, DJ?" Bob asked.

"Dad always says his favorite two beers are the last one in the first six-pack and the first one in the second six-pack."

Jack nodded vigorously. "Makes perfect sense to me. Marley, you should have figured that out immediately."

"Anyway," Marley continued, glaring at Jack, "it opened a web site that displays a prompt: ENTER PASSCODE. Naturally, I entered the code from the other sticky-note," her fingers flew across the keys, "and got this." She spun the laptop around.

ENTER 2ND PASSCODE

Marley looked around the table to see if everyone understood. "It's a multi-level passcode. The code on the first note is used as a modified URL to bring up the account website. The code on the second note is the first of two or more passcodes. There is at least one more passcode needed to access the account. Anyone have any ideas? DJ, can you think of another place where your dad might store really valuable information, like an empty pickle jar in the fridge, or stuffed inside an old tennis shoe?"

DJ didn't answer but pushed back from the table and stood, waking up Buster. "Stay!" he commanded, unclear whether he meant the dog or the group. He walked to the door and outside.

"Great stuff, Marley. Really nice work," Bob said. "We have to give Rafter credit; man knows how to do a web search and follow directions. He must have stored the rest of the passcodes somewhere else."

Betty pointed out the window behind Jonathan. "What's DJ doing?"

DJ crouched at the back of his truck for a few seconds, then walked back inside. He tossed an oversized pair of chrome testicles attached to a large chain on the table, fished a multi-purpose utility knife out of his front pocket and sat down without a word. He removed a screw from one of the nuts, gave it a twist and it separated into two pieces. A folded yellow sticky note fell out.

"Maybe this will help," DJ said, handing the note to Marley. "Found three notes inside the flashlight. Figured they must be important. Took one just in case, you know, Dad went ape-shit again. Thought it might come in handy so I hid it. Right?"

"Right," everyone agreed. Marley typed in the third passcode, another twelve-character random string. Her eyes opened wide and she slowly turned the screen around one more time for all to see. Bob let out a low, holy-cow whistle.

It was a digital currency ledger showing a long list of transactions. Most were transfer deposits of several hundred dollars each, a few were transfer withdrawals of larger amounts. Just below the header the current balance of the account was displayed in both crypto-units and the current U.S money equivalent: seven hundred eighty-three thousand dollars and change.

Bob pulled his cell phone from his pocket and found the number he wanted.

"Detective Bent, it's Bob Dodd. Would you mind driving back out to the lake and meeting us at Krager's Diner? My friends and I want to buy you a donut and a cup of coffee. And we have something to show you, something you're definitely going to want to see."

Chapter 83

Thursday evening

Bob dropped the sixth season of *Seinfeld* in the DVD player and sat down carefully on the sofa, taking care not to spill his scotch. He pressed PLAY on the remote and heard the chime of the doorbell. He pressed PAUSE, set his glass on the side table, and opened the door.

"Hello Betty," he said, thinking of cinnamon chewing gum. "Come in."

"Thank you." Betty's smile was tight and thin as she slipped past carrying a plastic grocery bag.

"I was just about to have a drink, may I fix you one? Vodka and soda, right?"

"Yes, thank you." Betty glanced at Bob's drink by the couch and sat in the chair on the opposite side of the room.

Bob handed Betty her drink and picked up his own before sitting down. "To what shall we drink?"

"To you, Bob. And to Jack, Jonathan, and Marley. For saving me."

"And to DJ and Buster too," Bob said. They clinked glasses and he sat down, once again careful to not spill his drink. He waited for Betty to speak first. He thought he knew why she was here.

Betty crossed one knee over the other and leaned forward, holding her glass in both hands.

"I, uh, need to say…" She stopped, took a sip, and tried again.

"I want to apologize to you for my behavior the last several weeks. Actually, for years. For getting with Denny, putting myself in…for everything. I sort of lost my mind again, and I feel awful." Her eyes filled with tears.

"Betty, you don't—"

"I want to. I talked to Ray for nearly three hours yesterday on the phone. I told him everything. He was upset, of course, but he still loves me, I think. Somehow. He even tried to make it sound like it was his fault. He's cutting his trip short and will be home tomorrow. He wants me to get professional help and I promised him I would."

"I hope you two can work it out. Ray's a good man."

"He is," Betty agreed. Her eyes seemed to lose some of their sadness. "You are, too. You've always been a perfect gentleman and I know sometimes I tried to challenge that. I'm sorry. You deserve better."

"Thank you," Bob said. "Really, Betty, everything is good between us. I hope you don't get stuck in the past too much, just learn from it and go forward. It's all we can do, right?" *And maybe try to avoid time-shifting psychedelic road trips with a verbally challenged alien stowaway hiding in your brain.*

"That's good advice," Betty said, sitting up straight and wiping her face. "Detective Bent told me yesterday they were charging Denny with unlawful imprisonment, or something like that, since he locked me in the bedroom. And some other charges, too."

"Bent told me too. The crypto-ledger Marley opened is going to help them bust up a lot of the drug activity in Casstown. In fact, two of Rafter's boys who were arrested a couple of weeks ago heard Rafter was locked up and are now cooperating completely. Might bring the whole operation down in just a few days."

"What about that horrible monster, Megan?" Betty asked.

"Behind bars again, no chance of bail. Lots of additional charges. I don't think she'll ever roam free again."

"Good," Betty said. She sipped her drink. "I called Marley this morning."

"Really?" Bob knew Betty didn't think much of Marley.

"To thank her. Did you know she's been spending time with DJ the last few days? With his father in jail she said she just wanted to make sure he was okay. I think she was impressed with what he did with the third sticky-note. Marley introduced DJ to a friend who is a recruiter for the navy and they hit it off. It sounds like DJ is interested in signing up, if they can smooth over the bumps in his record. He turns eighteen in a few weeks and won't need his father's signature."

"That's great news," Bob said, remembering DJ watering his mailbox just a few weeks ago. *People change.*

"Marley said DJ was worried about leaving Buster. I told her to let him know Ray and I will take care of him while he's away. I'm going to be a stay-at-home housewife and try to fix myself and my marriage, and Buster got us out of that awful situation. It's the least I can do."

"Good, I'll enjoy having Buster around." Bob had often considered getting a dog for companionship. Having the bulldog next door would be a good test run.

"One more thing," Betty said. "I called Jack to thank him too, and he told me a little bit about your trip, how you both tried lots of new things, and…anyway, I got you a little gift. Hope you like it." She leaned across and handed him the plastic bag.

Bob pulled out an object covered with several layers of tissue. He unwrapped it and broke out laughing. It was a George Costanza bobble-head doll.

"Jack told me about your opposite strategy," Betty said with her best smile of the evening.

"This is terrific!" Bob placed George on the table next to his glass of scotch, a perfect combination. "I love it, thank you very much."

"So, what's next for you?" Betty asked.

"I'm going on another road trip as soon as Detective Bent says it's okay to leave town. I've got some unfinished business in Albuquerque." Bob reached over and flicked a finger.

George Costanza vigorously nodded his approval.

Steve Moore

Epilogue

Two weeks later
Thursday afternoon

Bob replaced the nozzle in the gas pump and yanked the receipt from the slot. He stretched his arms and neck before getting back in the SUV and starting the engine. Another two and a half hours of road time and he'd be having dinner with Julie. Bob had traveled historic Route 66 many times before. It was still familiar, like running your fingertip over a scar you had on your arm since you were a little kid. Route 66 was mostly boring interstate highways now, but he didn't really mind. The anticipation made it all worthwhile.

He got back on I-40 and set the cruise control on seventy-eight. He rested his elbow on the open window and thought about his other trip, the not-that-long, strange journey of the last couple of months.

Let's see, it all started when I thwarted Fake Momma's kidnapping plan in Costco on my ninety-first birthday.

Thwarted? Holy crap, I am such a fogey geezer. Okay, what else?

Fistfights. Flashbacks.

Insight into thoughts and emotions of other people.
Hiding my boner from Mrs. Lindon.
Making fun of Frank and the CHUMPs, playing Spot the Hooker with Jack.
Battling a house fire with a beautiful woman, stuck in an elevator with another.
Reenacting a scene from a kung-fu movie I've never watched to take down a major-league asshole.
Scotches on Sofas and Coffee on Couches,
Truck Nuts and Passcodes and Slobbering Bulldogs,
These are a few of my favorite things!
Empty boots and Kowboy Karaoke.
Shocking pain from a zipper and painful shocks from a zapper.
Hell's Grill and Krager's Diner. Mooncups, The Waffle Box, and Nicky's.
Doctors, psychologists and spies, oh my!
A bobble-head Costanza and a card-slapping card slapper.
A fidiotic drug runner with a sociopathic cousin.
Alaxis and the Ancient Astronauts.
Jack, Jonathan, and Marley: my one-eyed buddy, my nephew-in-law, and my personal tech-wizard.
Ruthie, the taxi-driving ex-stripper.
Betty. Christine. Amy. Tracy.
Julie.
Blue men who don't speak and Blump, who only spoke once. And just in time.

Bob had to admit his life was no longer boring. He still had a ton of stuff to consider and important decisions to make. He'd been mulling over the Alaxis proposal and would meet Roger Kilmore on Monday to discuss all that happened and get his opinion. If they decided to pursue a deal with Alaxis, Bob intended to negotiate funding for a couple of special side projects he wanted to explore.

First, though, he would spend the weekend with Julie, and see if they picked up where they left off. He was anxious to find out if the magic was real or just an old man's foolish delusion.

And there was Blump, his psycho-freak twin, squatting peacefully in his mind somewhere. Dormant since the night at Rafter's trailer, Bob still sensed its presence and saw it clearly in his imagination: a moist, dark cocoon tucked into a small, warm crevice in the back of his brain. It was normal now, even comfortable.

Blump's *"left hand truck nuts"* message was perfectly timed. Bob had dodged the left-hand jab and punched Rafter hard in the nuts. Game, set, match. Later, he wondered about the word "truck," it was almost like Blump was telling him the missing passcode was inside one of DJ's truck balls. There was no way to know for sure, but Bob would have bet seventy-two dollars DJ hid the third sticky-note in the truck nut hanging on the left.

Thanks, Blump. You saved my ass. I owe you one.

Despite everything that had happened, Bob was still surprised to receive a reply.

YOU'RE WELCOME. AND PLEASE, DON'T CALL ME BLUMP. MAKES ME SOUND LAZY.

CALL ME BLOB.

Acknowledgments

Years ago, when I started tinkering with the ideas that eventually became this novel, a twisted alien presence appeared and established residency in an unused corner of my mind (some would argue there was plenty of space). In lieu of paying rent, the lump in my head contributed a multitude of bizarre story concepts, helped develop the characters of the Dodd Squad, dredged up forgotten memories from the Moorechives, and frequently interfered with my ability to avoid crafting long, tedious, run-on sentences. I am grateful for the inspiration, of course, but any errors, omissions, or deficiencies in the final manuscript are Stumpy's fault, not mine.

I want to thank my fellow writer, Deb, for years of friendship and steadfast support. Your suggestions, edits, and encouragements were spot-on brilliant. We've come a long way since I first spied a copy of *Writer's Market* on your vintage desk many years ago. Cheers!

Huge thanks to Buddy, my long-time friend, writer, and fellow traveler. From pan pizza lunches in Taft over three decades ago, to $15 margaritas (for the second time) in Santa Fe last year, our innumerable conversations helped keep my writing dreams alive. I greatly appreciate your friendship.

Thanks also to Casie, Jeff, Mary, Deniece, and Layton. Your support and critiques of early draft chapters improved my writing and helped me find my voice.

To Susan and Dewayne: thank you for taking the time to read an early draft, and for your valuable suggestions.

Special thanks to Indi Martin, my talented daughter, writer, and artist for creating a terrific cover, and blazing the family literary trail years ago by writing three excellent novels of her own. Please visit her website: www.tortoiseharecreations.com

And to my wife and sweetheart, Vana: Thank you for many years of unwavering encouragement, support, and patience. Every writer should be so lucky. I love that my wife likes to read as much as I do. SPT!

Steve Moore is a most-likely retired petroleum engineer and future dog owner. He and his wife, Vana, live in Broken Arrow, Oklahoma. *A Fortune of Reversal* is his first book.

Thank you for reading my novel. To read excerpts of other works in progress and sporadically published humor, please visit my website and blog:

TunnelWriter.com

Made in the USA
Coppell, TX
04 November 2023

23810246R00215